We're All Phoenixes

A Novel

By

Kashish Mandhane

We're All Phoenixes
Kashish Mandhane

Published by White Falcon Publishing
Chandigarh, India

All rights reserved
First Edition, 2024
© Kashish Mandhane, 2024
Cover Imaging and Design by Chaitanya Modak, 2024

No part of this publication may be reproduced, or stored in a retrieval system, or transmitted in any form by means of electronic, mechanical, photocopying or otherwise, without prior written permission from the author.

The contents of this book have been certified and timestamped on the Gnosis blockchain as a permanent proof of existence. Scan the QR code or visit the URL given on the back cover to verify the blockchain certification for this book.

The views expressed in this work are solely those of the author and do not reflect the views of the publisher, and the publisher hereby disclaims any responsibility for them.

Requests for permission should be addressed to the author.

ISBN - 978-93-48199-48-5

Dedicated to:

My mother, Nilima Mandhane, a fighter and the strongest person I know.

Contents

1. EVANDER – The Village of Bosque Tranquilo 1
2. EVANDER – The Stranger 20
3. EVANDER – The Poisoning 30
4. RUTH – The Warning 35
5. RUTH – The Murders of The Forbes 43
6. RUTH – A Forbidden Answer 50
7. EVANDER – The Beckoning 57
8. EVANDER – A Bizarre Blessing 68
9. EVANDER – A Leap of Faith 77
10. RUTH – A Mind-bending Surprise 82
11. RUTH – The Plea 88
12. EVANDER – The Promise 101
13. RUTH – Silver Linings 114
14. EVANDER – The Disappearance 125
15. EVANDER – Déjà vu 144
16. RUTH – An Essential Epiphany 153
17. RUTH – The Ghosts of A Lost Life 163
18. EVANDER – A Miraculous Guide 169
19. EVANDER – The Friend 177
20. RUTH – The Betrayal 184
21. RUTH – The Tables Turn (sort of?) 192

22. EVANDER – The Vision 202

23. EVANDER – A Compromise........................... 214

24. RUTH – The Encounter 219

25. RUTH – The Cage 228

26. EVANDER – A Ray of Hope in The Storm 237

27. EVANDER – The Farewell.............................. 244

28. EVANDER – A Deal with The Devil 253

29. RUTH – The Unspoken Goodbye 259

30. EVANDER – The Curse Comes Alive 272

31. EVANDER – The Kingdom............................. 280

32. RUTH – The Escape....................................... 286

33. RUTH – The Obelick....................................... 300

34. EVANDER – The Prison 306

35. RUTH – An Unattainable Memory................... 316

36. RUTH – The Jewel.. 323

37. EVANDER – The Verdict 328

38. RUTH – The Assassin 336

39. RUTH – The Afterlife...................................... 344

40. EVANDER – Back in Paradise.........................359

41. EVANDER – Someone called Home 367

42. EVANDER – A New Beginning........................375

Epilogue.. 391

Acknowledgements 403

1.

EVANDER – The Village of Bosque Tranquilo

He was doomed.

Evander knew this the moment his GPS showed that he was close to a river, even though he was surrounded by greenery. Sweat trickled down his neck in spite of the leafy canopy that shielded him from the sun.

His feet shuffled in the mossy dirt as he tried to figure out the path he should take. Evander thought he was well-prepared, but he hadn't even anticipated stumbling into an unknown part of the woods where technology would be useless.

What his family always told him was definitely confirmed now: he was worthless. Evander's father's harsh, corrosive voice rang in his ears – "You think we illtreat you, boy, but believe me, the real world would crush you like a bug." His dad, Julio, was one of the most successful businessmen in Mexico, but he hadn't been the best parent to Evander.

He shook his head to clear it; he could mull over his unfortunate life later on. Right now, he had to find a way out. But there was no way out. He was lost. Evander had a terrible sense of direction; there was no way he'd be able to retrace his steps. So, what did it matter? Maybe he could wander around and figure it out. Or he could've been more practical about the situation, but his logic evaporated as he registered the beauty around him. His feet began moving forward themselves.

The coarse tree trunks had an odd consistency. Their tops dripping with greenery, breaking the monotony of the beige of the trunks. Evander caught a splash of colour between the thick, lush foliage - blossoms of bright fuchsia flowers or a cluster of deep violet berries. He had never been in a forest before. He felt like a child, eyes wide open, eagerly absorbing everything he saw.

The forest was alive with sounds: a hoot of an owl here, a hint of a birdsong there and a persistent hum of the insects, some meandering on the bark of the trees, some scurrying on the soil. He could feel the

Chapter 1

presence of hundreds of creatures around him; it felt invigorating. But the thought that the forest had other creatures who were perilous and famished made Evander pace himself.

Hours passed and the forest floor turned from moss to plain dirt that felt scorching hot even through his boots. He looked up from the ground to realise the foliage was gradually thinning. As he continued walking, the canopy overhead disappeared, and he realised this was where the woods ended.

And a village began.

His mouth fell open as his eyes glided over the scene. A vast village spread out for miles, beyond which lay rocky mountain terrain. Cottages of all sizes seemed to have been sprinkled over the landscape. All covered with a layer of the sand that coated the ground, held upright with bricks, weak wood planks or straw, the huts all looked quite alike, except one – the one that was closest to Evander.

Evander had never been in a rural area before. In fact, he had spent 80% of his life in his house, because his father wanted him to be safe, far away from the dangers of walking down the street or going to school and getting a proper education; the only times he had left his house was when he had gone to places like New York, Toronto and San Diego with his father and brother to help out with their work (under his father's bodyguard's protection, of course).

So, when he realised that he must take shelter in one of these cottages, his stomach turned. He didn't want to, but the hike had tired him and he didn't know the route back anyway. He decided that he could rest for a day and maybe ask the villagers for the directions. Reassuring himself that it was the right decision, he began walking towards the cottage closest to the forest line.

The villagers came into clearer view, dressed in poorly sewn rugs or ill-fitting pieces of torn, soiled clothing. They stared at him, pots brimming with water in some hands and others clutching vegetation. They gawked at him as he made his way to the cottage, some even whispering apprehensively. Evander supposed they didn't have visitors often. But it had to be more than that. Because, otherwise, they wouldn't all drop whatever they were doing to watch an outsider walk to a cottage, would they? Even the

Chapter 1

kids – some flat out naked – stopped throwing rocks at each other and running around to turn and train their beady eyes on him.

Perhaps he looked like an alien to them, in his faded blue jeans, orange polo t-shirt and black combat boots, with a huge travel backpack, ruffled blonde hair and very piercing blue eyes. Even back home, he often found people gaping at him - Mexico didn't have a lot of blue-eyed blondes. He seemed so out of place here too. It was no surprise that his arrival had startled these people.

Evander tore his eyes away from the villagers and looked at the cottage he was walking to. It was different from the others, certainly. With grey concrete bricks instead of the usual brown mud ones, it seemed far sturdier. Right next to the door, was a wooden post, tied to which was a sleeping cow. He quickly glanced around and found none of the other villagers had one. This did make him a little sceptical, but Evander was already at the door, and before he could second guess it, his hands were gently rapping on the wood.

When the door opened, Evander felt startled himself. Almond-shaped eyes the colour of gold, green and brown peered at him – he had never seen such a beautiful shade of hazel; the girl who had opened the door had silky black hair that fell around her shoulders. Her skin was pale and radiant, unlike the villagers', who had spent many years tanning themselves under the burning sun, or so Evander guessed. She wore an off-white cotton blouse, embroidered with bright floral patterns, and a chequered brown skirt. After him, this girl was probably the one who seemed most alien to the villagers.

Her eyebrows lifted quizzically as she examined him. "Can I help you?" she asked amiably. Her voice was... different. It was unlike anything Evander had ever heard. He could only describe it as what grace would sound like if it were a sound.

"Yeah, well, actually I-I got lost in the uhh... the forest and I was, ummm... hoping I could stay at your place for some time till I figured where to go. W-would that be okay?" he stammered, as if he had lost the ability to speak, somehow.

Chapter 1

"Sure," she said, her eyes lighting up with ecstasy, surprising him. Evander could see that she was trying to suppress a smile. "You can come in."

Before he entered her home, he saw a glimpse of the villagers, muttering ominously and shaking their heads in disapproval. What the hell was their problem? He'd probably never know.

Inside the girl's abode was only one room, with a cot made of wood and straw in one corner and roughly crafted wooden cabinets in the other. The far side of the cottage had two large vessels, probably filled with water. There was a basket of fruits beside them and another smaller vessel. In terms of food, the girl had barely enough for herself, but he didn't mind. He had packets of chips and snacks he had brought with himself for the journey; that would have to suffice.

He realised he hadn't introduced himself yet.

"Oh, I'm sorry. I forgot to introduce myself," he began. "I'm Evander. Nice to meet you." He extended his hand.

"I am Ruth," the girl said, shaking his hand. "It's good to have some company. It's frustrating... having no one to talk to."

Evander took seat on a rug that Ruth had laid down for him and realised that the cottage – though not luxurious – was absolutely clean. There wasn't a speck of dust or sand in any corner. The rug wasn't torn or even grimy. Evander started to wonder if this was why Ruth didn't have any company. She was too different from the villagers and had a home far too better.

But he asked anyway. "Why? Do the other villagers not speak to you?"

She chuckled. "Well, ever since I got here, I've had a feeling that they don't like me. They're always whispering when I get out and flashing me distasteful looks. They still consider me an outsider, I guess. After all, I came here only about a week ago."

"And you have this house so soon?" he asked bewilderedly. "How?"

Ruth's face turned slightly pink before she stood up and suddenly started to cut some fruits. "It isn't actually a big deal," she said evasively and changed

Chapter 1

the topic. "Why don't you get some rest? You must have been travelling for long. Bosque Tranquilo is not close to anywhere else."

"'Bosque Tranquilo'? Is that this village's name?"

"Yes. It has been around for quite some time now. Some decades back, a bunch of people got lost in the woods and when they found this barren stretch of land, they decided to make it their home. With the fruits and vegetation from the forest and its river's water, surviving here was easy."

That was definitely one of the weirdest pieces of history Evander had ever learned. He briefly wondered how Ruth had gotten this information but was immediately distracted by another thought: nothing was really impossible. Because here was a good number of people, surviving entirely on their own, without any contact to the world outside this pygmy village. Without any support of electricity or technology or the modern world. He was in awe until yet another question occurred to him.

"So, how come you ended up here?" he asked Ruth.

"Well, that's a long story, Evander," she said, dodging his question yet again. "I have to feed my cow. I'll be back soon."

She handed him a plate of slices of apple and as she did, Evander noticed a tiny mark on her right wrist. It looked like a cross with little '3's at the end of each line; its centre had a circle and it had four dots in the space between the four lines. It was a peculiar symbol. Then, again, he didn't know much about tattoos in general. Just as he decided to ask her about it, she left.

As he gobbled the apple slices, Evander couldn't help feeling like Ruth was hiding something. Something about how and why she had arrived at this place. It made sense, though. Evander was a stranger; they had *just* met. Maybe she didn't want to reveal details about her life to a complete stranger. Even so, something about her didn't feel right.

However, eventually, over the course of 18 years of his life, Evander had learned that being too curious had its own disadvantages. For as long as he could remember, he'd had a predilection for mysteries, mainly because reading mysteries and writing them transported him to a completely different place; a

Chapter 1

place where he could feel safe from the guilt of his mother's death, safe from his siblings' attacks, safe from the fear that he'd never be capable enough to build the life he wanted. When he was immersed in any form of narrative, he could escape his daily life and focus on the characters, their hopes and dreams, their problems and their journeys. Sure, this form of escapism felt like cheating sometimes, but it was the only form of joy Evander knew.

But the real world didn't accommodate his wishes, and so, growing up, he was perpetually told by his father that he mustn't waste time on things that didn't concern him. Like why his siblings' birthdays were celebrated like festivals and his was treated as non-existent. And so, now, as he placed the empty plate back in a corner, he shut his eyes and ordered himself not to wonder even a little about Ruth, or her strange tattoo, or how her house smelled like lavender.

****

CLANG!

That was loud enough to wake Evander up from his stupor. He sat up and saw Ruth frantically closing the container whose lid had apparently fallen.

She turned to him, her face paler than usual and an expression of horror covering her face. "I am so sorry for that," she said as if she had committed a crime. "I didn't mean to disturb you, I was just drinking water."

"Oh, don't worry, it's alright," he said, wondering why him waking up had been such a big deal.

"Would you like to have something? You've been asleep for hours. It's evening, actually."

He hadn't realised that he had slept through the entire afternoon. But it explained his growling stomach and parched throat. After all, he had been travelling in the woods for a long time; he had been sleep-deprived.

As Ruth and Evander had dinner, which comprised of a large platter of delicious fruits – most of which were entirely foreign to him – and a glass of milk, Ruth casually asked about Evander's life back home.

Chapter 1

"Yeah, Mexico's a great place," he began. "Not for me, of course." He scoffed.

When Ruth's eyebrows lifted questioningly, he remembered she didn't know. How could she? So, rather reluctantly, he began telling her what life really was like – not focusing too much on the painful details – because even though she was a complete stranger, she was the closest thing he had ever had to a friend.

"So, they just torture you?" she asked, a demented look dawning on her face. "They just— just... imprison you and make you work like a slave? For no reason at all?"

"They don't *torture* me, Ruth. And they definitely haven't imprisoned me," Evander said, somehow feeling defensive and taken aback by how Ruth had framed his predicament. "It's for a reason. They're only trying to protect me."

"They didn't let you go to school, Evander!" Ruth exclaimed, horrified. "That's not protection. You don't leave the house, ever, except for *their* work. That's imprisonment. And all this work that they make you do... th-this is just all wrong!"

"It's not wrong…it's just a bit much at times. But they're only doing it to prepare me for the real world," Evander said and immediately realised just how meaningless those words sounded when put together. "They did let me come for this trip," he said.

"How?" she asked in disbelief. "I just assumed you must have run away."

"Well, like I said, they haven't imprisoned me. They were reluctant because they thought it'd be unsafe. But they agreed after I begged them," he said, recalling the heated argument he'd had with his family. "It was my 18th birthday, so it was slightly easier to convince them."

"If you're 18, why don't you leave them entirely? You are legally of age, right?"

The thought was tempting. But he dismissed it. He had spent years being told by everyone in his family how he was just way too fragile and needed his family's protection to survive. And now more than before, he was convinced that they had been right. Didn't he just lose his way three days into his little trip?

Chapter 1

Even if his family treated him like a castaway 90% of the time, he knew he needed his family, not only residency-wise, but financially too. Julio didn't talk to Evander as much as a normal loving father would, but he always ensured Evander had the money he needed; like for this trip – he had been given far more than he'd ever need.

But he didn't want to tell any of this to Ruth, because saying it out loud would confirm it, make it truly true – the fact that he was afraid and wanted to remain safe under the wing of his indifferent father. Besides, why should he be taking any advice from Ruth? Who was she, anyway? A frail girl living all by herself in an abandoned village, being treated like an outcast herself. He realised her suggestion had rubbed him the wrong way. He didn't like just how repulsed she was by his family. Suddenly, he felt angry at Ruth.

"Yeah, well, the world beyond these woods is a lot more complicated than Bosque Tranquilo," he said with an air of superiority. "I don't expect you to understand."

His response had caught her off-guard and her eyes became closed-off, her expression unreadable. She got up, scooping the empty platters, and began cleaning them.

"So, when will you be leaving?" she asked after a couple of minutes, her back turned to him.

So, what, she wanted him to leave now? Because of his comment? The villagers disliking her was making more and more sense by the minute.

"Don't worry. I won't be troubling you for too long," he said, as he wrapped his jacket tighter around himself and tried to drift into sleep.

Much to his dismay, he did, in spite of having slept for hours.

His dream started with his mother's hand slipping out of his and her veering off into the depths of an inky gloom. The dream changed, and he was ten, surrounded by his family. Each one of them took turns at chiding him, for not ironing the clothes right, for not cleaning the kitchen well enough, for licking the frosting on his brother's birthday cake, and for being born and rendering his mother lifeless. Their outraged, hateful voices overlapped in a blur of

Chapter 1

loathing. He fell to his knees, bawling his eyes out, wishing more than anything to get out of this pain.

He woke with a start, drenched in sweat, face slick with tears. Evander had never even seen his mother, except in pictures. But she must have been an angel if his family punished him for her death, even though he had been an infant when it had happened. His father had never said this to him, but he had learnt it when he was met with infuriated scowls every time he mentioned his birthday. And his siblings, of course. They were very explicit about why they hated him.

"A-are you okay, Evander?" Ruth said, her voice shaky with worry, as she appeared by his side. "It must have been a terrible nightmare. D-do you want some water?"

Before he could answer, she ran off to get him some. As he drained the glass, he realised Ruth was watching him carefully. Like she was concerned; like she actually cared.

"Are you alright?" she asked, taking the glass from him. "No, of course not. I'm sorry. Do you want something? Maybe milk? I could get you some of those special berries that grow in a thicket at the edge of the woods if you—"

"I'm fine," Evander said softly.

"Oh, well, okay," she said, as if confused about what she must do now. "Do you want to talk about it? Sometimes it helps."

"No," he said, amazed. "But thank you."

"Alright. I'll let you rest then."

She returned to her cot and resumed reading a black leather-bound book. He thought of asking her what she was reading, but she probably wouldn't tell him. Despite her strangeness, Evander felt a tinge of warmth towards Ruth. Never before had someone shown him such kindness. Come to think of it, he couldn't even recall ever being asked if 'he was okay'.

His mind wandered to the conversation they'd had earlier. Even though it had ended sourly, it had been the best one Evander had ever had. No one had ever considered him worth their time or had been interested in what he had to say, but Ruth had been. Maybe Ruth really was his friend, even if they had met such a short time ago. He was wrong to have been rude to her. He should have been grateful. She was

Chapter 1

letting him stay with her – how could he ever repay her for that?

There was a sharp, deafening cry of pain from outside the cottage that made Evander jump, but it didn't sound human. Ruth looked up from her book, as alarmed as Evander. The cry resounded again, and he realised it wasn't human after all. The howl had been a cow's.

"Lesly!" Ruth exclaimed in horror as she dropped her book on her bed and rushed out the door, slamming it shut behind her. So, the cow had a name. Lesly. Interesting.

But when Evander stood up, thinking it would be considered decent manners to go see what was wrong with Lesly, he found something even more interesting. The leather book Ruth had been reading lay ajar on her bed.

And its pages were blank.

2.

EVANDER – The Stranger

He knew he shouldn't have.

Evander knew what he was doing was wrong and he still picked up the book and flipped through its pages. Not a single word coloured any of the pages of the thick book.

Bewilderment flooding his mind, he heard shuffling outside and knew Ruth must be returning. He quickly placed the book like Ruth had left it and ran to the door, as if he had been coming outside. Ruth opened the door and was startled to see Evander right there.

"I-I was coming out to see what was wrong with Lesly," he said, trying to conceal the sweat that trickled down his temple.

"Uhh... i-it is nothing, Evander," she said, quite panicky herself. "She was just hungry."

Chapter 2

"Really? That didn't sound like it," Evander said, suspicious of Ruth now. "She sounded like she was in pain."

Ruth let out a breathy laugh as she got into her bed and pulled up her blanket. "She's always been rather dramatic. But really, she's fine. I'll take her to the meadow in some time."

Evander sat on his rug, and acted like he was writing in his little diary, while he was actually trying to observe Ruth, who was absorbed in her book. Her eyes moving from side to side as if she was reading words... non-existent words. What the hell was going on? What was her deal? Was she crazy or something?

As the night dragged on, Ruth continued reading. But *what*? It didn't make sense. Then, after what must have been an hour after Lesly's crying, she shut the book and placed it in a small backpack Evander hadn't noticed before. She walked up to the vessels and opened a container that she took water from and drained her glass. As she returned to her cot, Evander realised that the container she had been drinking from was different from the one he was getting his water from. Maybe he was getting paranoid now, like an apophenic. It could have been for a multitude of reasons, but given that the girl read a blank book with unbelievable concentration, trusting her was getting difficult for Evander.

****

Somehow, with his thoughts all muddled between the secret Ruth was hiding and the horrendous nightmares that Evander was slipping in and out of, he had managed to get through the night.

When he opened his eyes, pale yellow daylight streamed through the ajar door. Ruth was humming an unfamiliar melody as she poured milk from one vessel to another. Maybe she had just milked Lesly. There was something strange about that too. Was it even possible for them to give milk if they weren't pregnant? That's what he remembered reading in an encyclopaedia, anyway.

"Oh, you're up," she said cheerfully, interrupting his train of thought. "I was thinking I could go and get these really amazing berries from the forest. You'll like them a lot."

"Okay," he said, unsure why she was telling him this.

Chapter 2

"I'll have to travel a good distance, so I'll take time to return. Could you just keep an eye on Lesly while I'm away?"

"Uh, sure," he said, wondering why Lesly would need to be kept an eye on.

As Ruth picked up a basket and hurried out the door, Evander realised what an excellent opportunity this was to unveil Ruth's secret.

When he had confirmed that Lesly was asleep, he carefully shut the door, ran towards Ruth's cot, and found her backpack. He emptied it, and the only things that spilt out were the leather-bound book, a crystal bottle, and a necklace with a gigantic iridescent diamond for a pendant.

Evander stared at the necklace in astoundment. Surely, Ruth was smart enough to know how precious the pendant was. She didn't need to stay here, in this awful village in a tiny hut. She could sell the necklace and have enough money to live wherever she pleased. But it could have been something she had inherited from her family, something too invaluable to sell. But then what was the crystal bottle for? Water? No, the bottle was much too fancy and significant for that. It was made of real, expensive crystal.

All the three items were so inexplicably bizarre, Evander had to know their purpose, their importance. He just *had* to; it was one of those impossible mysteries that he just couldn't resist diving into. So, he quickly whipped out his phone and snapped pictures of them. Maybe when he got back home, he could find something out.

He dumped the items back into the bag and placed it back in its place. As he stared at the pictures he had clicked, another idea occurred to him. Maybe he could sneak a peek at the contents of the container from which Ruth got her water. It might not be different from regular water, but what did he have to lose? So, he walked up to the large vessel when the door burst open, and Ruth entered, making him jump out of his shoes.

"Geez! You scared me!" he exclaimed, trying to get his heartbeat back to normal.

"Well, did you think I wasn't going to return?" she asked, looking rather amused.

Chapter 2

"N-no, of course not, I— I just thought there was more time," he managed. He walked over to the container he got his water from, poured himself a glass and chugged it down as if that was what he had intended to do in the first place.

"I got those berries I was talking about," Ruth said and showed Evander her basket, filled to the brim with juicy berries the colour of blood.

"Wow. I don't think I've ever seen them. We don't get these elsewhere?" he asked, picking one up to examine it closely.

"I have no idea." Ruth dumped some of the bounty onto a plate and handed it to Evander. "Breakfast." She grinned.

Evander wanted to smile too, he really did, because Ruth seemed exactly like the kind of person he had always wanted for a friend. But she wasn't his friend. No, a friend is supposed to be someone you can trust. But Evander found himself growing more and more distrustful of this girl, so different from the villagers, so secretive, so friendly, so helpful, so easy to talk to, yet so strange. He had no idea who she really was. The only thing he knew about her was her name. Although, for all he knew, that wasn't true either.

"What?" she asked, a serene smile playing across her lips. "Are you alright, Evander?"

"No," he said. "No. I need to leave. I need to go back home."

"Why?" she asked coolly, filling her plate with the fruit, and pouring a glass of milk. "So they can continue to treat you like a criminal? So you can continue to stay unhappy for the rest of your life?"

He had to admit it – her response had been completely unforeseen. But it was also just the kind of thing that could set him off. And it did.

"Yeah, you're right. Maybe I shouldn't go." The sarcasm in his voice was glaringly obvious. "Maybe I should just stay here with a stranger who reads a blank book, has bizarre tattoos, drinks strange water and has weird diamond necklaces. Maybe I should just stay here with someone I know absolutely nothing about and pretend that we're friends. Yeah, that sounds like an excellent idea."

Chapter 2

"How do you know about that?" she asked in a measured voice, staring at him with an unreadable expression, all her cool pulverised.

"None of your damn business!" he hissed coldly. "You're a liar! And you're hiding some weird secret. I better leave this wretched place as soon as I can. Who knows what you're capable of."

Evander's fury was running so high, he didn't even feel sorry for implying that Ruth could be a murderer; he stuffed his things back into his backpack and as he tossed it over his shoulder, his cheek was met with a smack so powerful, he was knocked to his knees. Rubbing his cheek gingerly, he looked up to see that it was Ruth's palm that had delivered the blow that had numbed his cheek.

"I may be many things, Evander," she said, her hazel eyes burning with resentment, "but I am NOT a liar. I never lied to you about *anything.*"

Speechless as he was, Evander couldn't sit there and gawk at Ruth. That would make him seem weak. He somehow found both, the courage and the words.

"Fine. Then tell me what's *really* in that closed container." He waited for her answer, but she just glowered at him. She finally opened her mouth to speak but that's when a knock on the door interrupted her.

Ruth took a deep breath as if to calm herself down and went to open the door. Evander stood up, rubbing his cheek, certain that Ruth had bruised his face.

When the door opened, in came the person Evander had been least expectant to see here, in Bosque Tranquilo. His pepper-coloured hair was all messy. His face wore an arrogant look – like it always did – and his mouth was set in a permanent frown.

"Hi, is my brother Evander here?" he asked Ruth in a desperate attempt to appear polite. She gestured for him to come in.

"Diego!" Evander exclaimed, not because of happiness or relief. But because he actually couldn't believe his brother – the one who considered everybody else beneath him – was there. In Bosque Tranquilo. For him.

Chapter 2

"Yeah, yeah," he said apathetically. "You look like you're ready. Let's get out of this place." He wrinkled his nose in disgust as his dark brown eyes scanned the cottage, clearly unimpressed.

"How'd you know I was here?" Evander asked.

"We can talk about all of that on the plane," Diego answered coldly. "Now, let's leave." He turned and walked towards the door, where Ruth was still standing.

Evander followed him, trying to figure out what he should say to Ruth, when suddenly, his vision was all hazy. His mind went numb and then, the only thing visible was darkness and the only thing audible was silence.

3.

EVANDER – The Poisoning

When he came to, the only thing he could register was a sickening pain everywhere in his body. His body ached so horribly, he wanted to slip back into unconsciousness. He slowly opened his eyes and saw a weeping, gasping and then smiling Ruth.

Before he could even get up, she had trapped him in an embrace. It was hers. The lavender scent that embellished the cottage's air was hers. She released him, and the scent faded slightly.

"Oh, you're okay," she said, wiping her tears and sighing with relief.

Nothing was making much sense. Why had he fainted? How was he okay now? And why did Ruth even care?

He sat up to see he was lying on Ruth's cot. Beside him, was a glass and some bottles, filled with green and brown stuff that looked like plants. He realised

Chapter 3

his mouth tasted really weird, like leaves or something.

"Wh-what happened?" he asked with a shaky voice.

"You fainted like the hopeless weasel you are," Diego said from behind Ruth. "Let's just please get out of here now."

"Why did I faint?" he asked Ruth, whose look of worry was only getting graver.

"You were... poisoned." She whispered the word 'poisoned' like it brought her pain. "Luckily, I was able to rescue you. My herbs turned out to be useful after all."

"What kind of poisoning? Oh yes, my stomach is probably not used to the fruits you gave me."

"Unfortunately, that isn't it," Ruth said, wiping a tear that had just trickled down her cheek.

"Oh, you have *got* to be kidding me," Diego said with frustration. "Why don't you just come out when you're done?" He stormed out the cottage and slammed the door behind him, making Ruth wince.

"What do you mean? It isn't food poisoning?"

"No," she said. "And it could have killed you. It's a good thing you were still here when it happened. Nothing else could have saved you."

"So, what you're saying is... you saved my life?" he asked, although he knew that that was exactly what she was saying. But he still didn't understand. How could he have died? What kind of poisoning had he had?

"Can you just answer one question for me? Honestly?"

"What?"

"Did you touch my book? Or necklace? Or the bottle?"

Evander didn't answer because he was sure Ruth knew he had. Her face darkened and she sighed helplessly.

"So... I got poisoned because I touched that stuff?" he finally asked when Ruth hadn't looked up from the ground even after two whole minutes of being in deep thought. "You know how sketchy that sounds right?"

Chapter 3

"Don't worry 'bout it," Ruth said, the worry in her eyes dissipating all of a sudden. "Your brother's getting impatient. You should probably go."

"What? No!" Evander said, taken aback. "I am not leaving until I have answers. You need to tell me, Ruth. You owe me the truth."

"I saved your damn life," she said testily. "I don't owe you anything. Now get out of my house."

All his life, Evander had been ordered around. All his life, he had shut his mouth and done what he had been told to. All his life, he had refused his instincts. But at that instant, Evander wasn't wondering about what Ruth would do. He couldn't care less about how angry his questions made her. He *had* to know. Especially when it could have cost him his life.

"No," he said firmly, standing up. "I won't leave until I get an answer. You must tell me."

"I cannot!" Ruth screamed, tears building up in her eyes as if she really wanted to, but something was holding her back. "Would you please, for the love of God, leave?"

Even though it sounded like it, Ruth hadn't been requesting. Suddenly, she was shoving him out the door, and no matter how hard he retaliated, Evander was outpowered by Ruth. She thrust his backpack in his arms and gave him one last push, and the wooden door shut with a loud thud between them, inches from his face.

Evander turned to look at the gawking villagers, who whispered unpleasantly and rushed to their homes. There was a jeep waiting for Evander close to the forest line with his brother Diego inside.

There was a gap in his memory.

How had he gotten here? This vast expanse that seemed like a village. He remembered being lost in the woods, the edge of which Diego waited now, but how had he ended up here? Right outside the door of a cottage? He wondered if he should knock the door and ask the cottage's owner—

"I'm leaving!" Diego's voice echoed. "You comin' or not?"

So, with his mind more clouded than it had ever been, Evander sprinted towards the car.

4.

RUTH – The Warning

Perched at the windowsill, Ruth watched the snow that glistened in the silver moonlight on the pavement. Toronto looked like an urban heaven when covered with snow. That's why Ruth's favourite season had always been winter – snow could make anything look pure and beautiful.

Her eyes moved from the snow-washed pavement to the maple leaf that had just been delivered by the breeze. A gush of wind, and it had transformed into a man. The calm Ruth was feeling evaporated. As the man neared, her heart hammered against her chest more and more impatiently. He was almost at the door. This was not going to be good.

She straightened her floral white dress and tried to compose herself as she walked to the door and waited for the doorbell.

TING.

Mythil was pokerfaced, but Ruth knew better than to assume he'd be forgiving. In fact, the first time they had met, she'd had an intuition that he didn't like her. His bloodshot, downturned eyes looked tired and bored, as if he had been dreading this meeting. To be fair, so had Ruth.

He was wearing a gown patterned with galaxies, moons, stars and symbols similar to Ruth's tattoo; his silver hair and beard were close-cropped. Mythil had a very powerful aura. Whenever he entered a room, the energy he projected gave a clear message: he was not one to mess with. Even now, he stood straight and his expression hardened. His mere gaze made Ruth feel like she was in dire trouble.

"You're early, sir," she said politely, closing the door as Mythil walked into the house, scrutinizing it.

"Well, some of us respect rules," he said, his rumbling voice dripping with resentment.

He took a seat at the dining table. Ruth did too, and watched him take his time examining every inch of the living room.

It wasn't much, after all, she hadn't been there for too long, and décor wasn't high on her priority list.

Chapter 4

Still, she had managed to make it look minimalistic and gorgeous – the walls painted a lovely shade of violet, an L-shaped leather sofa stood against one side of the room, with a coffee table in front of it.

"Are you so incredibly irresponsible to keep the *Elixir of Death* right in the open?!" Mythil bellowed infuriatedly, gesturing to the pitcher filled with a golden liquid on the coffee table. "What if an undead enters? What are you going to tell them? That it's coloured water?!"

"Sir, I assure you it'll be hidden before any undead can enter. You needn't worry about it," she said calmly.

"Fine." He exhaled exasperatedly. "Then what should I worry about? Oh, I know. Probably the fact that you erased the memories of two undead boys in spite of knowing that it is absolutely FORBIDDEN!"

"Sir, I didn't have a choice," Ruth said defensively.

"That's complete nonsense!" Mythil said heatedly. "There cannot possibly be a situation grave enough to force you to take such a dramatic step."

"Evander had seen my book, and *Crystalvocatio*," Ruth explained. "He was even poisoned! He kept asking me what I was drinking. What could I have done?"

"You could've been... careful," Mythil said slowly in an attempt to mask his anger. "You shouldn't have let him in at all. When he asked for help, you should've said no."

"But sir, that would've seemed very suspicious."

"Well, you know what? The villagers of Bosque Tranquilo were very sceptical about you anyway. The way you arrived out of the blue, with a cow and a concrete house. They knew something was wrong with you."

"Yes, sir, but—"

"But what?" Mythil snapped. "Do you know how dangerous this could end up becoming? A trivial doubt in their mind can destroy our civilisation, Ruth. And your abrupt departure—"

"I was *ordered* to leave, wasn't I?"

"Well, obviously! Because of your incapability of making a single correct decision!"

Chapter 4

"I agree that I shouldn't have erased their memories, but sir, you know—"

"I know nothing except the fact that you have been unbelievably ignorant of The Kingdom's rules and if this continues, you shall find your case annulled!" He growled.

Ruth flinched, surprised and afraid of the intensity of Mythil's anger.

He stood up and composed himself. "It already would have been, had I been your supervisor," he said in a calmer voice. "But I'm not. Mr. Bundleheckles is. He has assured me that you shall not cause any more trouble. If you do, keep in mind, Ruth, that your case *will* be cancelled. There will be no third chance. *One* more mistake, and you will be sent to where you belong."

Ruth couldn't argue further. Despite his behaviour and the unexplained dislike for Ruth, Mythil was, of course, right.

"Your silence tells me you shall take care next time," he said, watching her carefully. "Do, whatever you must, but discretely."

He headed towards the door, and Ruth followed. Opening the door, he stepped out and turned to say, "Mr. Bundleheckles has an unfathomable faith in you. I just hope you don't disappoint him."

"I won't, sir," she said in a small voice.

Mythil walked away, and as he reached the pavement, a wisp of wind engulfed him, and where he stood before was a sparrow now. The sparrow took off, flying into the inky sky.

Ruth slammed the door hard.

The moment she had decided that she would go through with this insane plan, she knew it'd be hard. Ruth knew this mission would be the hardest thing she'd ever done, but at the time, there seemed to be no alternative. Every morning, it took every last ounce of her energy to get up and try, knowing she was somehow destined to fail.

Ruth plumped on the couch - exhausted by the scolding - staring at the pitcher of golden syrup. What would have happened had Evander actually seen the *Elixir of Death* in that large vessel? Would she have told him the truth? No, of course not. She couldn't have. That would've been preposterous.

Chapter 4

Besides, he wouldn't have even believed her; and if he had, he would probably have run for his life instead of staying to help her. And honestly, Ruth wouldn't have blamed him.

She had seen his life, the entirety of it the moment they had shaken hands. It was one of the many powers *The Kingdom of the Lifeless* had given her. The only things Ruth had seen in Evander's life were sorrow, loneliness and suffering. From the little time she had spent with him, she knew he deserved so much better; she knew he should have been able to escape his awful family's clutches and create his own identity.

Ruth felt a pang of guilt whenever she thought about him. Maybe, if she had been careful, more friendly and less shady, she could have convinced him to run. To live his life to the fullest; to pursue his dream of writing. Instead, what he got in return for trying to be her friend was poison.

In that moment, Ruth hated herself so much, she had to drain a glass of *Elixir of Death* to clear her head. It was a type of elixir, yes, but it burned her insides as it made its way down her throat.

It was all way too much – the time constraint, the unspeakable challenges and the guilt of her mistakes... Ruth's fatigue and distress had taken over her. Not wanting to think of anything else that upset her – which was pretty much everything – Ruth collapsed on the sofa and decided to get some rest.

Unfortunately, falling asleep wasn't equivalent to 'escape from troubles'. At least for Ruth.

5.

RUTH – The Murders of The Forbes

The dream was back. The exact same one that had tormented her for the past 15 days.

Ruth's mother, Veronica, was gasping, clawing at the hands of a woman dressed in all-black.

"TELL ME!" the woman hollered, tightening her grip on Veronica's throat. "Tell me where the jewel is hidden!"

"I-I c-can't," Veronica croaked between small ragged breaths. Her emerald eyes dilated in fear and her face was starting to turn purple.

Ruth reached for her mother but felt her hands trapped in the stiff grasp of the accomplice of the strangler. She was much smaller, but still quite strong. Her beady black eyes stared into Ruth's as she hissed, "You dare interfere, and it'll be your last day here."

The muscular woman kept yelling in Veronica's ear, threatening her to spill the jewel's location. But Ruth's mother didn't. She couldn't have: she was bound by way more than an NDA – she was sworn to silence by her integrity. But the strangler didn't know that. She only continued to hurt Veronica, wringing her throat till her hands finally dropped to her sides, till her eyes stopped blinking, till she had exhaled one last breath of air. Veronica's lifeless body thudded to the floor, her ajar eyes staring at Ruth accusingly.

Ruth felt paralysed. She couldn't move, she couldn't scream, she couldn't even breathe. All she could do was watch her mother's face. So unbelievably beautiful once. So unbelievably dead now.

All at once, thousands of visions flooded Ruth's brain: countless summers spent at the beach, sunscreen being lathered on her skin by her mom, lazy afternoons on the kitchen counter, talking her mom's ear off as she baked Ruth's favourite apple pie, weeping in her mother's lap after a silly nightmare, dancing with her mom after winning her very first painting competition.

Chapter 5

"She was useless," someone said, forcing Ruth out of her montage of happy memories.

She tore her eyes from Veronica's face. She realised it was the girl tying her hands who had just spoken.

"What will we do now, Astoria?" the girl asked the strangler, sounding worried.

"Oh, the man should come in soon enough. Don't stress, Maxine. I've got it covered," Astoria said, completely unbothered at her failure.

"My father doesn't know anything," Ruth said, realising this was her chance to do something helpful, be useful. She was desperate to save her father's life. "My mom went to all the meetings, and she was ordered not to tell Dad anything! He doesn't know anything about the jewel! I-I swear!"

"Oh, really?" Maxine asked, twisting Ruth's wrists.

"Maybe we should get some info out of this one," Astoria said, eyeing Ruth like she was a piece of meat.

Just when Ruth thought she could distract them, the door burst open and her dad, Dylan, entered. His eyes widened in disbelief as they landed on his wife's dead body, and he was about to scream when Astoria got hold of him.

She trapped him in a headlock, and pulled out a dagger from her pocket. She held it at Dylan's throat, gently pressing the blade into his skin.

"WHERE IS THE JEWEL?" Astoria thundered.

"I-I don't know," Dylan said, his hazel eyes more afraid than Ruth had ever seen. "The trust has my name only for namesake. Veronica ran it. Only she knew about the jewel."

"More lies," Maxine hissed behind Ruth. "Maybe he doesn't care much about his life. But we have this awesome gold mine right here," she said, giving Ruth a jerk.

Astoria grinned and let go of Dylan just as Maxine let go of Ruth. Before she could even blink, Ruth was imprisoned by Astoria's strong, muscular arms and the dagger was at her throat now.

"SPEAK!" She yelled at Ruth's father. "Speak, or your daughter dies a very early, unnecessary and painful death. Where is the damn jewel?"

Dylan's face contorted in suffering – he too, like Veronica was big on keeping promises and fulfilling

Chapter 5

one's duties. But Ruth was in trouble, and Ruth knew her father was having the biggest dilemma of his life. She wanted to tell him to run away and get help, to not utter a single word. But his little girl had a blade 6 inches away from her heart. He was not going to run away, Ruth knew that with certainty.

Instead of surrendering, her father chose a third option.

He grabbed a cleaver knife from the kitchen counter behind him and advanced towards Astoria. But she was faster. She hurled Ruth to her partner and before Dylan could attack her, Astoria jammed her dagger into his gut and there was a sickening sound of impact as she pulled it back out. Deep red blood poured from his mouth and a visceral scream escaped Ruth. His weapon clattered to the floor, next to his wife's body. Dylan collapsed on the floor, blood oozing out the puncture in his abdomen.

Ruth struggled against Maxine's hands, she yelled for her father and cried for her mother and she begged for Astoria to stop, tears filling her eyes and blurring her vision. But no one seemed to be able to hear her.

"Tell me where the jewel is," Astoria said, kneeling next to Ruth's father. "Tell me, and I won't touch your daughter. Hell, I'll even get you to the hospital. Just tell me where you've hidden that jewel."

"Y-you will p-pay," Dylan stuttered, his voice raspy and weak.

Then, he went still.

Something in Ruth went out like a light. She stopped thrashing and shrieking and bawling. She lost all her energy as it registered that she would never see them again. She had lost her parents forever.

Astoria turned to Ruth, her amber eyes ablaze with fury and irritation. Suddenly, she had Ruth in a headlock and her forearm pressed into Ruth's throat, crushing her windpipe.

"TELL ME WHERE THE JEWEL IS!"

"I don't know," Ruth answered as calmly as her hoarse voice allowed.

"She's saying the truth," Maxine whispered to Astoria. "The owners aren't allowed to reveal the jewel's location to anyone. It is classified information. She's a kid, anyway. They wouldn't risk telling her."

Chapter 5

"Fine," Astoria grumbled. "Let's get out of here. We'll have to search for the jewel ourselves."

"Not before finishing her," Maxine said. "She'll tell the police, Astoria! She's too dangerous to be left alive."

"Mmhmm," Astoria said and pressed Ruth's throat even more strongly.

Seconds passed, and Ruth breathed one last time.

6.

RUTH – A Forbidden Answer

She woke up, soaked in cold, biting sweat, terrified to the core.

Every day, the dream had come to her, more realistic than reality. Every day, she'd sleep, knowing she'd have to relive the worst day of her life. Every day, she'd wake up, tears having dampened her cheeks and pillow, her blanket balled up in her clenched fist.

The first time the dream came to Ruth, she was awe-struck by the vividness of every detail. Usually, dreams, no matter how realistic, feel vague and you tend to skip over the details. Usually, you wake up and forget some aspects of the dream. But this one was nothing like that. Ruth saw every tiny nuance, felt every sensory feeling – whether that was the harshness in Maxine's voice, or the helplessness in her mother's eyes or the impact of the wound that had killed her

Chapter 6

father. It was a very unique form of torture. At least that's what it felt like.

Ruth sometimes wondered if it was like this for all souls – if they all saw only one dream, the dream where it all ended and where it all began.

Ruth wiped her tears now, and noticed that the tip of her forefinger was turning transparent. She rushed to the pitcher and poured the gleaming *Elixir of Death* into a glass that she soon emptied. Setting the glass back down precariously, she watched her fingertip turn opaque again.

The burning sensation of the elixir helped her return to the present, and she realised that she was running out of time.

5 months was all she had been given to find Astoria and Maxine and return the jewel back to the rightful authorities. She had squandered 15 days already.

Moreover, all she had for help was Lesly, her dingle. Dingles were shape-changing animal spirits who aided the souls who returned to Earth for a certain purpose. Ruth had always suspected that the decision-makers of *The Kingdom of the Lifeless*, called Mentors, had conveniently given her one of their faintest dingles. Ruth was Lesly's very first assignment, so Lesly was quite weak and had a lot to learn. Still, she had been resourceful so far.

The assistance dingles provide can be invaluable, because they have a great sense of smell and intuition. This is how Lesly knew that Astoria and Maxine were hiding out in Bosque Tranquilo. Which is why Ruth had gone there in the first place. But when she couldn't find them and was ordered to leave due to the 'Evander' incident, Lesly had said they were here, in Toronto. So, Ruth had come running to Toronto.

But so far, the hunt for the murderers had brought Ruth no luck. Finding them would be difficult in a city this big and crowded. And something told Ruth she couldn't do it herself, aided only by Lesly. She needed a companion but there was no one she could ask.

A part of her wanted to give up, cancel her case and go where she needed to be going. Never before had she done something so immensely tough. She'd lived a very short and happy life. All she had ever seen was comfort and happiness. Come to think of it, the

Chapter 6

hardest thing she had ever done was pass her AP Calculus examination.

Ruth thought back to her old life, reaching across millions of miles in her head, trying to hold onto the past that was slipping away. She saw herself painting in her room, surrounded by tubes of paint and paintbrushes; she saw herself baking with her mother; she saw herself picking lilies in a garden with her best friend Gracie; she saw herself arguing over a maths question with Noah (the math genius in her group); she saw herself living her little life.

But that was gone. Forever. Because what lay ahead of her now wasn't just difficult, it was also a little morally grey. And that wasn't something Ruth had dealt with before. Or ever imagined she would need to.

Lesly bounded into the room – now in the form of a tabby cat instead of a cow. "I was just trying to look for Astoria and Maxine and I think they're in some kind of forest. I have a feeling that they aren't that far away. We should go and look for them."

"It's almost midnight," Ruth said, looking at the wall clock above the dining table. "Do you think we'll be able to look for them in the dark?"

"Well, we have to try, right?"

"Yes, yes, we do," Ruth said. "I'll get ready in a second and then we can go."

****

As Ruth and Lesly travelled back in the direction of her house, she was overcome with anxiety. No matter how many forests and cities they looked through, the girls were nowhere to be found, in spite of Lesly's help. Ruth felt like Astoria and Maxine were very close to the jewel, at least closer than she was to finding them.

"This isn't working, Ruth," Lesly said in a dejected voice. "My powers can only help this much, unfortunately. We've had no real luck in looking for them. I'm starting to think we need to do something else to better our chances."

"What do you mean? What more could we do?"

"Well, perhaps we need a fresh perspective. Another pair of eyes to look at our predicament objectively."

Chapter 6

Ruth thought about it. Maybe another person with new ideas could help them make progress. She certainly wasn't making any on her own. "Yeah, you might be right."

"But who would we ask? *The Kingdom of the Lifeless* won't allow any of their employees to assist us."

"No. No, we cannot use anyone from The Kingdom. We need to ask someone else. I think the only person who could help us is an undead."

"But that's strictly forbidden, Ruth!" Lesly said, alarmed. "Telling an undead anything at all will have a severe penalty!"

"I have no other choice, Lesly," Ruth said, realising just how true it was. "If I talk to anyone in The Kingdom, given my recent indiscretion, I would certainly get into trouble. And the two of us aren't enough to search for either Astoria and Maxine or the jewel. We're running out of time with each passing day. We need to do something."

"Are you sure about this, Ruth?"

"Yes," she answered with conviction. "We have to do this. We have to ask an undead for help. It's the only way we'll find my murderers."

7.

EVANDER – The Beckoning

Evander stared at the fluffy white clouds out the window. He was traveling back home after his little vacation, with his brother Diego.

"How did you know where I was?" he asked Diego.

Diego removed his earphones and looked up from his phone, rolling his eyes. "Your mobile has a GPS tracker in it, dummy. Also, we had Miguel following you until you disappeared in the woods and he couldn't find you. He called Dad and Dad forced me to come get you."

"Miguel?" Evander asked in disbelief. "Dad had his bodyguard spy on me? While I was on a vacation? What the hell?!"

"He was afraid you'd run away," Diego said. "Why would he trust you? You're a complete idiot. He couldn't just let you go wherever you pleased."

Diego returned to staring at his phone screen and Evander returned to looking at the clouds. He couldn't decide how he felt about being spied by his own family. They didn't trust him enough to go on a vacation by himself. But, a part of him felt nice. Maybe they were doing all of this because they were protecting him, like his dad, Julio said. They were protecting him from the horrors of the real world. With these conflicting thoughts swirling in his head, Evander drifted to sleep.

****

As he moved onto scrubbing the last pot, Evander wondered if his family was ever going to let him have his own life.

He was 18 already and the only thing he spent most of his time doing was cleaning around the house or helping with his father's and brother's business. He hated everything about his life, including how controlling his family was. But he knew he needed their protection, given how incapable he was. There was no way he could actually build a life for himself right now. Even though he was technically an adult, he wasn't great at decision making. He had no idea how the world worked, or how difficult being on his own could be. He hadn't even had an actual education, just stuff he'd learned from books and

Chapter 7

encyclopaedias his stepmother, Bella, left lying around.

Even though his family illtreated him, there were times he contemplated if he deserved it. There were times, late at night, when he would think if he did indeed deserve punishment for being the reason his mother was dead. Besides, his family wasn't terrible. It was only... not good. Things could be a lot worse. Like when Evander had requested to go on a solo trip for his 18th birthday, they could have denied him permission. But they let him go. Granted, he was being spied on, but that was just his father's twisted way of looking out for him. The actual problem was that he couldn't remember the last bit of his trip to Venezuela that had been pretty great otherwise.

He recalled trekking through the mountain terrain and the lush greenery of the woods outlining Venezuela. He remembered enjoying the splendour of nature whilst recording every detail in his diary. While he had read the diary many times, no part of the descriptions helped fill the gaps in his memory. Evander could even remember the moment he had realised how lost he was after making some wrong turns. He had come upon an abandoned village, and the next thing he knew, he was standing right outside a cottage's door. All the events that took place between these two instances seemed to have been sucked right out of his brain. In fact, after they had returned home, Evander had asked Diego about this.

"I came there to get you, and the next thing I remember is you appearing in front of that door," he had said, unbothered at Evander's unease.

Evander loved mysteries. He was naturally curious and loved asking questions. So, when this question wasn't answered with enough credibility to satisfy him, it drove him up the wall. He *hated* not knowing stuff.

"How long are you gonna scrub that pot, doofus?" Juliana asked, suddenly appearing in the kitchen doorway and startling Evander. She was his elder sister, the one who had helped his brother torment him all his life.

Ugh, her again, he thought, rinsing the pot and placing it with rest of the washed dishes.

He turned to look at her and saw her sneering at him, her eyebrows arched to show how much she

Chapter 7

enjoyed his misery. It was painful to look at her, not only because the sight of her face was followed by some form of torture, but also because she resembled Evander's dead mother, Elena, too much. She had those exact blue eyes and dimpled cheeks that made his mother look like an angel. Juliana was like a living reminder of the fact that Evander had caused his mother's death. There had been some complications with his birth, and his mother had passed away during the delivery. His family had always indirectly made him feel like he had murdered her and in moments of self-hate, it was easier to agree with them.

"What are you daydreaming about, loser?" Juliana asked snidely, giving him an arrogant half-smile. "Running away?"

"No," Evander said.

As he tried to escape from the kitchen, she grabbed his elbow tightly and shoved him backwards, her grin not wavering even a little.

"We're not kids anymore, Juliana," he said. "You should stop doing this."

"Why? Is Mom back home yet?" she asked, her grin disappearing and her eyes ablaze. "IS SHE?"

"N-no," he stammered.

"That's right. She's not and she will never be. Because of you. Don't you dare forget that, you little—"

"Juliana," someone said from behind her. It was Julio, Evander's father. "What have I told you about swearing? Don't let it happen around me."

He was wearing a turquoise velvet pant-suit and his hair was styled with a bucket of gel. His deep brown eyes had the same stern and indifferent look they always had. He looked at Evander and tried to mask his scowl but Evander had learned to read his father's expressions and decipher his mood over the years. Right now, he was pretty annoyed.

"We have to leave for that fundraiser event in an hour, Juliana," he said strictly. "Why aren't you ready yet? Go. Now."

Juliana nodded and left after shooting Evander a hateful look and whispering, "Be careful, or you might lose that little room Daddy gave you."

Chapter 7

Julio looked at Evander. "I know you're upset about me sending Miguel after you," he said, his face expressionless. "But you're not mature enough to be in a different country all by yourself, especially hiking in a forest. You're not exactly built to thrive in the wild. Surely, you know that."

"Yeah, because you've never let me leave the house alone."

"We've had this conversation a million times before. I am not going to stop protecting you just because you think I'm harsh. I'm not here to coddle you."

"Oh, I know that," Evander said bitterly. "But Diego and Juliana, them, you can coddle. Got it."

"They're different, Evander," Julio said. "You're more delicate. You need more time. If I go soft on you, you will never be able to make it on your own. And judging by the fact that you got lost in a forest with a map, I think you realise how right I've always been."

Evander didn't like his father but he had a point: he had always been right. He was also right about

Diego and Juliana being different from him. But everybody knew that Evander being delicate wasn't the reason.

"I'm taking Diego and Juliana out with me for an important work event," Julio said, supposedly ending their conversation. "Bella is out with her friends. Finish up your chores and go to bed by 10. None of us are going to be home before midnight."

With a curt nod, Evander's father was gone. As if this and Juliana's taunts weren't enough, Diego arrived to remind Evander that the "lawn needs to be mowed".

****

So, after spending the evening scrubbing pots and pans, mowing the lawn and completing a billion other chores, Evander had finally found time to die on his bed, with its decade old mattress and shredding bedspread in his enormously pygmy bedroom. In comparison to the rooms his siblings had, the room was a dump. He hated that no matter how many times he had sneaked in an air freshener, the room still returned to its original stinking self. Although, when he thought about it, the room was a big upgrade from the attic he used to live in when he

Chapter 7

was younger. Eventually, the spiders and disgusting insects that Diego and Juliana would release in the attic to torture Evander had gotten on his father's nerves. So, Julio decided to move him to the smallest room in the house because cleaning the area had become difficult. *That* was the problem with keeping his son in the *attic*. The *cleaning*.

He picked up his mobile phone (an ancient hand-me-down, courtesy of Diego, with a cracked screen and no audio), trying to remember the last time he had used it for leisure at home. He couldn't. He scrolled through the pictures of the forests and mountains he had clicked, his eyelids drooping with fatigue from the day's work. He was about to get some shut eye, when suddenly, he came upon an image that he couldn't place at all. It was of a black leather-bound book, a crystal bottle and a necklace with a diamond pendant that looked expensive enough to buy a small house in his neighbourhood. He couldn't believe his eyes. Where had this picture come from? Who took it? Whom did this stuff belong to?

Evander checked the date the picture had been clicked on and seeing '9th March' made him feel a stabbing ache behind his eyes. That was the day he had left that weird village with Diego.

Suddenly, a searing pain engulfed Evander's head and when it faded away to render Evander dizzy, he remembered. He remembered everything.

He recalled Ruth, and her strange little items, the different 'water' she drank, and how he had been poisoned because he had touched her book and necklace. He recalled how she had kicked him out when he had demanded to know the truth.

Had she... actually erased his memory? Nothing else could explain why Evander didn't remember meeting her or anything else that had happened after he found Bosque Tranquilo. So, it had been her. Ruth. She had actually erased his memory! She had erased her entire existence from his mind! It was an impressive feat, not to mention impossible. How had she done it? How on Earth had she actually erased his memories? Now, more than ever, he *had* to know. He had to know her secret.

He took out the diary he had taken with him on his trip and a pen and jotted down everything he could remember about Ruth. Maybe he could use this

Chapter 7

information in the future in case Ruth tried to erase his memory again.

A wave of exhilaration overtaking him – something people called 'adrenaline' – Evander found his backpack and emptied it. He then started stuffing in everything he could possibly need: packets of food, a dozen sets of clothing, a windbreaker, his phone, a compass, a flashlight, his passport, the diary, filled water bottles and a good amount of cash he had been saving up.

He took a quick shower, dressed in fresh comfortable clothes, tied up his shoes, got his gear in place and headed out the door. It was only 10.30 p.m. He'd be long gone before anyone even returned home.

Evander set off towards the closest airport to buy a ticket to Venezuela. He had to find Ruth to get his answers. Even if it was seemingly irrelevant, Evander needed to know the truth.

8.

EVANDER – A Bizarre Blessing

Retracing his steps was difficult but the compass helped. He did not dare make the mistake of looking at GPS after the disaster it had caused last time.

As he travelled, he found that the forest was much more horrifying at night. The auburn tree trunks looked almost black in the dark; wind whistled eerily through the shrubs; the foliage that looked so gorgeous in daylight cast ghostly shadows now. Add that to the lack of visibility with only the moon as a light source, and the entire thing felt right out of a horror movie. *Oh, the flashlight!* Evander remembered and pulling it out, switched it on. At least he could see better now. The sounds of all kinds of insects were overwhelmingly terrifying, but they motivated him to keep moving forward no matter how exhausted he felt. The dried leaves crunched under his feet, and he hoped desperately that there was no hungry carnivorous animal around. There probably wasn't,

Chapter 8

because none attacked Evander. He couldn't be more grateful.

Soon, he came upon a clearing in the woods, and though resting was the most dangerous of his options, he needed to. The forest air was so freezing, he could feel the cold in his bones. He knew stopping wouldn't warm him up but he was just too weary; his limbs couldn't go on. So, he found a rock to rest on, and arranged his gear to be able to flee if any hungry creature did find him. Although, if one did, it was highly unlikely that he could outrun it. Ultimately, fatigue defeated worry and he managed to drift off.

****

Evander woke up to find the forest bathed in sunlight. He got up, stretched and realised the weather had warmed up enough for him to strip off his windbreaker. As he resumed his little hike, he nibbled on some chips he had brought with him. Soon, the sun was high in the sky, and Evander was sweating like crazy. *Ugh*, he thought. *Will I ever reach the place before melting into a pile of Evander-flavoured ice cream?*

He did.

After losing track of the hours he had walked for, he found the woods were diminishing, and soon enough, in front of him was the village of Bosque Tranquilo.

The scene was much different from the one he had witnessed the last time he was here. Not a single villager was in sight – they were all in their huts, perhaps. Maybe because the white sun was beating down and the ground felt like lava.

Evander scanned the many cottages and found none that looked like Ruth's. They all had brown mud bricks, not the concrete ones. He couldn't spot a cow anywhere either. Had Lesly left? With Ruth? What was going on?

Bewilderment clouding his judgement for a moment, he wondered if he should return and forget about Ruth and her stupid secret. What did it matter anyway... how she had erased his memory. It didn't. Who cared about what she drank? Evander didn't. And he felt immensely asinine having travelled all the way from Mexico City to this rotten place just to quench his curiosity.

As he turned and started to walk back, he realised he didn't want to. He didn't want to walk all the way

Chapter 8

back in the scorching heat in the dangerous forest and then go back to his prison-of-a-home. Besides, who knew how he'd be treated when he returned home? He had removed his phone's sim card because he didn't want his family to track him. He didn't want to go back home and he didn't want to give up on the truth.

So, he turned again, and this time, headed towards the cottage closest to Ruth's. It was much smaller, and definitely much less clean. Pinching his nose to block out the stench of putrid things, Evander knocked on the dusty door. After a bunch of knocks, an old bald man with a tanned face opened the door. His dark brown eyes were circled with lilac rings and his wrinkles became more pronounced as he squinted at Evander.

"Oh, you are that boy," he said gruffly. "The one who lived with 'the mysteriously peculiar one'."

"What?" Evander asked confusedly.

"'The mysteriously peculiar one'," the man said slowly. "That's what we called that strange girl who just popped up out of nowhere and built a huge cottage all by herself overnight."

"Oh," Evander said; his suspicions were finally confirmed. "Can you tell me... about her? Like where she went? I mean, her cottage isn't here."

"Oh, I don't know that, boy," the old man grunted. "All I know is that she disappeared in the night the same day you left."

"What? Really?"

"Yes," the man said, yawning. "She left in the night, because when we awoke, there was nothing left. Not her cottage, not her cow and not her."

"Sir, do you know where she was headed to?"

"Like I said... all I know is that she disappeared sometime in the night. I don't know where she went or anything else. That is all the other villagers will be able to tell you, too."

Disappointment flooded Evander and he realised how hopeful he had been to see Ruth again. Almost how hopeful one would be to reunite with a friend. Now he'd never know where she had gone. He'd never know how she had erased his memory or saved his life or why he was poisoned. He'd never get his answers.

Chapter 8

"Can I go sleep now, boy?" the man grumbled and before Evander could thank him, slammed the door in Evander's face.

****

He dribbled a stone between his feet as he walked deeper into the forest, not thinking much about anything. All he really felt was discontent. Not only because his questions would remain unanswered but also because this had been his first real decision – the first choice he had ever made that could have changed the course of his entire life. But it hadn't exactly played out how he had planned.

Come to think of it, what had he planned, anyway? What had he thought Ruth would tell him? That she had powers? That magic was real? That she was a witch?

No, not that. When Evander gave it some thought, he realised he hadn't had anything in mind. He was simply... curious. But he had been hoping to meet Ruth. Probably because he just so desperately needed something different, something like an adventure, something, anything, that would get him out of his unrelenting nightmarish life. Or perhaps... because he just simply needed a friend.

The epiphany caught Evander off-guard and he pulled up short, staring at the stone he had been dribbling. That was it. All along, what had kept him going after Ruth was not only his curiosity but also his loneliness. He felt a pang of self-pity. How miserable must he have had to be to want a stranger who erased his memory for a friend?

Evander knew what he must do now. He *had* to find Ruth.

Except that she wasn't just waiting for him somewhere in the woods. For all he knew, she could be literally anywhere. None of the villagers knew anything about her whereabouts. There was no one else he could ask. It had been so many days since she had left this place, would anyone even remember seeing her if they had? Probably not. Hopelessness began strangling him as he dropped to the grass and buried his face in the soft grass blades. He just stayed that way until he heard footsteps.

He looked up to see a figure walking towards him from the thick woods. He watched and realised it was a woman. As she neared, she became clearer – she

Chapter 8

wore a violet blouse and a flowing yellow skirt patterned with flowers. She had auburn hair, with some strands of silver, and her eyes were a beautiful shade of emerald. She wore a tranquil smile and Evander instinctively knew she wasn't harmful. She wouldn't rob his possessions or murder him. She had an inexplicable aura of peace and happiness, and her smile was so contagious, Evander almost smiled back.

"Oh, what a beautiful place to be in, isn't it?" she said, her voice amazingly similar to something Evander had heard before.

"Uh, yeah, I guess," he said, examining the woman. "Who are you? Do you live in Bosque Tranquilo?"

"Oh, I live here, in the woods," she said, still smiling.

"Wh-what? How? How do you get food? How do you—"

"You want answers," the woman suddenly said – her eyes squeezed shut in concentration – cutting him off. "You're looking for something... yes? Or someone...a girl?"

"How did you—" Evander started, flabbergasted, but was interrupted again.

"Oh, I see it." The woman said, gesturing for him to be quiet, as she concentrated harder. "Snow... snow lies where your answers do."

"Snow? I— What's going on?!" Evander yelled in frustration, baffled.

"Toronto," the woman continued as if Evander's outburst hadn't happened. "That's where you must go, my dear boy. That's where you'll find your answers."

Before he could make sense of anything at all, the woman was walking back the way she had come, muttering something under her breath that only she could hear.

9.

EVANDER – A Leap of Faith

"Ma'am? Would you please care to elaborate?" Evander shouted across the woods, but the woman had vanished.

What the hell is happening? He wondered, absolutely bemused.

He stood there for many minutes, just trying to decide if he was dreaming or if this is how bizarre reality could get sometimes. Evander realised it wasn't a dream. Because a dream would eventually end. But this seemed interminable.

He plumped down onto the grass and as he gobbled up chips to quiet his rumbling stomach, Evander pondered over the day's events: Ruth having left Bosque Tranquilo; a strange middle-aged woman who lived in the woods appearing out of nowhere and telling him to go to Toronto to find answers, which is exactly what he was looking for. But how? Why?

He wondered about the woman he had just met. Perhaps she was a psychic or something like that, after all, she did have her eyes shut when she told him all of that. But he hadn't asked her about anything. She didn't even know his name. How could she have deciphered all that she had from the mere sight of his face? It was impossible. But then again, so was erasing someone's memory, and Ruth had done it.

Evander assessed his options: he could either walk to the closest airport and return to Mexico, where he was sure to have a horrible life, even more so, since he had just run off to another country without permission; or he could board a flight to Toronto, where he might or might not find Ruth, but the chances of finding her were far better than they would be if he left for Mexico.

He had enough money to be able to make either one of those two journeys but he didn't know if travelling all the way to Toronto was a good idea. What if Ruth wasn't there at all? Moreover, Toronto was a big city. Even if Ruth was there, it was very unlikely that he would actually find her. What would he do then?

Chapter 9

He realised it simply wasn't a possibility he was actually willing to consider. He *would* find Ruth. He would scour every nook and cranny of the city if there was even the slightest probability of him finding her secret and knowing the truth to how she had saved his life. Because, as far as mind-boggling mysteries went, this one definitely took the cake.

****

Evander wasn't exactly fond of his room, but it was worth its price. It was spacious – about 30 square feet with a single bed and a pygmy bathroom. He didn't care; he didn't plan on spending a lot of time in it.

His flight had been extremely long and tiring and for some reason, he had never been able to sleep on a plane. So, even though it was around 11 in the morning, when he was done washing up, he died on his bed.

He woke up many hours later and wolfed down the rest of his food packets. His legs felt sore and Evander remembered that he had walked from the airport to this hotel – 'The Comfort Hub' – as well, because he couldn't afford spending the rest of his money on cabs. Toronto was a great place, but it was expensive. Luckily, Evander had found a hotel cheap enough for him to stay in. What he hadn't been lucky with was the weather. Even though it was March, the snow was falling relentlessly here, and he didn't have any warm clothing except his puny windbreaker. The weather was a problem for another reason – he knew it would make finding Ruth even more difficult. The visibility was next to non-existent when he had arrived at the hotel and now, somehow, it was worse.

So, he decided to take another nap. The weather would take a good amount of time to settle anyway.

When he awoke, Evander examined the view outside; the visibility was a bit better; he saw a street lined with homes right in front of his hotel. The signboard was covered with snow but he managed to decipher its words – 'The Melkin's Street'. He was admiring the homes' simplicity when he noticed something. A figure in the snowstorm – it seemed confused about the path it must take and then, just as Evander placed a mane of black, the figure walked into The Melkin's Street.

It was probably just his mind playing tricks on him. Nothing was clearly visible. He shouldn't have been impulsive. But in his head, he didn't have a choice.

Chapter 9

Evander found his rucksack, stuffed his possessions in it and ran out the door, sprinting down the stairs and into the full-blown raging snowstorm. He could indistinctly hear the hotel's manager shout warnings about the weather but his feet were no longer in his control. The snow crashed into him like stabs of icy shards and the gale cut right through his clothes. Logically, he should've returned to the hotel's safety, but every fabric of his being told him otherwise. He couldn't give up. Not now.

A weak wisp of lavender scent forced its way into his nostrils along with the frozen air, and he suddenly knew what he had to do. He didn't need anything to be visible. All Evander had to do was follow the scent.

Following the scent, he came upon a beautiful house, painted an elegant and classy black. And before his mind could question the sensibility of his actions, his knuckles were rapping on the door.

10.

RUTH – A Mind-bending Surprise

Sharp cries jolted Ruth from her slumber.

She sprinted to the living room, startled by the intensity of agony in the voice. There she was. Lesly. Lying on the floor, still in cat form, holding herself awkwardly and groaning.

"Oh my god, Les—"

Lesly began to transform. Her black and brown cat fur changed into pale nothingness and in the next moment, she was a blob of white mist, just floating over the carpet. Ruth ran to her room, rummaged through her bag and found the bottle. Running back outside, she held the bottle an inch from the mist and watched as it slowly poured into the crystal bottle. She shut the bottle's lid and tried not to let her tears spill.

Chapter 10

Of course, this had been her fault. Seemed like everything was, these days. Things wouldn't have gotten this far if she had been more attentive to the sudden bouts of pain Lesly had had in Bosque Tranquilo and even after coming to Toronto.

After they had reached Bosque Tranquilo, Lesly had begun exhibiting some symptoms, but at the time it seemed trivial. Lesly assured Ruth that she was fine – probably just exertion. Ruth hadn't given it much thought either, because after Evander showed up, she hadn't really focused on Lesly. But now... now she had no choice but to go and get Lesly treated. She could go to *The Kingdom of the Lifeless*, but that would be like inviting trouble, given her history. Other than The Kingdom, there was only one person who could help Lesly out.

Mr. Bundleheckles.

****

She despised the snowstorm, mainly because it had arrived exactly when she had to go out to meet Mr. Bundleheckles with a very sick Lesly. This was the perfect time to leave, though – the less undead noticed her, the better. And right now, the streets were almost empty, except for the heaps of snow and a few pedestrians running to their homes.

Ruth wrapped a thick coat around herself, stuffed the crystal bottle filled with white mist (that was Lesly) into her bag and braced herself for the cold.

The chilly wind was almost tangible, impossible to push through and the snow seemed to be falling relentlessly, the temperature dropping by 2 degrees with each snowflake. Ruth rubbed her palms to return the feeling to her fingers but they remained numb as she walked towards the street where Mr. Bundleheckles lived.

It was quite a coincidence that she had come to Toronto, or meeting him would've been slightly harder. Not very hard, though; Mr. Bundleheckles always ensured he was easily accessible to Ruth. He had been incredibly helpful and kind to her since the day they'd met, to the point where you'd think it was more than just his job.

After the 10-minute walk, she had finally reached. Ruth glanced to her left and found a small building called 'The Comfort Hub'. *Probably some kind of hotel*, she thought and walked to the right, into The Melkin's Street.

Chapter 10

Soon, she was at his door. It was black and had a gold doorknocker. She knocked.

Mr. Bundleheckles opened it a moment later, greeting her with a genial smile that deepened his wrinkles. He was *old*. He must have been around 50 when he died. That explained his mane of well-groomed silvering hair and beard. He was wearing a red collared t-shirt and khaki pants. Mr. Bundleheckles didn't like wearing those gowns Mythil wore – he had told Ruth once, laughing. He'd said those make anyone look silly.

He welcomed her in, his warm amber eyes sparkling.

"This street is actually quite cosy," Ruth said, smiling. "Even in a snowstorm, it has a homey feeling to it. You must enjoy being here."

"Yes, I do," Mr. Bundleheckles said. "My neighbours are such kind people, they occasionally swing by to bring me pies and stuff. It's almost like I'm alive again, when I'm with the undead."

Ruth nodded, remembering his love for being around the undead – he had told her that it reminded him of his old life, when he was alive and happy and not a soul who governed other souls.

"So grateful to have some company, my dear," he said. "What with the snowstorm, I was reminiscing the old days. I would stay in with my little daughters and wife during cold, snowy nights and we'd play boardgames."

"Yes, winter is perfect for family time," she said, recalling the chilly evenings she had spent with her parents, watching movies and having popcorn, hot chocolate, apple cider and watching the snow glaze their neighbourhood in beauty. The memory jarringly turned painful when she realised that it was only a memory now – not a possibility.

"Well, we can pretend we're family and enjoy this lovely evening," Mr. Bundleheckles said, bringing a glass of *Elixir of Death* from his kitchen.

"Thank you." Ruth laughed, accepting the glass.

"So, what's urgent enough to get you here in that awful weather?"

Ruth's mood shifted and all warmth evaporated from her body.

Chapter 10

"Well, I didn't tell you on the phone, but Lesly is really sick," she said, gulping down the golden liquid. "She's been in pain since we entered Bosque Tranquilo, but I was too occupied to pay any attention."

"She's in the bottle?" Mr. Bundleheckles asked, his eyebrows creased in concern.

"Yes." She pulled out the crystal bottle and handed it to him.

He examined the white mist in it and Ruth noticed that it was growing denser. That couldn't possibly be a good thing. Or could it? Ruth was completely clueless about this stuff.

Just then, there was a pounding on the door that startled them both.

"Why don't you go get it?" he said and hurried off with the bottle to the kitchen.

Ruth opened the door, and almost jumped out of her skin. Because in front of her, were those electric blue eyes.

11.

RUTH – The Plea

Her heart stopped beating for a moment. It took her another moment to realise that this was reality and *not* one of her dreadful nightmares or unattainable daydreams. Evander was there. Right there. His eyes flooded with relief as he took her in; his hair was ruffled by the wind, like it had been when he had come to Bosque Tranquilo.

Ruth had a million questions, but she knew Evander had more.

"Who is it, Ruth?" Mr. Bundleheckles' voice called from behind her and she snapped out of her trace.

"Why don't you come in?" she told Evander and he entered. "Would you like some water?"

"I'd like some answers," he replied flatly.

"Who is this young gentleman?" Mr. Bundleheckles asked with an amused expression, smiling affably.

"Evander, sir," Ruth answered.

Chapter 11

"Oh, *the* Evander?" Mr. Bundleheckles frowned at Evander for a moment. "Well, what do you plan on talking about?" he asked Ruth.

She didn't know how to answer. Could she tell Evander everything and risk breaking the rules again? Except this time no one would really know about this, since this - unlike the spells she used - wasn't traceable. But Mr. Bundleheckles would know. If he allowed her to bend the rules a little, he would tell no one.

"With your permission, sir, I'd like to tell him everything."

She believed Evander deserved to know the truth - given that he had travelled all the way to Toronto and had almost died because of Ruth's carelessness. Another thought occurred to her: maybe she could ask for his help with the mission, since she had decided that she needed an undead's help anyway. She told herself not to pin her hopes on him saying yes, though.

"Everything?" Mr. Bundleheckles asked dubiously.

Ruth nodded.

"Alright. You have my permission. I'm sure you have thought this through."

He left and went to his bedroom, shutting the door.

Evander took a seat at the dining table and burst out. "Okay, I'm so lost. You like— like made me forget everything! Ho-how did you do that? I mean, I'm so glad I took that picture—"

"What picture?" Ruth asked.

"Never mind," Evander snapped. "Tell me. Everything. You *have* to. I came all the way over here. Ruth, you must tell me."

What astonished Ruth more than Evander somehow remembering and finding her was how desperate he sounded to know the truth. She found it baffling how intense his curiosity was.

"Yes, I will. But you need to understand the context first," Ruth said.

Evander nodded.

"One of most esteemed and renowned museums in New York have the custody of this one particular jewel. It's like a huge diamond and it's exorbitant, worth millions of dollars. Originally, it belonged to

Chapter 11

royalty but there are no records confirming the identity of its owners.

"There have been heist attempts when it was stored in the museum. People would often file complaints against the museum, claiming it was their ancestors whom the jewel belonged to. But since the museum didn't know the owners, there was no way to verify anyone's claims. Protecting the jewel was becoming more challenging by the day. So, it was decided by the directors of the museum that the jewel's ownership should be given to a trust capable of managing such an asset."

"How does this have anything to do with you and Bosque Tranquilo and—"

"If you waited, you'd get to know," she said crossly. "Anyway, so, about 2 years ago, my parents, Veronica Forbes and Dylan Forbes gained ownership of the jewel, as their trust was very successful, renowned and capable of guarding the jewel."

"Oh, so are your parents here too?" he asked, looking around.

Ruth sighed. Talking to Evander was like dealing with an impatient 5-year-old, and she wasn't enjoying it. "How about you let me finish?" she asked as politely as she could muster. He nodded and she resumed again.

"Then, on 27th February of this year, two thieves broke into our house, and tried to get my parents to spill the jewel's location. They didn't reveal anything, and the thieves killed them while trying to get the information."

Ruth paused, knowing Evander would say some kind of condolence. But he just stared at her, his eyes wide in shock. "I-I'm so sorry that happened to you," he said with a thick voice.

"Then they killed me."

The effect was immediate. Evander's eyes widened even more, and his mouth hung open. Then, his face relaxed and he smirked at her. "Using humour to deflect your sadness? Been there, done that."

"I'm not using humour to deflect anything," Ruth said. "I'm saying the truth. After killing my parents, the thieves killed me."

Chapter 11

Evander looked at her like she'd told him that 1+1=4. "You're really not kidding?"

"I wish I was," she said. "After I died, I entered *The Kingdom of the Lifeless*. It's like a government for souls who return to Earth for unfinished purposes."

"Nope," he said and then proceeded to do something so bizarre, Ruth actually let a giggle escape her. He slapped himself hard multiple times until his cheeks had reddened. "Wake up, you idiot," he told himself. "You're dreaming again. WAKE UP!"

"Hey, hey, hey," Ruth said softly, gently pulling his hands away from his face. "You aren't dreaming, Evander. I *am* dead. And *The Kingdom of the Lifeless* is real. And, yes, I erased your memory. As a soul, I have the power to do that to the undead, and much more."

"Undead?"

"The alive people who aren't souls. Like you."

Evander looked at her in a daze. "So you're dead and a soul. Okay. Makes sense. Actually, it doesn't. But I think I'm just gonna go with it. Because how else would you erase my memory, right?"

"Right," she said, smiling.

"What do you mean by 'much more'? What other powers do you have?"

"Well, for instance, I was able to see your entire life when I shook hands with you when we met in Bosque Tranquilo."

His eyebrows lifted in awe. "You've seen my entire life?"

"Yeah, more or less."

"But how can I see you, touch you, talk to you, if you're dead? I thought ghosts were supposed to be invisible."

"Well, souls *are* invisible. To appear opaque and communicate with the undead, *The Kingdom of the Lifeless* insists on us having what is called the *Elixir of Death*, whi—"

"So that's what you were drinking!" he said triumphantly, like he had solved the greatest mystery on Earth. "I knew it wasn't water!"

"It wasn't," she said, and couldn't help but smile. "Oh, and also, that man who was just here - his name is Mr. Bundleheckles. This is his home. He's my supervisor at *The Kingdom of the Lifeless*. He handles

Chapter 11

the details of my case and supervises me to ensure I follow the rules."

Evander nodded. "But where do you keep getting your elixir from? Is there like a coffee shop or—"

"No." Ruth laughed. "There's no shop. Our containers fill up magically when it's empty. That's why it's essential no undead even sees it."

"Oh. That's really cool."

"Also, the tattoo –" Ruth paused to show him her right wrist, where her weird tattoo was etched. "– isn't a tattoo at all. It helps identify us as souls."

"So every soul has it?"

Ruth nodded. "And the 'blank' book I was reading isn't actually blank. You just couldn't read it because you're undead. It has all my notes about *The Kingdom of the Lifeless* and my mission."

"Your mission?"

"So, when I died, I decided I must avenge my family's death. To do that, I must find and kill Astoria and Maxine, and return the jewel to safe custody."

"Astoria and Maxine?"

"They're the thieves who killed me and my parents."

"Oh," Evander said. "You're really going to kill them?"

Ruth thought back to the moment she had woken up after death and was told about what had happened and how she had a second chance at fixing things if she wanted to. She remembered sitting there, wondering what she could possibly do to 'fix things'. But there was no fixing to be done. No matter what she did, she couldn't resurrect her parents and herself from death. But she could still do one thing – avenge her family. By punishing the people responsible. By punishing Astoria and Maxine for how brutally they had killed her parents and her.

But when she thought about how she could punish them, she couldn't come up with anything at all. When the word appeared in front of her eyes. 'Murder'.

Ruth had been only 17 when she was killed. She wasn't fond of violence, but when one watches the people closest to them being assassinated and is then callously garrotted to death, they start to think of

Chapter 11

alternative ways of getting even, rather than 'leaving it to karma'.

"Yes," she told Evander. "Because I've lost everything I had and could have had in the future. And it's all their fault. They are never going to get caught. They deserved to be punished, don't you think?"

Evander nodded solemnly. "I'm really sorry about everything, Ruth. Your parents' death and yours. You were too young. Astoria and Maxine deserve however you wish to punish them." He reached out and squeezed her hand.

She realised this was the first time anyone had shown her any real sympathy regarding the incident. Before that, everyone had been talking only about the 'mission'; Mr. Bundleheckles had told her how it would be an easy one, Lesly had been all about the location of the girls and plans about the jewel, and of course, no one from The Kingdom had given a damn. But Evander – being an actual alive human being – actually cared. He was the first person to truly empathise with Ruth about what had happened. She felt a spark of warmth in her chest and it made her smile.

"Thank you," she said in a small voice.

"What about that necklace?" he asked after the pause got too long. "What's that for? And the crystal bottle?"

Ruth explained to him about *Crystalvocatio* and the bottle that held Lesly currently. The concept of dingles and Lesly being one of them surprised him, but he was absorbing all of this really well. He probably should have been more shocked, but maybe it was all those years of believing in the impossible that was holding Evander together.

"Okay," he said slowly. "So, that was a hell lot of information to process."

"I agree," Ruth said, smiling. "But I need to know how you got here. I erased your memory. How do you still remember me?"

He explained to Ruth how he had clicked a picture of her things back in Bosque Tranquilo and how looking at them had returned his memory. She was slightly disappointed to hear this - what it indicated besides Evander's brilliance was how incompetent

Chapter 11

Ruth's magic was. Had she done the spell perfectly, no kind of photograph could have ever revived Evander's memory.

"Okay, that's it, honestly." He sighed. "Then, when I was in the forest after visiting Bosque Tranquilo and finding out that you had already left, this strange woman appeared out of nowhere and told me to come to Toronto. She told me I'd find answers here. So, eventually, I came."

"You know how weird that is, right?" she asked him doubtfully, wondering who that woman was and how she knew what Evander wanted and where he'd find it.

"Well, you just told me you're dead, so by comparison, that seems normal to me now." He shrugged.

Ruth laughed but suddenly lost her glee. Because now the only thing that was left was asking Evander for help. She knew that even if he refused, she had to at least try, for the sake of her dead parents.

"Also," she began. "All of this is too much for me to do alone. Finding the two of them and killing them and returning the jewel... it isn't easy for me, especially with the time constraint. I have only a few months left before I have to depart to the *afterlife*. I need someone's help, and since no one from *The Kingdom of the Lifeless* can help me, I thought maybe you would."

She felt her eyes fill with tears and watched an expression of utter disbelief dawn on Evander's face. Of course, whatever he had been expecting, it hadn't been this odd request.

"Pl-please, Evander" she said, and her voice cracked as a tear ran down her cheek. "I really need your help."

12.

EVANDER – The Promise

Peculiar as it was, what Evander considered more unbelievable than Ruth being dead was that she wanted his help. He had lived his entire life thinking he was too incompetent to do anything that mattered, justifying his thought process by using his family's behaviour towards him as evidence. He used to think, *Maybe I really am useless, a defect produced in a sea of perfectly capable humans, because why else would my own family despise me this much, consider me so undeserving, treat me like I'm worth nothing at all?*

But now, he knew he hadn't been the problem. The only reason his family hated him and treated him so poorly was that they were all jerks. Because by asking for his assistance in a mission as important as this one, Ruth had indirectly told him that she didn't think he was unworthy. She didn't think he was incapable of contributing to something meaningful.

"Of course I'll help you," he told her. That's when a question popped up in his head. "Just, out of curiosity... what exactly would happen after you're done with this mission?"

"Oh, great." Ruth sighed, wiping her tears. Her shoulders relaxed and she leaned back comfortably in her chair.

Evander had a feeling that she had probably been wanting to ask that question for a long time.

"Sorry, what did you ask?" she asked, just realising he had said something after 'Of course I'll help you'. "I just... sorry. What did you say?"

"If you do succeed in your mission, what would happen?" he repeated.

"Uh, I'll go to the *afterlife*."

"Oh," Evander said, feeling disappointed at the idea of never being able to see Ruth again, which was stupid, because he had known her for, like, 15 minutes.

"Well, okay, so should we get started?" Ruth said.

"With what?"

Chapter 12

"Searching for Astoria and Maxine," Ruth said in an that-was-obvious tone.

"Right. Well, I think—" Evander began when the bedroom door burst open and out came a very worried Mr. Bundleheckles.

"Ruth, I-I— Lesly—" he stammered.

"Sir, what is it? Is she fine?" Ruth asked, her eyebrows knitted together and her eyes filled with concern.

"She isn't," Mr. Bundleheckles said, sighing tiredly. "But Alex is treating her. She should start to heal soon."

"What's wrong with her?" Evander asked. "Who's Alex?"

"Alex is my dingle," Mr. Bundleheckles answered. "Lesly... she's suffering with something that is called Numerphobia. It's a common disorder among new, younger dingles. It is caused by the dingle being constantly surrounded by a lot of negativity."

"Oh. Interesting," Evander said, and felt dreadful instantly.

Who says 'interesting' when someone is diagnosed with a disorder? He also realised that the reason of the 'negativity' was probably Ruth, so he decided to shut up.

"How long will it take her to be fully cured?" Ruth asked.

"I don't know, honestly," Mr. Bundleheckles said apologetically. "It could take a couple of months."

"But Ruth doesn't have that kind of time!" Evander said agitatedly.

"Yes, I know... Evander," Mr. Bundleheckles said with a weird emphasis on 'Evander' and he knew straightaway that Ruth's supervisor wasn't particularly fond of him. "But we need that time to figure out their location, anyway. So, we better get working."

"He's right," Ruth said. "Let's start."

****

Evander and Ruth had driven all the way to Crothers Woods from Mr. Bundleheckles' house at 7 in the morning, because this was the best time to be searching for two murderous girls. And since it was still snowing quite a bit, there were no hikers around.

Chapter 12

"Shouldn't you souls have a faster way to travel around than drive?" Evander asked Ruth as they got off the car and began heading into the woods.

"Yes, we do, actually," she said. "It's called Transformation. It's a form of soul magic that allows you to take the form of anything you want – a bird, a butterfly, a speck of dust. And then, you travel through air. It's about 20 times faster."

"Why don't you use it then?"

"I haven't learnt how to do it, yet," Ruth said sheepishly. "I haven't had the time. And if it's not done correctly, Transformation can be very dangerous. But Lesly knows it. Every dingle does. They're very good at it, and strong enough to carry souls with them. So, she was helping me travel, before she fell sick. I think she could carry you along as well."

"How would that even work?" he asked. "Would I turn into a sparrow too? That's so weird. And cool."

Ruth smiled. "Once she's better, we can ask her to do it."

As they walked on into Crothers Woods, Evander saw that the forest looked nothing like a forest when so much of it was covered in snow. The trees had hardly any leaves. The ground wasn't even visible through the thick carpet of snow. Evander wrapped his windbreaker tighter around himself as the frozen wind whistled past his ears. He realised his wardrobe choices had been questionable, because he was really close to becoming a human popsicle. Evander decided he didn't like the snow or winter at all. It made everything wet and cold and disgusting.

"You should've borrowed a coat from Mr. Bundleheckles," Ruth told him, chuckling.

"You think me shivering to the point where I can't breathe is funny?" he asked, his teeth chattering uncontrollably. "I'm glad you find my misery entertaining."

"Here, take mine." Ruth took off her coat and put it around Evander's shoulders. "It's not like I'm going to catch a cold or something."

"Thanks."

They walked for an hour, looking through every clearing, listening for the faintest of sounds, whispers, voices. But they didn't find anyone. Suddenly,

Chapter 12

Evander remembered that he didn't have an amazing sense of direction.

"Do you know where we are? And how we're going to go back?" he asked Ruth, panic taking over him. Last thing he wanted was to get lost in yet another forest when the temperature was dropping by the hour.

"Yeah. I'm using a map," she said, showing him her mobile phone, which displayed a picture of the map of Crothers Woods.

"I once got lost in a forest even with a map. I mean, how can someone possibly be that dumb?"

"You know, a lot of professional hikers often lose their way in uncharted sections of a known forest," Ruth told him. "Nature can be treacherous. Especially for someone who's had absolutely zero experience with being in the woods. I'm surprised your parents even let you go alone."

Except, Evander didn't have both his parents, and the one he did have didn't care about him that much.

"I-I am sorry, Evander," she said quickly. "I forgot about your mother for a second there. I'm sorry."

"No, no, it's alright," he said, shrugging. "You should know, though... they didn't let me go alone. My father sent his bodyguard to spy on me."

"Oh."

She looked at the ground, and Evander could almost hear her thoughts.

"You're judging my family, aren't you?" he asked her, smiling.

"Uhh, no," she said, her cheeks red. "I wasn't."

"Yeah, you were," he said, chuckling. "I understand. Honestly, I wouldn't blame you if you judged me too."

"What would I judge you for?"

"I don't know. I guess it would seem to you like I'm too much of a coward with no self-respect to still stay with them."

"No, I get it," Ruth said, surprising Evander. "You were scared. That's not cowardice. That's just being human. It's just the way you were raised, Evander. It's like you were so well-trained to be afraid of the real world, you forgot to be afraid of what your life would be like if you stayed with your so-called family forever."

Chapter 12

He thought about what she had said, and it clicked – the fear of the outer world was ingrained in his head since he was a little boy. It was easier to ignore his family's mistreatment when he thought about how much worse the world outside his home could be.

"Why do you think they did it?" he asked her. "Force me to stay with them even if they held me accountable for what happened to my mother. Why not just ship me off to a boarding school far, far away? Why not just get rid of me entirely, instead of keeping me imprisoned and manipulating me to think I need them?"

These questions had haunted him for as long as he could remember. He couldn't believe he was actually asking them out loud to someone else. And if it was anyone else in front of him, he might have hesitated. But this was Ruth. Something about their dynamic had changed. Once he had thought of her as a liar and now, he couldn't think of anyone he trusted more.

"I remember thinking this very thing the first time I saw your life," she said. "I thought, 'If they despise him so much, why even bother keeping him home? Why bother about him at all?'"

"And?"

"Well, since then, I have started to understand what grieving and loss actually feels like. Now that I think about it, I believe they did it simply because they're helpless."

Evander stared at her in astoundment. What did that even mean? Was she defending his family? Was she saying that they were innocent?

"They lost someone very important," she continued. "When your mother died, your family probably couldn't deal with being so helpless. They probably wanted to do something, anything. Even if that something was blaming someone innocent. And you were easy to blame. Easy to call a bad omen, label bad luck. I guess it was just easier to hurt you and punish you instead of accepting that your mother's gone forever and there's nothing they can do about it."

He had never thought about it that way. He had never assumed that it wasn't just because they felt vengeful, it was because they felt like it was the only

Chapter 12

thing they could do. Because, apparently, moving on after a loved one's death like a regular, rational human being was too much.

"So, they aren't horrible people?" he asked her.

"More stupid than horrible. But, yeah, they had no right mistreating you and punishing you for something that wasn't your fault. They were being sadistic, which was really wrong and not something you should forgive. Not everyone deserves a second chance. You can move on without forgiving or forgetting, you know."

Ruth was right. No matter what their intentions or motivations were, no matter how much pain they were in, no matter how helpless they felt, Evander was the one who had had to bear the consequences of their actions. They had taken his childhood from him; they had refused to be a real family to him; they had never shown him love or care. They deserved anything but forgiveness.

"You don't need to worry about them, Evander," Ruth said, wiping a tear he didn't know was trickling down his cheek. "You don't ever need to think of them again. Because you already made the decision to leave them when you came to Toronto. So, when I'm done with my mission, you better run away. For real. To a place you can truly call home. To a place where you can find a family who will show you love and cherish you for who you are. I want that for you. You deserve it."

Evander's throat was choked up with tears. He felt overwhelmed with too many emotions.

He had spent many nights crying himself to sleep, telling himself just the opposite - that he didn't deserve any happiness, or peace, because he had gotten his mother killed, that he shouldn't bother praying for anything better to come along because he simply wasn't worthy of it.

Growing up, voices in his head whispered that he might be mistaken about this, but there were several audible voices outside that proved them wrong. Today, the audible voice, the one that wasn't his own conscience, was telling him that he *had* been mistaken. Ruth believed he deserved happiness. She *wanted* him to find it. So, how could he not?

"You won't return back to that place, will you?" Ruth asked, concerned at his silence and probably tear-blotched face.

Chapter 12

He couldn't speak. He only nodded in response.

13.

RUTH – Silver Linings

Sunlight poured on the snow-glazed grass, making it shimmer. Ruth had never been inside a forest during the winter. The only time she had been in a forest at all was when she was trekking through the woods near Bosque Tranquilo. It was surreal, being in a forest. She felt so connected to nature: the Earth and the pleasantly cold air that made the branches dance and the snow that crunched under her feet.

"H-how are you not even cold?" Evander asked, his teeth chattering, nose red like a cherry, shivering in a thick coat Mr. Bundleheckles had let him borrow after hearing about his predicament when they had gone to Crothers Woods.

"I *am* cold," she said, trying not to laugh at Evander's terrible tolerance for low temperatures. "Guess I'm just more used to the cold than you are."

Chapter 13

"Yeah, let me give you a fun fact: there's not a lot of snow in Mexico City. Especially inside my house," he said with a completely straight face.

Ruth tittered.

"How could anyone ever camp in this place?" he asked, annoyed. "They'd freeze to death. Maybe you won't have to take the pain of killing them, after all."

"Well, they're definitely not hiding in a crowded place like the city," Ruth answered. "They could've stopped here for a couple hours or at least the afternoon, since it'll be warmer. If we're lucky enough, we could find them here."

"How did Lesly know they're here?"

"She's a dingle. They have special magic. It can help track people, if you have a strong enough memory of them."

"Well, I'm pretty sure Lesly is kind enough to give us their current location if we ask her nicely. I don't think she wants us to die because she wasn't in the mood to use her magic."

She laughed. "Yeah, that would've been ideal. But, the thing is... Lesly is weak. Not only because of her illness, but also because she's a brand new dingle. Her magic isn't powerful enough to be very accurate. So, she can tell us where they were in the recent past, but not after that."

"God, that's some bad luck," Evander said. "Did you really look through the entirety of Bosque Tranquilo like this?"

"I spent a week just searching the woods," she said, remembering the days she camped in the woods for the very first time; even though she had had magic, it had been quite difficult. If she weren't already dead, she would've died because of at least a dozen infections. "When I still couldn't find them, I had to take the risk of going to the village. We are ordered to stay as far away from the undead as possible. Of course, I messed up with that."

"Yeah, you messed up pretty bad." Evander chortled. "How did you even tell me the truth? Won't it get you in trouble?"

"Revealing anything to an undead is a huge offence in *The Kingdom of the Lifeless*. But, as long as Mr. Bundleheckles doesn't rat me out, no one will find out."

Chapter 13

"How can you trust him so much?" Evander asked. "He has no reason to help you this much. He's only your supervisor, after all. Right?"

"Well, yeah," Ruth said. "But he's always been very kind to me, way more than he needed to be as a part of his job."

Ruth recollected the very first time she had met Mr. Bundleheckles. She had just received the instructions regarding The Kingdom's rules from a guide named James at *The Kingdom of the Lifeless*.

She was waiting for Mr. Bundleheckles in his office. It was a very cosy place, full of pictures of two young girls and a beautiful woman – probably his family. Ruth recalled now how anxious, scared and dejected she had been feeling then. When he arrived, he treated her with such benevolence. She was still grieving her parents, and she felt so alone; she had no faith about whether she'd succeed in getting her revenge.

When they met, he told her that her case was one of the easiest ones he had ever dealt with. He assured her that it would take her a maximum of 2 months to kill Astoria and Maxine and return the jewel to the rightful authorities. She was probably having the worst panic attack of her life, but he had cheered her up and made her feel so confident. He had promised her that he'd help and assist her in every possible way.

"Hey," Evander said, and the memory drifted away, returning Ruth to the present. "You just got lost in thought."

"Oh, sorry. I was just... I was thinking of the time when we met. I was a complete mess, and I-I probably wouldn't have gone ahead with my mission if he hadn't encouraged me to do it. He's the reason I'm even here right now. Or I would've given up and gone into the *afterlife* long back."

Evander nodded in understanding. "Come on. Let's keep looking."

They continued into the Glendon forest. It was a big place, full of dense trees and clearings that were easily concealed. If they were vigilant enough, maybe they would find Astoria and Maxine there, but that was a big 'maybe'. Ruth suddenly realised she had lost a lot of time looking through large expanses of land for the elusive criminals. They were good at hiding and had escaped her before in Bosque Tranquilo. Maybe they had gotten away this time too. Besides,

Chapter 13

even if they were in Toronto, the city was gigantic. There were many forests and parks where they could've camped for a day and moved on. There was no way to search all the forests and find them, given how less time Ruth had. She had to find the jewel as well. This method was proving to be very inefficient.

"Why don't we split up and look for them?" Evander suggested after they came across yet another completely vacant clearing in the forest. "We'll cover more area."

"I can't risk that," Ruth said. "Astoria and Maxine are ruthless. They'll go to any lengths to erase evidence and stay hidden. For all I know, if you find them, they'll kill you on sight. I'll be able to defend us if we find them."

"Right."

As they walked, Ruth allowed herself to indulge the other reason she didn't want to split up, the first thought that had popped up in her brain before logic kicked in.

She didn't want to split up because she didn't want to be alone in a forest, looking for her murderers, again. Of course, Lesly had been with her in Bosque Tranquilo, but she wasn't human. Or alive. In fact, Lesly's very presence was a deafening reminder of the predicament Ruth was in, of the life she was living. Of the life she had lost.

Being with Evander was different. There were times in the past week when they were walking in some woods together and while talking, laughing and shivering in the cold, she had completely forgotten about the fact that she was dead. She had realised that with Evander, she could be more than just a ghost trying to avenge her parents. She could be a normal, happy, innocent 17-year-old girl. Someone she should have been all along.

****

"So, you lived in New York?" Evander asked. "Before all of this. You said the jewel was in New York. So is that where you lived with your parents?"

"Yep. Born and raised."

"So, what was living there like?"

Ruth tried to remember her life in New York. It felt like many lifetimes ago. "I was in paradise," she said, mystified by the memories flooding her mind. "I

Chapter 13

loved my parents. We would go to malls, water parks, amusement parks with huge roller coasters. We would gather to watch a movie every single Sunday, and we'd eat my father's infamous blueberry pie. I would go to school and enjoy every minute of it, because I so loved learning new things. I was actually a bit of a nerd."

She laughed, thinking of the times she had freaked out immensely about her term tests and assignments. "I had this group of friends," she continued. "We've had every kind of party imaginable and mocked every teacher in our school. What I wouldn't give to go back."

"I wish you could've had all that again, too," Evander said, wearing a sad smile, his eyes sparkling with tears.

"Oh, I'm so sorry, Evander," Ruth said, immediately realising that he had never experienced any of this. How could she have been so ignorant?

"Come on, Ruth," he said, shrugging. "Don't apologize for having a happy past."

When he said that, Ruth realised something she had never had to think about before. Even though the ending had been beyond awful and devastating, Ruth had been fortunate enough to live a full, happy and beautiful life. Her life had been free of hardships, melancholy or struggle; she'd had loving parents who would've brought her the moon, she'd had amazing friends who she'd enjoyed with so much and she'd had everything anyone could've ever asked for.

Evander had never had any of it. All 18 years of his life, he'd lived in pain, misery and loneliness. And now that she knew how unfair life could be to some people, for the first time, it dawned on Ruth that amid everything that had happened since her death, she hadn't been very grateful for everything she did have, or at least had. She had been so busy thinking about everything she had lost, she had forgotten to take a moment to be thankful for the incredible life she was lucky enough to have lived.

"Hey, you okay?"

"Yes," Ruth said, looking up at Evander's bright face, smiling wide. "For the first time in a long time, I'm good. Really good."

Chapter 13

He smiled at her. "We're going to find your killers, Ruth."

"Yes," she said with an unprecedented certainty. "Yes, we will."

****

"This isn't working," Evander said. He looked at his watch. "It's almost noon. We've been looking for 6 hours and we haven't found them yet."

"You're right. But what else is there to do? Lesly can't help us more than this. She's still ill. What can we do?"

Evander sat on a fallen log, and stared at the ground, deep in thought. After a couple of minutes, he snapped his fingers in triumph. "We could use their past locations to track where they are now. We already have the necessary data. All we need to do is find a pattern."

"Do you really think that would work?" Ruth asked sceptically. "That sounds like a plan in one of those thriller spy movies."

"That's where I got the idea from!" he said excitedly. "We need to at least try it once. It'll be far more efficient that whatever we're doing here. I just know it'll work!"

Evander was beaming at her: his eyes full of zest and a big grin spread on his face. Ruth had her doubts; after all, Evander had no experience with this. But then again, neither did she. In fact, there were probably very few people in the world who had any experience with coming back to life to kill their family's murderers. So, really, what difference did it make? Besides, a new approach could be just the thing that could lead to a breakthrough. She couldn't just stick to the ordinary; she was a literal ghost: there was nothing ordinary about the situation.

"Alright," she told him. "Let's give it a shot."

Evander jumped in the air. "Oh my god, wouldn't it be so extremely cool if this actually worked?! It would be awesome!"

"It really would be." Ruth laughed. "Come on, let's get going back now. We need to get back home before the snowfall starts again."

14.

EVANDER – The Disappearance

It had been two weeks since Evander had moved into Mr. Bundleheckles' house along with Ruth to help her find Astoria and Maxine. Mr. Bundleheckles' place wasn't too extravagant, but it certainly was elegant and put-together. He lived in the living room, since the guest room was Ruth's.

The living room had a huge beige leather couch off to the side of the room, and a couple of bean bag chairs opposite to it. The chairs were an odd choice for a 60-year-old ghost, but Evander loved plumping down on them. There was a huge wooden showcase next to the dining table filled with gorgeous décor like glass vases, and he loved glancing up to see a turquoise tinted glass tortoise looking back at him. It was a huge upgrade from the hotel, and free too.

But that wasn't the reason he was sticking with Ruth. There were multiple reasons, actually. The first obviously being that those killers deserved punishment. They deserved to be as viciously murdered as Ruth's parents were. And Ruth was. Somehow, Evander kept forgetting that detail.

This mission was also very important to him because it was the only way he could prove to himself that he wasn't a worthless moron. He had to succeed to have the satisfaction of knowing that he was perfectly capable of taking care of himself and building his life. He had to succeed in helping Ruth. For his own sanity.

Besides, as it was turning out, this work wasn't that difficult either. Evander had noted down all of the past hiding places of the two murderers with Lesly's help, who had assisted them as much as possible despite being unwell. He had been working with those coordinates for a week because he knew there must be a certain pattern to where the girls went. They couldn't just pick random places for hiding. That would be careless. They probably couldn't afford being careless if it meant getting caught.

"You're not going to find anything," Mr. Bundleheckles said one morning, as Evander chugged down a strong brew of coffee. "You're wasting your time. We just need the jewel's location."

Chapter 14

"But Ruth wants to kill Astoria and Maxine," he said, slightly surprised.

"We'll find them too. But we need to find the jewel first," he said authoritatively, and Evander felt a sneaking suspicion.

"Mr. Bundleheckles does know best," Ruth said, entering the living room, sipping *Elixir of Death* from a glass. "If he says to search for the jewel first, maybe that's correct." But she didn't look much convinced herself.

"Of course, it's correct," Mr. Bundleheckles said. "Evander, why don't you go get some rest? I can help out Ruth till then."

So, it was confirmed. Not only did he dislike Evander, but he also didn't want him helping Ruth, or more specifically, he didn't want Evander finding Astoria and Maxine. That sounded ludicrous, though. He was Ruth's supervisor at The Kingdom of the whatever. He couldn't possibly be trying to sabotage her mission, could he?

To hear Ruth tell it, Mr. Bundleheckles was the very reason she was even going through with this entire thing in the first place. He had encouraged her and supported her and whatnot. Why would he try to harm her mission in any way at all? Evander convinced himself that he was being paranoid. *Maybe I should just take a damn nap*, he thought and died on the couch. Given his fatigue from the brainstorming and the all-nighters he had pulled recently, sleep came to him instantly. Strangely enough, though, no nightmares did.

Evander woke and saw the clock ticking to 12.30 pm. A sharp smell of something burning assaulted his nostrils. It was coming from the kitchen. He ran to the kitchen, praying the entire thing wasn't on fire. It wasn't. Ruth had apparently just burned a dish.

"Well, it's a good thing you aren't going to be a chef," he joked, taking the pot from her and putting it in the sink under running water.

"Oh, shut up," she said, flushed and embarrassed. "I didn't cook one day in my life."

"Mmhmm." Evander found a brand new pot and set it over the stove. He washed carrots and began chopping them up swiftly. "I can teach you. But I will require a fee."

Chapter 14

"I'm letting you stay here rent free. That should suffice," she said, grinning.

"Let's start with stew. It's simple," Evander said. "You basically just boil a ton of vegetables in a pot of water and add black pepper and salt. It's really tasty."

He washed a bunch of vegetables and gave a couple to Ruth. "Think you can chop them up?"

"Think I can cut my finger off in the process." Ruth laughed. "Oh, wait, I can't. I'm dead."

Her saying that startled Evander. For some time there, he had forgotten about that. Like he did so often. And it hurt him every single time he remembered that his first friend ever was dead. But she was laughing; her laugh was as rare as a comet, and for some reason, he loved seeing her laugh. Something about her was so pure, so untarnished, in spite of everything that she had faced. Evander felt like she was proof that you could walk through hell and still be an angel.

"Well, then, you're going to learn cutting vegetables really quickly."

As Ruth started chopping, he poured water in the pot and started the stove.

"I burned my hand the first time I made this stew," he told her. "That's how I learned how to *not* hold the pot."

"Oh, no," she said. "Why were you cooking in the first place?"

"You saw my life, didn't you? You should know this stuff," Evander said, because he didn't really feel like talking about it.

"Seeing a person's entire life is a lot," she told him. "Honestly, I think I forgot most of it in Bosque Tranquilo itself. So, tell me."

"Well, we didn't have cooks, even though my father could easily afford 3," he began. "My father thought his new wife would do it. Except she was lazy. So, she gave 11-year-old me a cookbook and left me to do it all by myself."

"Oh my god, Evander, that's dreadful," she said benevolently. "I'm so sorry that happened to you."

"Yeah, but get this," he said. "Since I didn't botch up the stew, my stepmother made me make every single meal henceforth. I burned my arm, I cut my

Chapter 14

finger, and I've thrown a lot of bad food in the trash. But no one really noticed or cared."

Ruth's eyebrows creased in pity, and he knew he'd said too much. So, he tried to dial it down. "Anyway. The good thing is that all of that helped me learn the art of cooking. It can be fun too, once you understand how to do it properly."

Ruth nodded and resumed cutting the vegetables. Once they were done with the chopping, they put the pieces into the boiling pot of water, and he turned up the heat. He added salt and began stirring.

Soon, the aroma of the vegetables had filled the kitchen. It reminded Evander of the last time he had made the stew in his house. It was for his stepmother, Bella's birthday. It had been really tasty, but no one had expressed any appreciation. The thing was, by that time, Evander had stopped caring.

"I don't think a hoard of vegetables and hot water is going to be yummy," Ruth said, snapping Evander to the present.

Evander turned off the heat and poured the contents of the stew into 3 bowls. He added a bit of black pepper as seasoning and gave a bowl and a spoon to Ruth. "Try it."

She did, and her eyebrows rose in surprise. "It's really good." She grinned, and began wolfing down the stew. "We've got to make this again tonight for dinner."

Evander brought the other two bowls to the dining table, and as he took a seat, he noticed Mr. Bundleheckles wasn't with them.

"Where is he?" Evander asked, looking around. "I thought he was helping you."

"He is, but as a supervisor he has many other responsibilities, and he isn't allowed to be helping me. So he needs to be doing everything else as well as this work, and discretely too," Ruth explained.

"Well, I am here to help you now," Evander said, finding an opportunity to get rid of Mr. Bundleheckles. "I bet he's too stressed. Maybe he should solely focus on his other work."

Ruth looked at him like he was crazy. "What are you talking about? His help can be invaluable. Do you know the kind of sensitive data he has access to? I think we can directly get Astoria and Maxine's

Chapter 14

location from the database in *The Kingdom of the Lifeless*. They keep track of all the undead."

"Okay," he said, observing Ruth carefully. "Why hasn't he done that yet, then?"

"It isn't that easy, Evander!" Ruth said, suddenly irked. "Not everything is a cakewalk. If he gets caught, he'll be tortured in the *afterlife* for eternity."

"Fine, I get it. I'm not accusing him or something. You don't have to be so defensive."

"I'm not being defensive," Ruth said in a measured voice. "Just stating the facts."

"Okay," Evander said, but something about Mr. Bundleheckles didn't sit right with him.

"Hey, listen," he told Ruth after a long pause in which he had finished his bowl of stew. "I still honestly think we should look for Astoria and Maxine first, before the jewel."

"We've been over this, Evander," she said in a stern voice. "If Mr. Bundleheckles doesn't want us to do it, we shouldn't. We've already lost so much time trying to find them. Maybe his way will be faster."

"Yeah, I get that he's older and has experience and everything, but would you just hear me out once? You asked for my help, didn't you? So that's what I'm doing, Ruth - trying to help."

"Fine."

"Okay." He sighed with relief. "Now, two things are possible - either the girls have the jewel, or they don't. If they do, finding them and interrogating them could lead us to the jewel. Then you can kill them. If they don't have the jewel, it means it's in its original safe place. So, we find and kill them so they cannot reach it and the jewel remains unharmed. Either way, finding Astoria and Maxine first is essential."

Ruth sat there, and Evander could see the wheels turning in her head. She was considering his plan. *Of course, she is*, Evander thought. *It is the right one.*

"You make sense," she replied after a couple of minutes and Evander jumped with glee. "But I'm not going against Mr. Bundleheckles. Let's carry on with his plan for another week or so, and if we still haven't made any progress, I'll ask him about your idea."

Chapter 14

He was disappointed but not surprised. Wait, no. He was neither. Because he knew exactly what he was going to do now. He didn't need Mr. Bundleheckles' permission. Or even Ruth's. The important thing was finding the murderers, and Evander was going to do exactly that, even if it meant doing it all by himself, clandestinely.

****

Drawing the embroidered cream curtains open, golden light streamed through the glass panes in the living room. Dawn was here, and the melting sludge that was the snow looked less repulsive bathed in warm sunlight. He watched the sun rise till it was glaring at him and he had to turn away. That's when he saw Ruth, watching him silently. He flinched.

"Oh, sorry. I didn't mean to scare you," she said. "You've been working through the night." She gestured at the dining table, where there was a large world map, some books with his notes and scrap papers he had torn out of frustration.

"Yeah," he said. He remembered that he had to act like he was searching for the jewel. "Don't you think if you went to that museum and told the authorities about what has happened they'd protect the jewel themselves?"

"Oh my god! That's such a great idea, Evander!" Ruth exclaimed, her voice filled with extreme ecstasy. "I just didn't think of that, did I? I'm such an idiot."

Evander realised that Ruth was being sarcastic. And unnecessarily mean, of course.

"Don't you think I thought of that?" she said, annoyed. "You think they'll just believe me? Didn't you hear me when I said that millions of people are after that jewel? Anybody could just lie like that."

"But you have proof that your parents were murdered!" Evander said.

Ruth sighed like he was just not getting it. "Yes. And do you know who else was murdered? Me. They have my death certificate. They have my body buried next to my parents'. I am dead. I cannot return to New York or to that museum. My parents had friends there. Friends who think I was killed with my parents. And I was. So I cannot just go marching back, saying that they need to relocate the jewel because two murderous thieves are looking for it!"

Chapter 14

Evander was stunned. Obviously, he had – for the hundredth time – forgotten that Ruth was dead. He hadn't factored that in. Her explanation made plenty sense to him, so he nodded in agreement as she exasperatedly disappeared into the kitchen.

"What's all that shouting about?" Mr. Bundleheckles said, emerging from his bedroom. His bloodshot amber eyes had dark circles under them. His shoulders were slumped and he seemed jaded, but why?

Mr. Bundleheckles seemed like a real diva to Evander; he'd rest shamelessly throughout the night in his room and was conveniently busy with Kingdom work most of the day. Whenever he *was* available, he'd tell Ruth that he had something big planned, and that she had nothing to worry about. He hadn't exactly 'helped' them a single day ever since Evander had arrived. In fact, his only contribution was allowing them to use his house and letting Alex treat Lesly.

Evander took a seat at the dining table where Mr. Bundleheckles was having a large cup of *Elixir of Death* and rubbing his temples like they hurt. Like souls could experience pain! Evander chuckled at the thought.

"Something funny?" The old man looked up and glared at Evander like he had committed a crime.

"N-no, nothing. I-I just thought that maybe you have a headache. But that can't be correct, right? Like, you're a soul. You can't feel pain."

"Well, actually, that's not true," Ruth said, as she brought three plates filled with toast and three mugs of coffee in a tray. "*Elixir of Death* is designed to make our bodies as undead as possible."

"What?!" Evander said, choking on his coffee. "S-so you mean... you're alive?"

"She obviously didn't mean that," Mr. Bundleheckles said, rolling his eyes. "You're quite slow, aren't you?"

"Sir, please, calm down," Ruth said gently as she took a seat beside Evander.

It was better that she had intervened, because Evander was sure his response wouldn't have been polite.

"Look, the elixir only makes my body appear mortal, so that it's easier for me to blend in with the

Chapter 14

undead. It makes my body opaque and allows me to feel pain, hunger, tiredness, everything. Although, I am not completely alive, so I cannot die. We can't be injured either, and if do somehow get hurt, it heals really quick."

"Oh. Cool."

Evander picked up his toast, and saw Ruth devour hers. Boy, she really could feel hunger. And Mr. Bundleheckles really could feel pain. Evander turned back to him and had the urge to ask Mr. Bundleheckles more about himself. He had to know more about the dead man before drawing any conclusions.

"So, Mr. Bundleheckles, I don't know much about you," he started but the man didn't even look up from his plate. "I was thinking maybe we could start with your first name...?"

"Caleb," he said dryly, still nibbling on his toast.

"Oh, mind if I call you that?" Evander asked.

"No, he actually prefers his last name," Ruth said, guzzling down coffee.

"But Caleb's so much faster to say."

"Yes, but—"

"ENOUGH!" Mr. Bundleheckles suddenly roared, making Evander shudder and Ruth lose grip on her cup that plummeted towards the floor and cracked into sharp shards of ceramic. "Enough with the unnecessary chitchat already! This is my home and I expect there to be some damn quiet when I'm tired!"

Before Evander could apologize, the man stormed into his room, slamming the door so hard, it made Ruth wince. So his intuition had been right. Mr. Bundleheckles had something else going on, and it wasn't something that was helping Ruth.

"He never behaves this way," Ruth said in a small, deflated voice. "He's always so calm and... he has never yelled at me before. Ever. I don't know what has gotten into him."

"I think he doesn't like me," he admitted. "Hasn't exactly been very nice to me since I arrived."

"Oh, come on, Evander. That's not true at all," she said, defending Mr. Dumb-old-dead-man *again*. "He hasn't told you but he admires you very much. The

Chapter 14

day you came, he told me that he thinks you are very brave."

"Whatever," Evander said and got back to work.

****

Two more weeks passed by and Evander realised that living there wasn't so great, after all. In the two weeks, Mr. Bundleheckles had been nothing but inexplicably infuriated and fatigued. He had been mean to Evander, yes, but he had behaved rudely with Ruth too.

And as Evander had begun to gauge, Ruth was pretty delicate. So, she started breaking down every time Mr. Bundleheckles said anything cold to her and the worse part was that Evander had to console her.

He empathized with Ruth - he really understood how terrible it must be to have to avenge your parents' deaths when you are dead yourself with nothing but a mean old jerk for a guide. But one thing he couldn't handle was someone crying.

Evander had spent years bawling all by himself - no one had ever shown up to wipe his tears or hear him vent. Evander simply didn't know how to comfort someone because he had never been comforted himself! If the circumstances were different, he'd probably find the irony amusing. But he couldn't, because it was so damn difficult to sit there and watch Ruth be in pain. Yes, it was awkward to see someone cry when you're unable to console them. But watching Ruth cry was a different kind of torture. He hated it.

Evander watched the clock drag to 2 o'clock and decided to have lunch. He hadn't figured anything out about the jewel or about Astoria and Maxine yet. As he had actually begun working, he was starting to understand that there was some truth to what Mr. Bundleheckles had told him. Finding a pattern was proving to be impossible. He only had 5 locations, and there seemed to be nothing that connected them. Each day that went by without any success was making him more and more frustrated with everything.

As he and Ruth sat down for lunch, Evander reminded her that Mr. Bundleheckles was probably still napping.

"Oh, yes. I'll just go get him."

Chapter 14

She got up but he had a feeling that she didn't have that same eagerness in her voice. Maybe she didn't want that mean dingus around, after all.

He heard her knock 5 times. The door stayed shut and her calls of "Sir, can you open the door?" were met with silence.

Evander arrived and stood beside Ruth. She exchanged a concerned look with him and finally, pushed the door open. They scanned the room and found there was no one inside.

15.

EVANDER – Déjà vu

He had been in multiple situations that had blown his mind away. Back when a stranger in the woods told him to come to Toronto to find Ruth and he did; when Ruth told him she was dead. But this was different. This was different because it made perfect sense and *still* surprised Evander.

Immediately, Evander realised that while the incident was just 'bizarre' to him, it was downright devastating for Ruth.

She stormed into the room, searching every nook and cranny, desperately clinging to the hope that Mr. Bundleheckles was still there, helping her, guiding her, maybe even looking out for her. But he wasn't.

"Ruth, I'm sure he's just gone to that kingdom place," he said, rushing to her side as she started to hyperventilate, sweat beads trickling down her temples and tears swelling in her gorgeous hazel eyes. "He'll be back soon. Don't worry."

Chapter 15

"No, Evander." A whisper escaped her trembling lips because her voice was too fragile to be completely audible. "He isn't at work. He's gone."

There they were. Thick, salty tears gushing down her face. Her knees gave way and she sunk to the floor; Evander crouched beside her, holding her and stroking her hair as she bawled silently.

"No. O-of course not, Ruth. He'll be here soon. I- I am sure." But he wasn't, and his stammering voice wasn't helping.

As she continued to weep – probably still trying to process what had happened – Evander stifled a groan. He hated this: Ruth sobbing uncontrollably. He wasn't good at consoling, mainly because it involved saying a lot of white lies like 'It'll be alright' or 'You're going to be fine'. He just couldn't do that, especially with Ruth. The girl needed constant reassurance – she had next to no confidence.

Then, like a smack in the face, Evander remembered that neither did he. He was no one to judge Ruth. He had suffered, yes, but he couldn't even imagine going through whatever she had. And it wasn't like she was a mature 30-year-old woman either. She was young, probably even younger than him. No, Evander couldn't be harsh with her.

So, he helped her the best to his abilities. He brought her tea and tried to reassure her that Mr. Bundleheckles had probably left for some emergency and would return soon but Ruth was inconsolable.

Then, after about 20 agonising minutes, a squeaky voice said, "Ruth! Are you alright?"

It was Lesly in rabbit form now, all healed, not showing a single sign of sickness or discomfort. She hopped over to Ruth and she stopped weeping at once.

"Oh, Lesly!" she choked out. "A-are you okay? Have you healed?"

"Yes! Alex's magic was quite strong and I have been taking my medicine regularly. I still have to keep taking it, though."

"Alex? Oh, yes, of course! Where is he? Is he here? Did he tell you anything about where Mr. Bundleheckles went?"

"No, he didn't. He left about a couple of hours ago. But he didn't go with Mr. Bundleheckles, Ruth.

Chapter 15

He went back to *The Kingdom of the Lifeless*. That isn't where Mr. Bundleheckles is, though."

Lesly's news only upset Ruth more. But luckily, since her dingle was here, Ruth didn't really need anyone to comfort her, or so Evander thought was safe to assume. So, as Ruth continued to feel sorry for herself, Evander guiltily left Lesly to look after her.

****

A week had passed since the disappearance and Ruth still hadn't recovered from the shock. She still hadn't been able to wrap her mind around the fact that Mr. Bundleheckles had left her to her own devices. She had spent the last three days locked up in her room, doing nothing but crying or sleeping uncomfortably as Lesly brought in meals and the elixir.

He understood that Ruth believed that her supervisor at The Kingdom was genuinely trying to help her and she felt betrayed by his abrupt departure. But did she need to sit and be upset about for a week? *7 days*? Really? She had barely known the man for a month. How could she possibly be this upset about him giving up on her? Ruth had been through a lot, but being this emotionally volatile was not going to get her anywhere. And her nature was really starting to get on Evander's nerves.

He had ceased to make any attempts to hide his frustration after the first 4 days. He had stopped trying to get Ruth out of her room and work with him. He was focusing on only one thing now - finding Astoria and Maxine. And that fine, lovely afternoon, at 4.38 p.m., he did. Unbelievably, he had found an intricate pattern and found the murderers' current hiding spot, and he even had a hazy idea of the next one. If he went there immediately, they wouldn't get away. They couldn't.

His exhilaration knew no bounds and the success from his hard work was sweet. Now all he had to do was tell Ruth all of this so they could go and kill Astoria and Maxine.

As he gathered the map and his notes to show to Ruth, he realised he had perhaps never felt this zealous about anything before. Although, when he thought about excitement, he instantly thought about that time when he was 10 and had started in his diary what was supposed to be a book. He did write quite a lot of it too. But he could never quite get the ending. Eventually, though, he stopped trying

Chapter 15

to figure it out, thinking that finishing the book wouldn't change anything about his awful life.

The thrill he had found coursing in his veins back then ran through him now, and before he knew it, he was eagerly beating Ruth's door.

"I've got it, Ruth! I've got it!" he yelled breathlessly. "I've found their location. Now we just have to go there."

After a couple more knocks, the door finally opened, and if it was possible, Ruth looked much more miserable than she had the last time he saw her. Nevertheless, Evander was determined to tell her his achievement. Even though she didn't look the least bit interested, he explained how he had decoded the murderers' location.

"Why wouldn't you say something?" he finally asked, giving up. "Do you not care? How can you not care, Ruth?"

"I-I... I'm just tired, Evander," she managed in a weak voice.

Maybe she was. Maybe she was shattered. Maybe, no matter what, Evander could never truly understand her situation. But suddenly, he didn't care. He could feel his child-like glee and gusto ebbing into full-blown fury. Fury that probably wasn't entirely Ruth's to endure. Because what he was witnessing here was something he had witnessed a hundred times before.

****

He's five. Five and happy. Happy with the way his drawing has turned out after days of hard work. Five and naïve. Five and excited. Excited to show Dada how beautiful the lake he has drawn and coloured is. So, he's running down the corridor to Dada's room where he works all the time. He's there at the door, grinning ear to ear holding up his paper and running towards Dada – who is still staring at his laptop. And there is Dada – scrunching Evander's drawing in his strong fist into a crumbled-up paper. He is shouting now. But Evander doesn't understand. He doesn't understand what 'packed with work' means and he doesn't understand why Dada isn't happy about his drawing. All he understands is that tears are pouring down his face now. But he knows Dada doesn't like the sound of him crying, so Evander obediently leaves, trying to wipe off his tears. He leaves to make a better drawing that he knows Dada will definitely like.

Chapter 15

****

Evander returned to the present with a jolt and realised his face was burning with red-hot anger, irritation and agony all at once. The way Ruth was treating him right now was how he had been treated his entire childhood. His entire life. And in a fit of rage, he decided he didn't want it anymore.

"Yeah?" he spat, the word dripping with hate. "If diva Ruth is oh-so tired, maybe I'll do this whole damn thing myself! I mean, sure, it's *your* mission. And *you* wanted to avenge *your* parents' deaths but you're so incredibly tired, aren't you? So tired to travel to a place where *your* murderers wait to be killed. I get it. Totally."

His reaction rendered Ruth wide-eyed, taken aback. "Evander—" she began but he'd had enough of her nonsense. He had tolerated enough weeping and cowardice and the blind trust that Ruth had for Mr. Bundleheckles.

"I'm leaving!" he announced loud enough to make Lesly hop into the living room. "I'm leaving to get those two. And if you don't come, I'll get them locked up or something. Because I'm not stupid enough to wait here even when I know where they are. Unlike you, I just cannot afford to be that weak, Ruth."

Ruth pleaded for him to stay, but he tuned her voice out. He gathered his notes and maps and everything that belonged to him and thrust all of it in his backpack and tossed it over his shoulder.

"Evander, please," she said, sniffling, and he heard her now. Her face was a mess of tears and snot, too painful to look at. "Please, don't leave me alone. I'm sorry I didn't cooperate. But I'll do it now. We'll go there together. Just please—"

"It was nice knowing you," he said bitterly, cutting her off as he headed towards the door. "You and your little secret. I'll take your leave, then."

Before she could implore some more, he swung the door open and stormed out, his heart hammering against his chest. He headed towards the closest airport.

16.

RUTH – An Essential Epiphany

Weak.

All the energy that had been sucked out of her body by Mr. Bundleheckles' and Evander's departure returned to her in a powerful wave.

He had called her weak.

A powerful wave of anger. The wave washed over Ruth. And she felt her eyes drying up and something shutting down inside of her. The way she had felt when she had watched her parents die.

Before she knew it, Ruth was hurling stuff around, like she used to when she was a toddler and wouldn't get her favourite treat in spite of being promised she would. She picked up a crystal vase, and flung it towards the wall; it exploded into a million shards that rained down the living room like shrapnel. Then Ruth picked up another showpiece, a large glass tortoise and thrusted it towards the same wall. It shattered. She found the fancy wine glasses from the kitchen and broke them too. And then she used her powers to overturn the dining table and the couch and then demolished the entire living room: every picture frame and every embellishment lay on the floor. The room was a wreck. Like her.

The wave of energy disguised as anger vanished and left Ruth feeling more exhausted and hopeless than ever before. She was back at square one. All alone, and clueless as ever. She didn't know where the jewel was or where Astoria and Maxine were, either. Maybe she would have, had she listened to Evander but she just hadn't had the energy for it. And he should have understood that instead of walking out on her when she so desperately needed a friend.

She felt betrayed.

Mr. Bundleheckles was like a mentor to her; since the moment they had met he had been extremely helpful and supportive, so much so, that she had started to see him as a father figure. And Evander. She knew him better than anybody probably ever could. She knew he wasn't good at consoling, and she knew seeing her cry was awful for him but he hadn't understood the magnitude of sorrow that Ruth felt. Or he wouldn't have turned his back on her.

Chapter 16

"Ruth," Lesly said jumping over the fallen things and making her way to Ruth. "You'll be fine. We can work our way to their location. Then we—"

"No, Lesly," Ruth said and found her voice was hoarse. "We aren't doing that."

"What do you mean?"

"What I mean is... I am sick and tired of trying to go on when some force clearly doesn't want me to. I won't go. Evander will find them and send to prison. And frankly, I don't care about the stupid jewel. Let them steal it. I don't care. I'll just exist here until it is time to go to the *afterlife*."

"Prison? Is that what you want for those horrible monsters?" Lesly asked, hopping right in front of Ruth. "By law, a convicted murderer is executed. Those two murdered not only your parents but also you - how can you let them go to *prison*? They don't deserve to live, Ruth. You know that. You cannot give up."

"Why?" Ruth asked the rabbit. "Why can't I? Who cares? Mr. Bundleheckles doesn't. Evander doesn't. And The Kingdom certainly doesn't. Nobody gives a damn, Lesly! So why should I? Why should I keep working and working even if it's the last thing I have the energy for? Why should I keep going on when everything is always against me?"

Lesly had no answer. She just looked at Ruth with sad rabbit eyes.

"I've been a complete idiot all this while, thinking I could do this myself," Ruth muttered under her breath. "I've been a fool. I wasn't built for this. I was never strong or capable enough. I was simply stupid to think I was. I give up."

Much to her own dismay, Ruth found herself crying again. She sobbed as Lesly tried to comfort her; the fatigue had taken a toll and Ruth was pushed into the hazy, murky world where dreams lived.

****

Her dream was different this time. Very different from the usual dreadful one. It wasn't about her parents or about her old life that she found herself often longing for. It was also far more realistic than any regular dream feels, more so, even, than the flashback of her death.

Chapter 16

Where Ruth stood, everything seemed foreign and... otherworldly. She watched the sky and as the sun made its way to the horizon, the sky seemed to have been ignited a blood red. The colour faded, changing to a pink that dissolved into a picturesque violet. She looked at the army of lofty trees standing in front of her. She entered the forest, and soon, came across an auburn tent that was perfectly camouflaged among the sunburnt trees. So much so that it was surprising she had even noticed it. But she had. And it was because there was someone inside the tent, making a commotion.

Someone stepped out of the tent, and Ruth's heart leapt. It was Astoria! It had to be Astoria, with her muscular build, dirty blonde hair and tattered, soiled camouflage jacket. She was shouting at someone in the tent. Ruth wasn't surprised to see Maxine get out of the tent next. Maxine looked the same skinny girl she had been when she had helped Astoria murder Ruth's family. Her eyes were the same indifferent black, and her skin was the same ashen that made her look so alien.

"You have no idea what you're doing, Astoria!" she yelled. "That's the truth. Admit it!"

"Don't you dare talk to your elder sister that way!" answered Astoria, matching her sister's level of anger.

Ruth stood there, flabbergasted about why they hadn't noticed her yet.

"Stop playing that sister card. God!" Maxine huffed exasperatedly. "Just because you're older and more buff doesn't mean I should listen to you all the damn time. We both know very well that I'm the brains of this operation."

"I think we both know very well... who the *real* brains of this operation is," Astoria said slowly, lingering too much on the word 'real'.

Ruth wanted to listen to more of it, but everything suddenly began to fade. The trees, the tent, the sisters, the sky, everything... and Ruth was floating in blackness.

****

She awakened, gasping for air, her mind overwhelmed with thoughts.

"Lesly!" she called and found the rabbit was right next to her, in the heap of the mess Ruth had created

Chapter 16

earlier. Lesly was lying like she was about to have a nap, looking drained.

"Lesly, I— Are you okay? Are you sick again?"

"No, I'm fine," the rabbit managed but her voice was strained. "I just had to show you that."

"Show me what?"

"You did see it, didn't you? The murderers... at their current location."

"*You* showed me that?" Ruth asked in disbelief. "Bu-but that's impossible! You don't have that kind of powers, do you?"

"No, but everything can be learned. So I begged Alex to teach me. Because I couldn't bear you giving up on your mission, Ruth. Yours was the first case that was assigned to me. If you fail... well, so do I."

Ruth was speechless. She had never pondered what a dingle must have to face if their soul fails to accomplish their mission. Because souls depart to the *afterlife*, but the dingles are reassigned to other souls and the cases they are given depend largely on the help they provided on their previous case, and a failed first mission must not look great for them. Ruth had been so selfish to have declared that she wouldn't continue the mission; she hadn't given Lesly a second thought.

How could she possibly give up? How could she give up when the only reason she and her parents weren't together, living their fantastically normal lives was that Astoria and Maxine had been so blind with greed, they had killed three people without ever considering the consequences?

No, she couldn't give up. She had to bring justice to her parents. And herself. Because Ruth had had dreams too. Just like Evander's dream was to be a writer, hers had been to become a doctor and save lives, help people. She had friends she loved dearly; she had cousins who she'd never talk to again; she had so many things in her life that she had wanted to cherish forever. Ruth was just like any other 17-year-old girl, with dreams and hopes and a passion to make her life whatever she wanted. But she had been robbed of that opportunity when she was - by absolutely no fault or involvement of her own - brutally murdered.

Ruth knew in her soul that she could not give up.

Chapter 16

"I won't, Lesly," she finally said. "Thank you for helping me realise that."

"Well, you know where the sisters are, then? Evander told you?"

Hearing his name brought another wave of regret. He had left, yes, but before that he had tried his best to help her, and she had shown no interest. The vague memory returned: Evander had been showing her a lot of notes and a map and talking about coordinates but she hadn't listened because she was too busy being a cry-baby. Ruth felt such immense hatred for herself she wanted to punish herself somehow.

"Oh, you must have the elixir!" Lesly said suddenly.

"What?" Ruth asked, snapping out of her train of thought. "Why?"

"Your arm," Lesly said, pointing at Ruth's left arm with her paw.

Ruth looked at it and found that it was completely invisible! The only thing she could see was her elbow and that was translucent too. She rushed through the mess and found the pitcher of the golden syrup in the kitchen, and as she gulped down a large amount, the liquid scorched the inside of her throat. *Good*, she thought. *I am getting punished, after all.*

She watched her arm turn back to normal and walked back to Lesly, who had drifted off but was awakened by the sound of Ruth's footsteps.

"Why don't you go get some rest, Lesly?" Ruth asked the rabbit. "Have your medicines too. I'll get this place in order. And after that, we've got a mission to complete."

17.

RUTH – The Ghosts of A Lost Life

Finding the location wasn't easy, but with Lesly's extensive help, Ruth had managed it within four days. The difficult part was learning to transform. Transformation was a method of transportation for souls and dingles: it was fast, free and – more often than not – easy. But Ruth had never done it before and learning it well and as quickly as possible was crucial.

Even though Lesly was proficient at it, and could easily carry Ruth along like they had done before, Ruth had understood that Lesly was fragile, and shouldn't be pushed past her limits. Transformation can be draining, and if Lesly exerted herself too much, she could end up getting sick again.

She and Lesly spent another couple of days preparing for the journey while Ruth tried her best to learn the skilful art of Transformation. The key, she realised, was deep concentration. You have to truly think of the thing you wanted to turn into – whether that was a bird or a leaf or a speckle of dust. After that, the journey is pretty simple.

"We'll just take breaks," Lesly said exasperatedly – in hamster form now – one evening as Ruth practiced. "You're doing good but too long a stretch at a time and you'll have no energy. We'll just have to take breaks."

****

So, a week after Evander's departure, Ruth was finally ready to leave herself. She had her stuff packed, along with the *Elixir of Death* and the medicine for Lesly. Luckily, Lesly was in far better shape than she had been in a long time. That was at least one less thing Ruth had to worry about.

As Ruth started to assemble her gear at 9.30 in the night, Lesly took off to get some rest before the journey. Done with her packing and everything else, Ruth took a moment to sit down and reflect upon everything that had happened and would happen in the near future as she sipped the *Elixir of Death*.

Chapter 17

She thought about the progress she had made – she would soon kill her assassins. *If only I hadn't met that jerk Evander, things would've gone so much faster*, she thought. The thought made her feel smug but after a moment, she started to wonder if this was really true.

She had been unsuccessful in finding the sisters in Bosque Tranquilo and as much as she could remember, her plan then had been to use Lesly's powers to basically chase and catch Astoria and Maxine. In hindsight, this plan of hers didn't make much sense; especially with Lesly becoming as sick as she had, Ruth would never have been able to hunt for Astoria and Maxine. Had she not met Evander, and had he not returned to help her, she would've been completely alone. It dawned on Ruth that it was because of Evander's idea of decoding the pattern that she knew now where the pair was, because Lesly could only provide information of the past – which is why showing that glimpse of Astoria and Maxine had also been challenging for her. So, basically, she owed all her progress to Evander.

But Evander had done way more than just help with her mission. He had been a friend, a real friend;

he had made her see the light in her past through the darkness of her present; he had given her happiness, even though that was the last thing someone in her place would've felt. Even in death, Evander had managed to make her feel alive.

She wondered about him. Had he reached the sisters yet? Had he confronted them? Suddenly, she was worried - had they killed him too? Maybe he was already dead and the sisters had fled. The mere notion was so unbelievably perturbing, Ruth guzzled down all of the remaining *Elixir of Death* in one go to bring herself back to reality.

This is why Ruth didn't believe in reflection. In Ruth's case, even before she had died, introspection of any kind always resulted in an unhealthy amount of overthinking that only doubled her anxiety and heartrate. She remembered what her friend Gracie used to tell her before any important event - like an exam or competition - 'Just don't think too much about it, okay?'

Gracie's sweet voice played in Ruth's head and suddenly, she felt homesick. She missed her friends - Gracie, Avery, Steve and Noah. She missed their conversations, which could be anything from 'how

Chapter 17

lousy some fanfiction writers are' to 'why Ms. Pembroke wouldn't give them a single day off.' (Ms. Pembroke was their AP Calculus teacher.) Ruth longed for her home, her room - which she had recently gotten painted to aqua (her favourite colour) - and she longed for her parents. Her heart ached.

"Is everything okay? What are you waiting for?" Lesly's squeaky hamster voice asked as she bounded in the room ardently, making Ruth jump.

She had a million things on her mind. But telling them to Lesly wouldn't change anything. So, she didn't. "Nothing. Let's go."

Soon enough, Ruth was with Lesly and her backpack in her backyard. She gazed up at the sky. Toronto was blessed with many things, but stars weren't one of them. That's when the clouds drifted and an ominously large and ghostly moon hung in the sky. The wind was suddenly too strong, and there was something unpleasant in the air that Ruth couldn't place. The sky, the moon, the wind... they seemed to be warning her of something, but she had no idea what that was.

"Ready?" Lesly asked.

"As I'll ever be." Ruth steeled herself as she gripped her backpack and tightly clutched Lesly.

She knew she wouldn't fail; she couldn't. She concentrated hard and felt a strong gust of wind engulfing her. Soon, she was a sparrow.

18.

EVANDER – A Miraculous Guide

He couldn't even recollect the last time he had felt this unruffled.

In the tranquillity of the woods, Evander had nothing on his mind, so it was inevitable for it to get lost in the beauty of his surroundings. This place was very different from the forests outlining Bosque Tranquilo.

That place was wilder, more like a jungle. Here, the ground was just dirt and fallen tree limbs or the occasional creeper, not any kind of moss. There were patches of shrubs and thickets loaded with berries and fruits of all colours: Evander actually saw a sky-blue fruit the size of an apple. He hadn't eaten any of it though – gorgeous foreign fruits were the most dangerous thing he'd probably encounter here. There seemed to be no being here except for the insects. The tree trunks were large and towered over him, their thick foliage seemed sort of comforting as it shielded him from the sun and the underbrush was excellent to use as pillows or blankets when he had to rest.

It was amazing to find some solitude after being locked up with two insane dead people for a month.

Was he exhausted? Without a doubt; his calves, knees and feet were unbelievably sore. Was the sun baking him in spite of the greenery? His t-shirt was drenched with sweat. Was he upset, though? Nope. Not even a little bit.

Standing up to Ruth had been one of the most difficult things he had ever done, and he had single-handedly cleaned an entire house at the age of twelve. As he had been travelling, Evander had had a lot of time to ponder why that was. It had occurred to him that it was because he hadn't just stood up to Ruth - in his head, he had stood up to his father, brother, sister and stepmother. The words were different from the ones he would have used with his family but the sentiment had been the same. But remembering how he had stormed out of Mr. Bundleheckles' place made him think of Ruth, and at the moment, that was the last thing he wanted to do.

So, Evander switched gears in his head.

Chapter 18

He found it astounding how he had made it this far. Not only had he taken a flight all the way over to this rotten place, but he had also been on foot in these woods that lead to his destination for around two days now. No, wait. It was three. With the flight and the resting, it had been five days since he had left Mr. Bundleheckles' place. Now, he was heading there – right there, where he'd find Astoria and Maxine.

The thought pulled him up short. He'd find them and then... what? What would he do if he actually encountered the murderers? He couldn't kill them. Not even if it meant his own death. Helping Ruth was one thing but committing murder himself was something completely different. And no matter what they had done, Evander didn't have the right to kill Astoria and Maxine. They were Ruth's to kill. Besides, 'killing' was such a diabolical word, even thinking about it made chills run down Evander's spine. What would he do, then? Maybe he could call the police and... and what? How would he get them arrested? He didn't have any solid evidence to prove the sisters' crimes. It wasn't like he could just say – 'Well, they murdered my friend and her soul returned and told me to get them arrested'. After a long time, Evander felt helpless. *Ugh*, he thought. *I'll figure it out when I actually find them.*

He plumped down on the ground and devoured a bag of chips and found he had only one left now. His water supply had majorly dwindled too. He'd have to find a stream to drink from; he had actually found one when he had arrived but with following the compass and the necessity of staying on track, Evander had lost the stream.

All of a sudden, he realised that he had so much to be worried about. He was running out of food and water; the travel was still not over; he had no idea what to do after he found the murders; and he was extremely jaded.

So, he decided to act on the last one and took a nap. Probably not the best decision - one would think - while in the woods, but the few days he had been there, Evander knew he was safe. And incredibly sleepy. So, when he had fashioned some vines into a pillow, he instantly drifted off.

****

Chapter 18

He awoke a couple hours later, grateful, so immensely grateful to see the blazing sun had turned its brightness down a notch. But this also meant he had to get moving. He avoided travelling in the night. He had only one flashlight and he wasn't sure how long it'd last. So, energized by the food and the rest, Evander got up and moving and continued to travel until night fell. It was the same then: a sip of water and dozing off. This time, his eyes opened to bright sunlight and he was glad to get going because now he was getting really thirsty and within a single swallow, his bottle had emptied. He had to find a stream. Or, Evander was well cognizant that dehydration could cost him his life. Not that he was particularly fond of his life, but lately, it hadn't been so bad.

Evander continued walking at a steady pace until he came upon a crossroad. The wide forest path divided into two different ones. His compass would point the same way until much later and the coordinates weren't helpful at this point.

The two paths could lead to two completely different places, and only one of them would lead Evander to Astoria and Maxine. *Man*, he thought.

Why does everything have to be so damn hard? What the hell am I supposed to do now?

"Ah, an outsider," said an unfamiliar voice from behind him.

Evander literally jumped out of his shoes, his heartbeat skyrocketing and his skin crawling and somehow, he found the courage to turn, his eyes squeezed shut with terror. *Please don't kill me, please don't kill me, please don't kill,* was all he could think.

"Ah, boy... what brings you to my woods?" the voice asked and Evander knew he must open his eyes.

He was astonished to see a middle-aged man in front of him. He looked decent – wearing beige pants and a pale blue t-shirt, his beard trimmed with streaks of silver and his hair was black, except specks of grey here and there. The man didn't look harmful to Evander. His gregarious smile and twinkling hazel eyes certainly didn't tell so. But then what was he doing here, in the middle of nowhere?

"What do you mean... your woods?" Evander asked.

"I mean I live here," he answered with a smile. "My entire tribe lives here. This is our home."

Chapter 18

"Oh, alright," Evander managed as his breathing returned to shallow again.

But there it was again. Déjà vu. Hadn't something similar happened before? He had met that strange woman in those other woods and she had said she lived there too. *How bizarre*, he wondered. But then again, what wasn't these days?

"Where do you wish to go?" the man asked him. "Maybe I can guide you. I know this place in and out."

Evander wasn't sure what his answer must be. He didn't want to say anything about Astoria and Maxine. That would sound too weird: him trying to find two girls in a forest. No, he couldn't say the truth.

"Oh, I get it. You don't want to tell me. Well, I'm sure you'll find it helpful to know that the right path leads to nowhere, actually. It just ends in a large pit. If you're going somewhere and you're sure you're on the right track, you should take the left path."

The advice actually being useful surprised Evander. For all he knew, the man had to be right. He lived there. Who was Evander to question him?

"Sir, thank you so much," he said. "I am very grateful for your help."

"No problem!" the man replied cheerfully. "Take the left path. It is the right one."

The man broke into a guffaw at his pun. When Evander turned to glance at the paths, the laughing suddenly vanished. And when Evander turned again, so had the man.

19.

EVANDER – The Friend

He stood there, staring at the empty space where that tribal man had just stood. He took a moment to feel flabbergasted and confused but then relaxed. Maybe the tribal man didn't want to be here with him; maybe he was scared of Evander. But why? He had a lot of people with him and Evander was all alone. Besides, how had the man just disappeared? Evaporated into thin air? Evander hadn't heard any shuffling or footsteps. It was strange, yes, but far less strange than that encounter Evander had had with that woman who had told him to go to Toronto. Not only was this tribal man's advice practical, but the entire thing was also far more realistic. Tribals could be living in this place – and they would know it better than anyone else.

I should've asked about a stream, Evander thought with regret as he took off on the left path like the man had suggested. 100 metres into the walk and he remembered the man's attire – t-shirt and pants.

Tribals didn't wear things like that. Did they? The man's beard and hair had been groomed too - that was definitely impossible for a tribal man.

Evander eventually decided that wondering about the abnormal instances in his life could take a long time of wondering and didn't benefit him in any way, so he let his mind wonder instead when he'd get water. As he treaded, he registered the painful dryness in his throat and the parchedness of his tongue. The energy was draining out of him faster, now that his body knew it wasn't getting water any time soon. He persevered on, though, listening intently for any sound of water trickling, any din of water running through rock crevices.

As time passed, he was glad for the forest sounds - he saw brightly coloured birds bouncing from branch to branch, tossing hints of birdsong and melodious harmonies back and forth. The birds helped him stay awake and distracted him from his increasingly dehydrating body. After about 2 hours of strenuous walking and dryness etching every part of his body, Evander found he had reached the end of the forest line.

Chapter 19

What? He thought as he looked out at the large expanse of bone-dry, barren and bleak ground. In the distance, about 500 metres away, Evander could hazily see the line of something dark – probably trees.

I hate my life, he thought and started off. And immediately knew he wouldn't be able to make the journey. Out of the protection of the foliage, the searing sun was right above him, its heat causing blisters to form on his neck and fresh sweat to trickle down his back. His entire existence felt like it was melting into nothingness. The dehydration symptoms were kicking in – he was too fatigued and suddenly even standing appeared as impossible a feat as flying.

He had been strong for too long. Evander could feel his energy ebbing, his body shutting down, refusing to continue going forward until its demands were met. It was literally the last thing he wanted to happen at that moment, but surely, he fell onto the scorching ground and lost all consciousness.

****

When Evander came to, he had the vague feeling of cold air enveloping him – it was comforting, really.

Before he could even open his eyes and look around, someone pressed a glass of water to his lips, and he was so grateful to be able to gulp it all down in one go. He gasped for air and hopefully another drink of water, but when he opened his eyes and gained a steady vision, his world veered out of focus.

Concerned hazel eyes were staring right into his. He jerked back, startled.

"RUTH!" he exclaimed loud enough for the entire country to hear.

"Now that you're well, I can resume being mad at you," Ruth said, her face turning a gentle shade of red.

"What?" Evander said, still in a state of shock. The last thing he could remember was being jaded and dehydrated and collapsing on the ground and now suddenly Ruth was in front of him. What the hell was going on?

"I'm mad at you." She huffed angrily and walked away to sit on a couch.

That's when he actually noticed his surroundings. They weren't in a forest or in the baren land where he had fainted. They were in a big white tent – it was

Chapter 19

about 8 feet tall and big enough for two huge cars to fit inside. There was a couch and a bed in the tent and a small pillow on the ground on which a hamster was fast asleep.

"What's all this?" he asked, getting up.

"I've been learning more advanced magic. I was able to conjure this. I can conjure food and water too now." With that last statement, Ruth almost sounded cheerful. But her voice lost its verve again. "Enough," she said sternly. "I'm done with you and your nonsense. How can you shamelessly act all normal after betraying me?"

"'Betraying you'?" Evander asked, taken aback. "What are you talking about?"

"Oh, so you didn't walk out on me?" she asked, matching his level of surprise with just the hint of sarcasm. "That wasn't you? Yeah, you're right. I must have been dreaming or something, like the dumb weakling I am."

"I didn't betray you, Ruth. I just left when I thought you didn't need me anymore. Because I was sick of being treated the way you were treating me. To be honest, you were acting a little too much like my family."

She took a pause before speaking again. "I needed you. In fact, even more so than I did before. I understand that I wasn't exactly helpful—"

"You weren't just unhelpful, Ruth. You were downright indifferent! I showed you the coordinates of this location and you didn't even care!"

"I know, and I have felt awful about it ever since," she said, tears returning to her eyes. "But I was just so vulnerable. I didn't have Mr. Bundleheckles. You don't know how much I had been relying on him."

"Well, I hadn't. I didn't even trust the guy," he admitted.

"What do you mean?" Ruth asked, her defence mode turned on again. "He is—"

"You don't know him, Ruth," Evander said as calmly and definitively as he could muster. "You don't actually know him. You only know the version he chose to show you."

She seemed to have been stunned, for she stopped arguing. "That isn't the point," she said after a minute. "I am mad at *you* for leaving! How could you

Chapter 19

have? When I trusted you? When I thought that we had finally become friends?"

He felt like he had been smacked right across his face.

'Friends'.

No one had *ever* called him their friend.

"I'm sorry," he said, feeling embarrassed about his rash decision of storming off. "I probably shouldn't have. It's just that..." He couldn't think of any reasonable justification for leaving. Because there wasn't. "You just... cried a lot."

"Excuse me?!"

"That's enough!" said a third voice, and Evander realised it was Lesly's. The hamster had awoken. "Do you idiots *ever* stop fighting? We have to go and find those sisters."

"They're sisters?" Evander asked and looking at Ruth's and Lesly's expression, immediately knew the detail was irrelevant. "Yeah, okay, fine. Whatever. Let's get going."

"We're not done yet," Ruth told him warningly and all he did was roll his eyes in response.

20.

RUTH – The Betrayal

As they stepped into the dense forest, Ruth noticed something odd – the sand beneath their feet, the tree trunks and the sky were all the same colour – beige. The entirety was almost seamless if one ignored the leaves. Which was quite easy to do since the foliage wasn't very thick and was high off the ground – the trees towered over them, threateningly, as if they were protecting something. Which, of course, they were. Here, somewhere among these woods, they'd find the killers. The monsters who, without hesitation, had assassinated Ruth and her parents. She'd find them today. And it would be their last day on Earth.

"Can we stop for a little bit?" Evander asked, panting. "I have been walking for like 5 days now. I need some rest."

"We've been walking for only an hour," Ruth answered impatiently. She was still mad at him. She

Chapter 20

didn't care if he was tired. "Besides, you had enough rest when you were passed out."

"I passed out because I had been walking continuously without food and water for hours," he explained, grinding his teeth. "Come on, Ruth. Don't be heartless."

"Oh, *you* wanna talk about heartless?" she spat. "Okay. What about the time you abandoned me? I don't know if I have the right to judge but that sounds pretty heartless to me."

"Would you stop?" Evander said pleadingly. "I know for a fact that you probably didn't even care that I left. Let's be honest: you're just dragging this out because you're actually mad at Mr. Bundleheckles and this rubbish you've been telling me about 'abandoning' you is actually the stuff you want to tell him but can't, so you're taking it all out on me."

What Evander had just said hurt Ruth in a multitude of ways. Firstly, that comment about her not caring about him leaving was far from the truth. Of course she had cared. He had become more than a mere accomplice for her mission. And him leaving her *had* hurt her. But what Evander had said about

Mr. Bundleheckles was partially true. She did want to say that stuff to him – about how he had left her with nothing but fear and sorrow. But she couldn't and maybe that was why she was being harsher with Evander. Her head felt heavy with all her thoughts. She needed to sit down.

"Well, well, well," said a familiar voice from behind Ruth and her head spun.

From some distance away, there was ripple in the air and that's when she noticed the tent – brown and flawlessly camouflaged, exactly like it had been in the dream Lesly had shown Ruth. From the tent, out came Mr. Bundleheckles.

"I believe I just heard someone say my name," he said coolly, walking towards Ruth.

Ruth was simply dumbfounded. What was Mr. Bundleheckles doing here? Had he found Astoria and Maxine's location before either Ruth or Evander? Why hadn't he told her about his plan before? It would have saved her so much pain and worry.

"You piece of crap," Evander said harshly, glowering at Mr. Bundleheckles.

Chapter 20

"Evander!" Ruth hissed at him indignantly. "How dare you talk to him this way!"

"Oh my God. You're still siding with him?" he asked in disbelief.

"Of course I am!" Ruth said. "Why wouldn't I? He's still helping me. He came here to finish off Astoria and Maxine. I bet they're already dead."

"Dad, we're cutting some fruit—" said someone as they appeared out of the tent and stopped midsentence as they realised Ruth, Evander and Lesly were there too.

"Astoria!" Ruth said, her mind too bewildered to process anything.

It was Astoria. Right there in front of her. *Not* dead.

Ruth wasn't thinking.

She lunged at Astoria, using her powers to try and shove Astoria and pin her to the ground, and throttle her like Ruth had been.

But when Ruth came within two feet of Astoria, she was thrust backwards with such power, she landed on the ground far away, pain enveloping her entire body. And she wasn't even supposed to feel pain.

"What the hell!" she heard Evander shriek as he ran to her side. "A-are you okay, Ruth?"

When she managed to nod after he'd helped her sit up, he turned on Mr. Bundleheckles. "What on Earth is wrong with you? Why are you trying to sabotage her mission?" he hollered, fuming.

"Wh-what are you saying?" Ruth got out in a weak voice. "He isn't sabotaging anything."

"Oh, really? Cause I just saw him use his powers to throw you away from his daughter."

"Daughter? He didn't attack me, Evander."

But that's when she realised that Mr. Bundleheckles had, indeed, attacked her. No one could outfight her except him, because he had powers too. But what daughter was Evander talking about? And then it dawned on Ruth. She hadn't paid much attention before but when Astoria had come out of the tent, she had said 'Dad'.

"I can actually see the wheels turning in your head," Mr. Bundleheckles said, mockingly. "It's quite amusing, really."

Chapter 20

"So you've been trying to protect your daughters all along? Is that what your 'help' was? Is that why you didn't want me looking for them?" Evander asked.

"Right you are, boy," the old man said, smiling. "It's fascinating how much smarter you are than Ruth here. Honestly, she should've guessed it ages ago. But then again, she couldn't."

"This isn't possible," she wondered aloud.

"Oh, but it is," Mr. Bundleheckles said. "The moment I found out that you're after my daughters, I knew I had to be more involved so I could sabotage your mission. Now, you're nowhere near the jewel, and with me on their side, there's no way you're killing my daughters. You're doomed, Ruth."

How strange it was to see a sneer on a face Ruth had once thought to be of an angel's. She simply couldn't believe how deep a wound Mr. Bundleheckles had given her. She had never been betrayed before – not like this, at least. After what Mr. Bundleheckles had done, Evander leaving seemed nothing in comparison.

"Your wretched daughters are killers," Evander said.

"Even so... they're *still* my blood." The man smirked arrogantly. "Telling them about the *Kingdom of the Lifeless* was essential the moment Ruth entered. They've known about her ever since. I've been helping them escape. Ruth wouldn't have gotten here either had you not shown up."

"Of course," Evander said like everything was making sense to him. "That explains you disliking me. I messed up your evil little plan."

"I must admit: your genius is appreciable," Mr. Bundleheckles told Evander playfully. "I cannot help but think of Ruth's incompetence – not only is her magic mediocre but she's been quite worthless from the beginning. Couldn't find Astoria and Maxine for the longest time; couldn't save her parents' lives; couldn't escape alive. What a shame... what a shame for her dead parents."

"HOW DARE YOU!" Evander bellowed, as he charged towards Mr. Bundleheckles but was thrown off course effortlessly. Evander landed with a thud on the ground and groaned as Ruth rushed to him, snapping out of her paralytic daze.

Chapter 20

"Evander, are you okay?" she asked, knowing he wasn't. "I-I'll get you something, I—"

"I'm fine," he managed. "My back... hurts, though."

"I have some medicine, you can have that." As Ruth turned to reach her backpack that she had dropped on the ground, she saw that Mr. Bundleheckles and Astoria were gone. She strained her eyes and realised the tent was still there. "I'll just be back," she told Evander and rushed to the tent. Peeking inside, she found it completely empty.

So they had escaped, then. Ruth's and her parents' killers had escaped. So had their malicious father. Without the slightest wisp of a sound.

All Ruth knew was that they'd have to repay.

21.

RUTH – The Tables Turn (sort of?)

Ruth paced in the tent that Astoria, Maxine and their traitorous father had left behind. The tent was no less than an apartment, with two areas separated by curtains and with sofas and food. This was Mr. Bundleheckles' magic's creation, surely. Nothing else could be this perfect.

While one half of her wanted to accept what Mr. Bundleheckles had said – 'You're doomed' – the other part wanted something more intense. To brutally and mercilessly punish Mr. Bundleheckles and his daughters. He had deceived her; he had made her trust him and misused that trust to his advantage; he had made her think he had her back. As it turned out, all of it had been an act, a façade, an Oscar-worthy performance. Ruth felt disgusted and furious. At herself, too. If she hadn't been so gullible and trusting, none of this would have happened.

Chapter 21

"Don't be so hard on yourself, Ruth," Evander said as if reading her mind. "I would have done the same thing."

"Probably not," she said. "You can read people so flawlessly. You knew something was up with him the moment you met him, didn't you? You warned me too. I was just foolish to not have listened."

"That part's true. Every time you didn't listen to me, you were being really foolish."

"Evander, I'll go to the afterlife in less than 3 months. We won't be able to catch them," she said, letting her dejection colour her voice.

"Not with that attitude, we won't," Evander replied cheerfully.

"How can you possibly be so happy? You're hurt. And we're not exactly in the best predicament."

"I am relieved, Ruth," he said. "Now we know exactly what we're up against. First, we had this grey area with Mr. Dumb-old-man but now, we don't. We know exactly what they're going to do and we just have to act accordingly."

"I don't get it. What do you mean?"

"You cannot defeat Mr. Bundleheckles but you do have a fighting chance. Besides, he won't stay by their side forever. I say, we find their next location and you can go there, and while you finish them off, I can look for the jewel. If you find its location first, we'll be all done."

"It's that easy?" Ruth said, chuckling wryly and sitting down beside Evander.

"Probably not," Evander said, returning her smile.

"Why are you guys laughing?" Lesly said, popping out of the blankets she had nestled in. "None of this is funny."

"Probably not," Evander said again, laughing this time.

Somehow, for no real reason, Ruth felt a giggle bubble in her throat and after weeping and feeling sorry for herself for months, she simply couldn't control it. Soon, she and Evander were guffawing. Probably because whatever had happened had been too much for the both of them. Lesly didn't chime in, though. Instead, she just looked at them sternly until their laughter had died down.

Chapter 21

"Now, if you are done, I believe we should find their location," she said.

"Uh-huh," Evander said and Ruth nodded.

For the first time in months, Ruth finally felt hopeful. And part of the reason was Evander. Because when she would normally have been bawling her eyes out, crestfallen irreversibly, he had managed to make her laugh. And that was a mystery she'd probably never unravel.

****

They sat in the tent for hours as Evander meticulously continued his research, working with their current coordinates and the previous ones.

"What if they break the pattern altogether?" Ruth asked. "They know we're on their trail now. They could pick any location in the world for a hideout. It wouldn't necessarily follow the pattern."

"Yes, but they cannot just go anywhere," Lesly explained. "They're criminals. Apart from murders, they've committed many other felonies. They wouldn't risk going somewhere they haven't researched about well in advance. A crowded place is the last one they'd choose. For them, the safest option is to lie low in their decided place and hope that we don't find them."

"I think it's a risky plan," Ruth said, unsure now, and feeling odd that she hadn't thought about this before. "We may not find them or the jewel."

"Well, alright," Evander said. "Then we can just sit here and have a lovely picnic till your 3 months are up and then you can depart to the afterlife and I..." Evander trailed off.

"That isn't what I meant," Ruth told him.

"Well, I don't care if this plan turns out to be completely useless. Because I cannot give up, Ruth. Not now. Not when this is the only thing you want."

His response gave her a start. Evander was sticking around only to help her. Only because this mission was her death wish. The more time she spent with him, the more she found herself being clueless about who he really was. Quarrelling with her unstoppably at times, and being selfless and supportive all of a sudden.

Chapter 21

"Besides, I don't have any other plan," he added, sensing what he'd said had just the hint of awkwardness. "And I know you don't either."

"He's right," Lesly said, eyeing the two of them. "Why don't you go rest till we find the place? You need to save up your energy."

So, Ruth did.

****

After she had freshened up from her nap, Evander told Ruth that he had found the place Astoria and Maxine should be hiding currently. It was in a sequestered desert, far from where they were. It would be a long journey, even with 'Transformation'. So, Ruth stuffed herself with the food she had conjured until she couldn't hold another bite and drank *Elixir of Death*.

"Hey, Lesly and I are going to stay here for a bit," Evander told her when she was ready to go. "We need to figure out where to start."

"Yes, and if we find something, we'll get to you," Lesly said. "If you need our help, use *Crystalvocatio*, and we'll come wherever you need us to, as soon as possible. If we find the jewel, we'll tell you too."

Ruth nodded and bid Evander and Lesly goodbye and stepping out of the tent, summoned all her concentration to turn into a leaf.

****

When she landed on the sand and turned back into human-form, Ruth couldn't help but admire the desert's beauty. Silent, calm and minimalistic. No trees, no huts, nothing at all – just golden sand dunes. It must have been close to evening, judging by the dimming light of the orange sun as it neared the horizon. It was a beautiful place to be in – the sky was ombre with all possible shades, from orange to peach to pink to purple.

Realising that the soothing wind that caressed her face now could get really chilly really soon, Ruth quickly got down to work. Conjuring a tent and a jacket, she decided to rest for a little bit, after all, she had been travelling for many hours. Soon, she would go looking for the trio.

Two minutes into the nap, she woke up to the sound of light footsteps. She was instantly ready to

Chapter 21

get into action-mode; she braced herself and got out of the tent to see a figure walking towards her, slowly, not evading her but not attacking either. As the figure neared, Ruth recognized it.

"You traitor!" she hissed at Mr. Bundleheckles, whose face remained as unreadable as ever. "You dare return after what you did? You're here to fight me? You know I won't die. You know I won't stop the pursuit of your daughters until the very last second."

"Yes, I do, my dear Ruth," he said pleasantly, like he hadn't attacked her some hours ago.

"'Dear'? How stupid do you honestly think I am?" Ruth asked. "I'm not falling for your lies again. You can try your best but I will find your daughters and kill them."

"And what about the jewel?" he asked her.

"What about it? I'll snatch it right from your daughters' hands and return it to its rightful place!"

"But my daughters don't have it," Mr. Bundleheckles said simply. "Although, I do know where it is."

"This is just another one of your lies! You don't care about the jewel. You just want to save your daughters. You're tricking me into leaving their trail. But I'm not dumb enough to do that. Not anymore."

"I could show you," he said, pleadingly. "I could show exactly where my daughters are so you can get to them. Believe me, I never intended to assist them. But I knew that there was something dubious about the search of the jewel. Why would they kill your parents when they knew very well that they were the only thing that could lead them to the jewel? It was obvious – something else was at play. And they knew exactly what that was. Now I do too."

"You were the only one I trusted besides Lesly," Ruth said, ignoring his monologue. "You betrayed me."

"But I didn't!" he said, his desperation mirrored in his frail voice. His bloodshot amber eyes were almost pitiable. "All of that was just a set-up so I could get information from my daughters that could help you in finding the jewel. I swear! I was on your side this entire time! I know it's hard. I really do. But I could show you proof. Please, just please give me a second chance to help you fulfil your mission."

Chapter 21

She wasn't going to let Mr. Bundleheckles manipulate her again. "You know I won't."

"I cannot help you if you don't agree, Ruth," he said. "And I cannot give up helping you. This is very, very important to me. Please. Maybe, look at it as a compromise. Just give me one last chance to prove my innocence."

Ruth wasn't stupid. But she wasn't heartless either. Mr. Bundleheckles' imploring voice had melted the hard coating of hate around Ruth's heart. She wanted to believe him, she really did. Because it'd mean she hadn't been wrong to have put her faith in him. Him saying the truth would mean she wasn't the naïve fool Evander probably considered her.

Alas, she wasn't made of stone. So, with much reluctance and caution, she nodded 'Yes'.

22.

EVANDER – The Vision

Just as he sat down to scan the world map again, Lesly – now a puppy – bounded into the room.

"I've received a message from Ruth," she told him.

She handed to him a small piece of crystal, almost the size of Ruth's *Crystalvocatio*. It was glowing a pearly white, and on it were shining the words – 'This is extremely important. You two must come where I am as soon as possible.'

"That's very ominous," Evander said, returning the crystal to Lesly.

"Yes. She has probably found them and needs backup," Lesly said, worried. "You're packed, right? Let's leave right away."

"How are we going to go? Transformation?" he asked Lesly.

"Yes." She took a moment to think about it. "Although, I have never taken an undead along. So, I'm not aware of how that's going to go."

Chapter 22

"Why don't we try transporting a small distance first? So, you know, you don't accidentally kill me or something?"

"It's not going to kill you." Lesly laughed. It was weird seeing a puppy laugh. "It might weaken you a little bit. But we'll just have to take that risk. Come on, let's get going. Ruth could be in trouble."

"Well, please do help her when I'm dead."

"Ugh. Fine. Let's try going outside the tent," Lesly said. "Then we can leave."

"Okay, great."

Lesly jumped into Evander's hands. "Here goes nothing."

Suddenly, wind enveloped Evander, making him shiver. But when it was gone, Evander opened his eyes and found he was an insect, with 3 pairs of legs, two pairs of wings and antennae. It was the strangest feeling in the world; no, probably stranger than that. He realised he was riding on top of a bird. The bird flapped its wings and they were moving. His surroundings were too huge for him to make sense of anything. But he didn't have to. Soon enough, wind wrapped around him again, and when it vanished, he had turned back to a human, holding Lesly in puppy-form in his hands. They were back in the tent. Had they even left it?

The puppy jumped back onto the ground. "How do you feel? Are you alright? Or are you dying?"

"I am not dying," he said with smile. "I'm okay. Except a little dizzy. But I think I'll be fine."

"From what I know, as long as you are in contact with me, you'll be okay. It's very similar with souls too, except, it's slightly easier to carry them since they're dead too. But we'll take breaks. So, don't worry."

Evander nodded and stuffed the world map in his backpack. They stepped out of the tent and before he knew it, he was a tiny bug again.

****

When they finally landed, it took a good 5 minutes just for Evander's vision to stabilize. Even when it did, the world seemed to be dancing around in curves in front of him. He felt disoriented and couldn't understand if they had reached or not.

Chapter 22

"Evander," he heard Lesly's voice say, but it sounded distorted and muffled. "Are you okay?"

He fell to the ground and saw the sky above him. The sky's many colours swirled around and looked like paint being mixed together with a brush by an artist. It was gorgeous. His eyelids drooped.

Evander's eyes opened and he was surprised to see his vision was perfectly clear. He sat upright and found there was dizziness.

"Oh, thank goodness!" he heard Lesly shout with relief. "You were asleep for like an hour. How do you feel?"

"Alright. Let's get going. Ruth must be waiting for us."

As they began walking, Evander had the ambiguous sense that trouble was close. The sky was pitch black now and the shimmering stars looked beautiful, but the sight of the ginormous expanse of sand dunes with nothing but the sound of his own breathing and footsteps was giving him a bad feeling. If that wasn't bad enough, the cold air froze his sweat and made him shiver. *Oh, must I always be scorching or freezing?* He wondered irritably.

He pulled out his windbreaker and wrapped it tightly around himself, hoping they'd find Ruth soon and he could warm up in the tent. That's when he remembered this wasn't some cosy reunion - Ruth had called them for help. She was in trouble. And if she was, so were him and Lesly.

"Evander!" he heard Ruth's voice call from his right and momentously, he was relieved because her voice didn't sound anxious. But then he turned and found something much worse than anything he had imagined.

Mr. Bundleheckles.

Just sitting there, beside Ruth on a mat, wrapped in a blanket, peacefully sipping something from a cup.

"What the hell is he doing here?" he asked Ruth from a distance, not even wanting to go near the wretched man. "You don't think he's on your side, do you? Because he had no problem attacking either of us some time before."

Chapter 22

"I am not asking you to trust him," she said, standing up and walking towards him. "But, just... just hear him out. Please. He knows where the jewel is."

"I see," Evander said, scoffing. "He's managed to fool you again. Don't you see how selfish he really is? Ruth, you always see the good in everyone because you're too good for the world. This man is a liar! I'm not going to hear him out. Not after the way he betrayed you."

"How devastating it is to see how easily hate fills a person up," the old man said philosophically, clucking his tongue, as he walked towards Evander. "I'll be honest, son. I have wronged you and Ruth in many ways. But it was all for a good cause. I never meant to support my daughters. They are in the wrong and Ruth should punish them however she wishes. I must not keep you in the dark anymore. You have the right to know the truth—"

"Oh, I know the truth!" Evander shouted with certainty. "The truth is that you are manipulative and evil! You can convince Ruth but not me. I know this is all pretence. I bet your darling daughters are hiding somewhere around here right now, waiting for your signal to attack."

Mr. Bundleheckles looked disappointed as he turned to Ruth. "We don't have any other choice," he said, shaking his head.

Ruth nodded as if heeding a command and charged, clutching Evander's hands so tightly, it hurt. He tried to break free but now Ruth's gentle hands were as tough as ropes glazed with iron. Mr. Bundleheckles was slowly walking towards him, expressionless. Evander was terrified and puzzled. For all he knew, this jerk had convinced Ruth to kill him and that's what was happening now. Evander screamed at the top of his lungs - his afflicted voice echoing around the desert - calling for help, but Lesly didn't come to his aid. No one did.

Mr. Bundleheckles placed his right palm gently on Evander's forehead, and with a twinge of pain attacking him, he slipped into a gloomy oblivion, where he had a vague sense of being trapped.

Slowly, an image floated into his view and replaced the darkness. He was forced to pay attention to the image, and he decided to ignore his bewilderment for

Chapter 22

a moment as he tried to focus on what was happening.

He could see a beautiful blue-green sea, glistening under the sunlight, waves rippling across the water's surface. As Evander watched, a small boat veered into focus. He recognized one of the two girls on the boat – she had broad shoulders and blonde hair. It was Astoria; and the girl next to her – with beady black eyes, ashen skin and jet-black hair – must have been Maxine, her sister. There was a man on the boat too – Mr. Bundleheckles. The girls appeared to be arguing when their father bellowed angrily for them to shut up. They did, and watched their father as he sat down, enraged.

"Oh, this messes up everything," he said. "The whole plan's going to go down the drain."

"What plan, Dad?" Maxine asked. "We're safe now."

"How did they find us, Dad?" Astoria asked furiously. "I thought you were misleading that good-for-nothing girl."

"I was! Until that boy showed up out of nowhere!" he was so vexed, his face turned a shade of red. "I'm just going to have to do it this way now." He sighed.

"What do you mean?" Maxine asked.

"Tell me where the jewel is," Mr. Bundleheckles said.

"We obviously don't know that, Dad," Astoria said, surprised. "If we did, we'd have sold it by now."

"I know you have it!" her father exclaimed, making the girls flinch. "I know you do! SO STOP LYING! Do not mistake me for a fool. You two have no idea what I'm capable of."

Maxine was shuddering, taken aback by her father's behaviour. "Da—"

"ENOUGH!" Mr. Bundleheckles hollered, cutting her off. "Out with the truth right now! Or the consequences are not something I want my daughters to face."

"We can't!" Astoria said finally, tears starting to fill up her eyes. "I just can't. Or she'll kill us. She told us she'd kill us if we told anyone."

"*Who* will kill you? I won't let them do anything. Just tell me where the jewel is."

Chapter 22

"W-with Mom," Maxine choked out, tears spilling down her pale face. "She has the jewel back in Ravenwood."

"Iris?" Mr. Bundleheckles said, so shocked, all his anger had evaporated. His eyes widened as he stared at Maxine in disbelief. "Iris is still—"

"Yes," Astoria said. "She has gone absolutely nuts! All she thinks about is money and power and herself. She sent us in the pursuit of the jewel – she is the mastermind of this entire heist."

"This isn't possible," Mr. Bundleheckles said, dazed.

"It's the truth," Maxine said. "Then, when she was lucky enough to stumble upon the jewel herself, she told us to continue searching for it anyway, so people wouldn't know she has it. We have to pretend to keep looking for it for another month or so. Or she threatened to kill us."

Mr. Bundleheckles sighed exhaustedly. "Looks like I'm going to Ravenwood with Ruth, then."

"'Ruth'?" Astoria asked. "What are you talking about, Dad?"

"What, you actually think I'm on your side?" he asked. "I had no choice but to pretend to help you because I knew you'd lead me to the jewel. You really thought I'd protect you after you callously assassinated three innocent people? I loved you both because you were my daughters, but you aren't anymore. The girls I raised could never have chosen this path. Killing people in cold blood is just not something one can come back from. Ruth deserves to avenge her family by punishing you however she wishes."

"She wishes to kill us!" Astoria said, weeping like a little girl.

"Which - if you can remember - is not much different from what you did to her."

As Astoria and Maxine cried and implored for their father's help, Mr. Bundleheckles simply waved his hand, and they fell unconscious.

His hand hovered over their bodies and after a moment, he sighed heavily. "Oh, I hope they don't remember this," he whispered anxiously. "It'll be easier for Ruth to reach them."

Chapter 22

The image zoomed out and dissolved into blackness as abruptly as it had appeared, and Evander was lost in the dark once again.

23.

EVANDER – A Compromise

As his eyelids slowly lifted, all he could feel was agony and weakness pulsating through his body.

"Oh, you're finally awake!" Ruth hugged him so tightly, she knocked all the air right out of his lungs. "How do you feel?"

A groan escaped him. "Terrible."

"Right, of course," she said, a crease appearing between her eyebrows as she helped him sit up. "This should help."

Ruth brought a glass filled with something green and even though it smelled disgusting, Evander didn't push it away - mainly because he didn't have the energy to. Ruth held the glass to his lips and he managed to take gulps of the bitter liquid.

"You might feel ill for a couple of days," she said, placing the glass on the table next to the bed Evander was on.

Chapter 23

"I don't understand what happened," he said, rubbing his throbbing temples.

"Mr. Bundleheckles used his magic to show you what had happened. That vision you saw was real. It was his memory. It happened right after he and his daughters fled from those woods."

"You let that fraud use his magic on me?" he asked, horrified.

"Well, you weren't believing Mr. Bundleheckles so we had to find a way."

"I refuse to believe that that vision was real."

"Well, son, it was," Mr. Bundleheckles said, appearing behind Ruth. "I know it's hard for you, given that no one you grew up with could be trusted. But, I swear, that vision was my actual memory."

Evander didn't like that Mr. Bundleheckles knew that detail about his past, but he had to admit it: the vision had appeared pretty realistic. It didn't seem like an act or a dream. Now he wasn't so sure. But he knew that Mr. Bundleheckles had certainly done a lot to earn his distrust.

"I don't know," he told Ruth. "I don't want to put my faith in him and then be betrayed like you were."

"Evander, please stop being so stubborn," she said.

"I'm being *wary*," he snapped. "It's probably not something you're familiar with."

"Enough!" said a squeaky voice. Lesly the puppy jumped onto Evander's lap and glared at him. "Do you realise that you have been unconscious for 3 days? Do you realise how much time we have wasted here? When we could have been searching for the jewel in Ravenwood?"

"Ravenwood?" he asked, scared of the puppy.

"The jewel's there. With Iris, my wife," Mr. Bundleheckles said.

"So, she's like... a criminal?"

"Yes, Evander," Ruth answered, sighing. "In fact, she was the one who got Mr. Bundleheckles killed."

"WHAT? Why? Is she crazy?"

"We'll find out soon enough," Mr. Bundleheckles said. "Only if you agree to come."

Evander scoffed. Like they needed him or cared if he came. "Ruth doesn't need my help anymore, does

Chapter 23

she? She trusts you again. I am sure she'll go with or without me."

Mr. Bundleheckles only rolled his eyes.

"I won't go if you don't come," Ruth told Evander, her face somewhat pink. "If we do this, we'll do it together."

He was taken aback. Firstly, because what she had just said didn't make sense. And secondly, because it didn't make any sense at all.

"But why? Going there could get you to the jewel and Astoria and Maxine."

"Yes, but I trust your judgement. If you think it isn't worth the risk, I won't do it."

"You'd go against Mr. Bundleheckles if I told you I am not coming?"

"Yes."

He was speechless. How could Ruth possibly trust him that much? And why did she trust his judgement? This meant only one thing – she didn't trust Mr. Bundleheckles at all. And if she didn't, she would surely remain cautious and alert. Her not blindly trusting Mr. Bundleheckles made the entire situation so much more manageable. The truth was that Evander wasn't a trusting person; he'd never had any reason to rely on anyone but himself. He hadn't trusted Ruth when he'd met her, and only after learning her secret did he truly believe she wasn't bad news. He wasn't willing to let his guard down with Mr. Bundleheckles. But, did he really have a choice now?

If they didn't go, they would be choosing a much harder path that probably wouldn't lead to their destination. They could search for the jewel for years and still not find it. Or Astoria and Maxine. Dangerous as it was, going with Mr. Bundleheckles was probably the best option for Ruth's mission. And that, after all, was all that mattered, right?

He sighed. "Fine. I'm in."

"Really? Oh, that's excellent!" The relief in Ruth's voice was proof enough that Evander had made the right decision. "We can get going, then."

24.

RUTH – The Encounter

The ominousness that coloured the air was so thick, Ruth couldn't help but feel perturbed. Everything in Ravenwood was eerily silent. Was that some kind of sign? An omen that something bad was coming their way? Ruth had never been one to believe these nonsensical superstitions, but she had also never believed that she'd be able to return to Earth after death, so what did she know?

As the group moved through the empty streets, Ruth noticed the damaged ruins of the city, which, evidently had been abandoned a long time ago. A fine choice for Iris, as Mr. Bundleheckles told them, given her long list of felonies (she was wanted in more states than he could remember). The smashed-in edifices, the yellowing grass in the backyards of houses with broken, dusty windows and parks with rusted swings that seemed to be glaring daggers at Ruth: the entire place wasn't exactly welcoming. She had a horrible feeling about the way things were going to go down if they did meet Iris. She wasn't just going to give away the jewel she had worked so hard to get.

"This is stupid," Evander mumbled almost inaudibly.

"Why?" Ruth asked him, stopping at once.

He looked up at her in surprise, probably wondering if she was being sarcastic. She wasn't. If Ruth had learned one thing, it was that even with his quirks, Evander had better judgement than her - every plan of his had panned out well. If he questioned something, she knew she should too.

"How are we gonna find her? Look through the entire city like a bunch of morons? Even if we had months to do that - which we don't - we'd probably never find her."

"I bet that's what you thought when you arrived at Toronto to find Ruth," Mr. Bundleheckles said.

"Then, not finding Ruth was an option I was somewhat okay with. Here, not finding Iris is unacceptable. We need to find a faster way to get to her."

Chapter 24

"Well, I'm out of solutions, so maybe you could take the trouble to think of one," Mr. Bundleheckles said harshly.

"You cannot talk to him that way," Ruth said, making Evander and Mr. Bundleheckles both look at her with a look of surprise. "Not after the things you've done. You're here to help us. That is all. If you don't wish to be here, you can leave."

"Ruth!" Lesly said. "He can still help us."

"How?" she asked.

"He has powers!" Lesly reminded her. "I'm sure he can use them some way."

"Can you?" Ruth asked Mr. Bundleheckles.

He frowned. "I might. But I don't like this new attitude of yours."

"Uh-huh. Tell us if you can be helpful," Evander barged in.

Mr. Bundleheckles sighed heavily as if thinking – *I brought this upon myself*. "I suppose, if I really try, I can find Iris' location."

"Whoa, really?" Evander asked, intrigued, and the child he was internally surfaced again. Ruth couldn't suppress her smile.

"Yes. I just have to concentrate hard enough on her memories, and maybe... we could find her. But it isn't fool proof."

"It is the best option we have," Lesly said. "Do it."

Evander scoffed. "You obviously could have done this for your daughters and helped Ruth finish them. But you didn't."

"Oh, for heaven's sake!" Mr. Bundleheckles yelled exasperatedly. "How many times must I explain to you buffoons that I couldn't have them killed before extracting information about the jewel?!"

"You're such a diva." Evander rolled his eyes, clearly enjoying punishing Mr. Bundleheckles.

"That's enough," Ruth said, trying hard to stifle her smile. "I'm sorry for our behaviour, Mr. Bundleheckles. Please help us."

"'Please'? Really?" Evander said.

"Evander, stop. We need his help."

Chapter 24

So, after much bickering and walking for about a mile, they finally found a bench where Mr. Bundleheckles sat in peace and concentrated. He sat there, and the rest of them stood next to him for about half an hour as the sun's heat baked them and made sweat trickle down the nape of Ruth's neck.

"How much longer is he gonna take? Jeez!" Evander whispered.

"You talk far too much for my liking," Lesly said from Ruth's hands.

Finally, after around 45 minutes, Mr. Bundleheckles stood up and stretched. "The place isn't much far from here. We must keep going North."

The group walked for another hour before coming upon a house that Mr. Bundleheckles found worth stopping in front of.

The broken forlorn building that stood before them looked unnerving – like the haunted houses in horror movies. The house was so old, every inch of it seemed to have been glazed with a thick layer of dust and spider webs. The blackened wood of the house made it look worse. Ruth didn't want to go inside. But she didn't have a choice.

"Do we really need to go in there?" Evander asked, grimacing.

"Yes. There's a good chance Iris is in there," Mr. Bundleheckles said.

Lesly jumped out of Ruth's hands and the group slowly walked towards the door. The door's hinges creaked as Mr. Bundleheckles pushed it open. The inside of the house was far more terrifying – not only because it was completely dark, but also because there were a million scorpions and other foreign insects meandering on the ceiling and on the floorboards and their ticking and clicking noises filled the air like a horrifying chorus. Ruth tried her best not to gag as she pinched her nose to prevent the effluvium of rotten wood from entering her nostrils. In the light that entered through the door, Ruth could make out a sofa, orange and tattered, with its springs and stuffing visible. There were a couple of doors too; they probably lead to the bedrooms or the kitchen. But the most important part of the scene was the set of staircases that lay in the far corner of the living room. There was a flight of stairs leading upwards and

Chapter 24

downwards. There was an underground level in the house. That was probably where Iris would be hiding.

"I'll go check the above floors," Mr. Bundleheckles said. "You both can check the bottom ones."

"No," Ruth said. "You and I will go together so I can keep an eye on you. And we'll go down first."

"Fine."

Evander nodded and moved up the stairs with Lesly. Ruth and Mr. Bundleheckles proceeded downwards – every step making the weak wooden stairs screech – and after going down 5 flights of stairs finally ended up in front of a freshly black-painted door. On the door, in white paint were the words – 'DO NOT ENTER'.

"This must be it," Mr. Bundleheckles said with sureness.

He looked at the door apprehensively, and Ruth couldn't help but wonder how he must feel to reunite with Iris, his wife. She had gotten him killed. They weren't exactly #CoupleGoals at the moment.

"Guys," Evander said, appearing behind them and making Ruth jump. "I didn't find anything upstairs, just some old, really dusty rooms. Did you—"

He noticed the door and his expression darkened. "She's in there?" he whispered.

"Must be," Lesly said from his hands. "We need to go in."

Ruth pressed her ear to the door and tried to gauge what the indistinct murmurs and hushed hisses were. She wasn't sure if they were an animal's or human.

Mr. Bundleheckles knocked on the door a couple of times. Then a couple more. But no one opened the door. Ruth's chest was tightening up with anxiety. Was Iris here? Was the jewel here?

"Let's just go in ourselves," Evander said.

As he reached for the polished doorknob, it turned itself.

The group moved backwards warily, soundlessly. They watched the door squeak as it opened and when it did, they saw nothing but blackness. Then, they saw the man. He would have been perfectly camouflaged with the black door and the interior, had his green eyes not given him away. His face had probably been

Chapter 24

painted black because nothing except his eyes was visible.

"What do you want?" the man asked in a deep, rumbling voice.

They just stared back at him, totally dumbstruck and petrified.

"What do you want?" the man grunted again, more irked.

"We wish to meet Iris," Mr. Bundleheckles said, and Ruth found it astounding how his voice was as confident as it always was.

"There's no Iris here," the man said. "Leave now. And do not return."

"We know she is in there," Mr. Bundleheckles said, unwaveringly. "Let us in."

The man's green eyes looked furious and just as he raised his painted fist to attack, a voice from inside the room spoke - "Lucius, lay off of them. I don't want any fights in my house. Let them come in."

25.

RUTH – The Cage

Instantly, Ruth knew the voice had to be Iris'. Even though she hadn't met Iris before – the voice was old, but powerful and authoritative, exactly what she had imagined Iris would be.

"IRIS!" Mr. Bundleheckles bellowed and stormed into the room past Lucius, and following him, when Ruth entered the pitch-black room, she squinted – nothing was visible. Suddenly, there was a faint light – probably created by Mr. Bundleheckles – illuminating the room and Ruth realised just how ginormous the place was. It was a hall, like the ones where you could hold parties or weddings or stuff. With polished, shimmering white tiles, a mirror for a ceiling that was about 30 feet above them, the place didn't look like it was a part of the house. The walls were an elegant cream and the pillars in the four corners of the room were engraved with convoluted patterns and coated golden.

Chapter 25

"Wow," Ruth heard Evander mutter.

And wow, the place was. In fact, Ruth was so wrapped up in the hall's décor, she had completely forgotten to notice the gigantic throne in the far end of the room. She did now, and beautiful as it was, in comparison with its owner, the throne was forgettable. The woman had ashen, no, porcelain-white skin. Pale and ghostly, as was her silk-embroidered white gown. Her eyes, however, were so black, they seemed to be all pupils. Her blonde hair with streaks of silver fell graciously around her shoulders in perfect uniformity. As she registered the presence of the outsiders, Iris' wrinkled face changed to bewildered and shocked.

"Caleb? Is that really you? But how? H-how is that po-possible? How did you survive?" she asked, flabbergasted.

Of course, Ruth thought. *She thought Mr. Bundleheckles is dead.*

"Oh, you needn't worry," he said. "I assure you I am dead."

"Then how on Earth are you here?!"

"Never mind all that," he said. "Astoria and Maxine told me the jewel is with you."

"Ah, you broke them?" she asked, losing her confusion. "Pathetic, dolt girls. Never should have used them."

"Yes. You shouldn't have. How could you use our daughters to do your dirty work? Thanks to you, they have the blood of three innocent people on their hands!"

Iris scoffed. "Oh, who cares."

"I do," Ruth said, finding her voice somehow. "I lost my family and life because of you. And you and your daughters will have to pay."

"Oh, will I have to, silly girl?" Iris laughed and the awful sound echoed around the chamber, making shivers run down Ruth's spine.

"Enough chit-chat," Mr. Bundleheckles said. "Give me the jewel, Iris."

"Oh, Caleb... how long will you be this naïve?" Iris heaved a sigh. "I have worked for years to get hold of that jewel. What makes you think I'll just hand it over to you? Like some fool? That jewel's mine! Once I

Chapter 25

find someone who can handle it without dying, I'll find a good dealer and have it sold."

"What do you mean by 'handle it without dying'?" asked Evander.

"Uh, who are you, again?" Iris asked.

"He's with us," Mr. Bundleheckles said. "Answer his question."

"Well, not that it's any of your business, but the legends about the jewel are true. It has magical powers. It cannot be touched by anyone who has sinned in any way. If this happens, that person is cursed, and will soon be met by some terrible fate. I know this is true because I lost many of my men while getting the jewel, because, you know, they've committed many felonies. Like myself. Which is why I haven't touched the jewel yet. We have been trying to find someone sinless to help us, but we just cannot."

A silence fell upon the room – everyone was probably deep in thought. How horrible must it be to realise that sinless people were as rare as three-headed dogs.

"EVANDER!" Ruth burst out before thinking about the consequences of her actions. His name resounded around the quiet room.

"What?" Evander asked her vexedly.

"Evander...you're sinless," she told him.

"I'm a decent person, Ruth. But I'm sure that's an overstatement," he said, scoffing.

"No, Evander. I have *seen* your life. I know for a fact that you haven't ever done anything wrong."

"Oh, well, this is absolutely excellent!" Iris declared ecstatically. "Evander, here, can help us with the jewel then!"

The next moment was a blur of many things happening all at once. The guards that had been standing beside Iris and at the hall's door dashed towards Evander and picked him up, trapping him in their strong bulky arms and bolted from the hall before Ruth could do as much as blink. Evander's calls for help snapped her to act.

"YOU NASTY DEVIL!" she shrieked at Iris, her mind focusing on nothing except the image of Evander being dragged away. "YOU GET HIM

Chapter 25

BACK RIGHT THIS INSTANT OR I'LL RIP YOUR THROAT OUT!"

Iris looked back at her expressionlessly. She wasn't afraid of Ruth. But she needed to be. Because Ruth couldn't let her harm Evander under any circumstances. Not when he had come all the way to this place only for her. She couldn't.

"You'll...rip my throat out?" Iris had the audacity to chuckle as Ruth glowered at her. "You think you're so invincible because you are dead? Need I remind you that being a soul makes you so much weaker than me?"

"Iris, we'll talk about the jewel later. Let Evander go. He has nothing to do with any of this. Please," Mr. Bundleheckles said.

"Oh, but I'm not harming him, Caleb," she said innocently. "I'll only wait patiently till he agrees to help with the jewel."

"YOU AWFUL—" Ruth was about to attack Iris, when a large iron cage dropped onto the floor out of nowhere, trapping her and Mr. Bundleheckles inside.

When Ruth tried to pound on the iron bars, Mr. Bundleheckles stopped her. "It's cursed, or something. I can feel it. It cannot be touched by souls. Or escaped. It'll incinerate us on contact."

"That's right," Iris said pompously, grinning from ear to ear. "While you were chit-chatting with me, my brilliant men found a way to trap you. They may be sinners but they're very good at research. Who knew this nonsense would actually work!"

Iris smirking at them made Ruth's blood boil. But there was nothing she could do. She was trapped. And so was Evander. Everything was falling out of place. They were doomed.

Soon, Iris left with her guards, probably bored looking at them defeated.

"Can't we transform into a mouse and get out or something?" Ruth asked.

"NO! Ruth, please. Don't even try it. We don't know how dangerous this thing is," Mr. Bundleheckles warned.

"I can get out," Lesly said.

She had been right by Ruth's feet. Ruth had forgotten about her when they had entered the hall.

Chapter 25

To prove her claim, Lesly jumped through the gap in the bars without touching them and landed safe and sound on the floor outside the cage.

"OH, YES!" Ruth exclaimed with joy. They weren't doomed. Lesly could help them get out and rescue Evander. Everything was falling back into place.

"Ruth, look," the puppy said gravely. "I've grown quite weak in the past few days. I think I might be getting sick again. I'm losing some of my powers. I cannot conjure anything at the moment. I need to go to *The Kingdom of the Lifeless* and get some help."

"How long will you take?" Mr. Bundleheckles asked as Ruth's hope ebbed away.

"About a couple of weeks," Lesly said. Ruth's heart sank. They didn't have that kind of time. "But, I swear, I'll be back as soon as possible. Just hang on."

"You take care, Lesly," Ruth managed as her tears threatened to spill.

"You too." Lesly bounded towards the door and disappeared.

"We're gonna fail, aren't we, Mr. Bundleheckles?" she asked, thinking of her parents, who loved her more than anything in the world, who she couldn't ever imagine living without, whom she wouldn't be able to avenge.

"Perhaps," he said, his eyebrows furrowed. "But you must know, Ruth... I will not stop fighting until the very last moment."

26.

EVANDER – A Ray of Hope in The Storm

When Evander awakened from the stupor a guard's strike to his head had put him in, he tried to make sense of his surroundings. He was in a dimly lit room, not much bigger than the hotel room he had stayed in at Toronto. Its grey walls were covered with cobwebs and dust and the single tube light that illuminated the room was dim and had flies buzzing about it. Evander realised that his feet were wet. He looked down to see that he was tied to a chair with stiff ropes and had water reaching his calves. There were wires placed in the water tub. What was going on?

Was Ruth alright? Or was she in trouble too? Suddenly, a feeling of relief settled over him. The only good part about Ruth being dead was that she couldn't be killed, or even harmed. Knowing that Ruth was safe made Evander so happy, for a second, he forgot his own predicament. He was relishing the reassurance of Ruth's safety when he heard a rattling behind the door of the room. It sounded like someone was rummaging through keys. Then, there was a loud thud of something heavy dropping to the floor.

The door flung open, and Iris sauntered in, looking as ghostly as she had been before, with her snowy dress and wrinkled albino skin. She smiled at Evander, although, the look in her menacing black eyes was unsettling.

"Look at you," she said in a falsely honeyed voice. "What a handsome boy you are! It would be such a shame...such a shame to have to slash your head off."

"What do you want, Iris?" he asked with a hoarse voice.

"For you to help us retrieve that jewel," she answered. "I have lost quite some of my men and I simply cannot afford to lose more. I get that you probably think this is a heinous act, but I assure you... I only want the money. I do not intend to harm anyone at all."

Chapter 26

"Your daughters murdered Ruth's family," Evander reminded Iris.

"Ah, yes." She sighed. "I'm sorry for that. It wasn't really my decision, though. I'll make sure my daughters don't repeat that. So, what do you say? Are you in?"

Evander's answer was obviously a loud and resounding 'NO', but he knew that would make things so much harder for him. And Ruth. She'd be trapped here with him – she wouldn't get the jewel or be able to kill Astoria and Maxine. What could he do? What could he possibly say to get him out of this situation?

"Very well then," she said after about a minute of silence from Evander.

Iris walked to the door – far away from Evander – and a guard placed a black remote in her palm. She was glaring at Evander, but her face was triumphant, like she had won the battle already. She grinned and her eyes gleamed with callousness as she pressed the single red button on the tiny remote.

A cry escaped him as a wave of ineffable anguish coursed through his veins. Evander had never, ever experienced this kind of affliction before, even when his sister had pushed him into a giant trough of boiling water. As the current swam through his blood, his nerves felt like they were being scorned. A burning sensation spread through his entire body. Evander couldn't think of anything, except how tranquil death would be; he just couldn't bear the pain anymore.

"KILL ME!" He yelped somehow. "KILL ME NOW!"

Agonizing moments passed and the fiery excruciation slowly seeped out of his frail body. The current had probably been turned off, but he still felt like he was being roasted for Iris' dinner. With the current, all his energy seemed to have left his body too; he felt so terribly drained, so colossally impaired, he couldn't remember what not being electrocuted even felt like.

"Oh, you poor boy!" Iris' voice dripped with pretence concern. "I hate to see people in pain." She laughed. "Just kidding. It brings me such an amazing pleasure!"

Chapter 26

Evander used every ounce of his energy to raise his hanging head and look up at Iris and couldn't help feeling disgusted when he saw her beaming at him.

"But you, Evander, are valuable. So, I decided to cut you some slack – you know, electrocute you only 2 times a day instead of the usual 5." Her smile vanished and her expression hardened. "I'm telling you, boy," she said, dropping the honey-voice. "Help me and you can live. Otherwise, you're as important to me as a bag of rotten food."

"I-I need some time… to think," he got out and was surprised by the effort it took to say those few words.

"You better think fast," Iris warned and left, nodding to her guards.

What was that nod for? The second electrocution for the day?

As an answer, Ruth appeared in the doorway. The moment they had locked eyes, she was running at him full speed and stopped only when they had embraced. She hugged him so strongly, the little energy that his body had salvaged left him too. Her sweet lavender fragrance was comforting, though, and made Evander feel a bit better.

"Oh, I'm so sorry!" she said, sniffling, as she pulled away.

Her eyes were bloodshot and swollen and her face was etched with trails of tears that were still spilling down her cheeks; her nose was a deep rouge, and she was trembling. Evander had just been electrocuted but looking at Ruth in that state was somehow more painful.

"Th-they made me s-see the entire thing." She snivelled. "They made me see your electrocution. How are you? Does it still hurt?"

"I'm alright," he said, trying to sound reassuring, but his strained, fatigued voice didn't help.

"No, no. You are not. And it's all my fault."

"Don't be stupid. None of this is your fault, Ruth."

"Do me a favour," she said, wiping her tears. "Just... just help Iris. Do whatever she asks you to. Sell the jewel. I don't care."

"WHAT? No!" Evander said. "We've been through so much to get that jewel. I'm not letting all of that go down the drain."

Chapter 26

"We'll figure something out," Ruth said, lowering her voice now. "Just lie to them for some time so that they stop torturing you and me both. We'll find a way to get the jewel from them and turn them in."

Evander didn't know what to say. Ruth was being stupid, risking the jewel. But when he truly thought about it, what choice did he even have? He couldn't just stall Iris forever. What he could do was say 'Yes' and then formulate a plan while Iris was busy celebrating her victory.

He sighed. "Fine. I'll tell her that I'll do it. But I'll request that she let me meet you until we get to the jewel so that we can come up with a plan in secret."

And for the first time, Evander could see hope in Ruth's eyes, and that glimpse was enough to give him the strength to keep going.

27.

EVANDER – The Farewell

The week that followed had been the most difficult in Evander's life, and his life had been pretty terrible even before he had met Ruth. Every electrocution rendered him with unbelievable pain and fatigue and burns that itched and hurt like hell. He hated having to go through it, but it was necessary because every day he'd get half an hour with Ruth, which was essential so that they could discuss their plan.

"I think Iris is growing suspicious of our meetings," Ruth told him one day, right after he had been shifted to a bed after his day's second electrocution. "What if they're listening to our conversations?"

"I honestly don't think they'll bother," Evander told her with much effort. "They can overpower us in any way if need arises. Besides, I bet Iris is too busy with the jewel. I think she is going to have us leave tomorrow."

Chapter 27

"'Us'? You think she'll bring me and Mr. Bundleheckles along? Come on, Evander. You're smarter than that."

"Well, I'll plead with her," he said. "I'll say I won't go if y'all don't come along as well."

"I'm not sure if that would work."

"What about Lesly? Has she returned yet?"

"No, still no sign of her." A crease appeared between Ruth's furrowed eyebrows. "I'm very worried, Evander. About everything. Lesly, our plan, you, the jewel—"

"I know," he said, placing his hand on her shuddering one. "I promise once I get hold of the jewel, I'll flee. If only there was a way to be sure that you'll escape from that cage thing…"

"Well, we don't know if I am even coming yet. We can worry about the cage later."

All Evander could do was nod grimly.

****

Later, in what he assumed to be the evening, when Iris had finally come to inform him about their departure the following day, Evander told her.

"Let her go free?" She gasped incredulously. "Don't be an idiot. I cannot let her go. Not until I have the money, that is."

"Well, then at least let her and Mr. Bundleheckles come along in their cage. That wouldn't be a problem, would it?"

Iris eyed him carefully for an entire minute before answering. "Look, boy, if you and your girl are trying to plan any kind of nonsense that'll make me lose my jewel, let me be clear – I will, one way or another, find you and have you punished in ways far worse than death. You and your entire family. You'll wish you were never born."

Evander stifled a laugh. If only Iris knew the number of times he had wished that already, she wouldn't be using it as a threat. And that thing about his family too - Evander wanted to think he loved them in spite of all that had happened, but at that moment, as he visualised Iris torturing them, he realised guiltily that he didn't care as much as he should.

Chapter 27

"Are you listening to me, you imbecile?" Iris hissed and Evander nodded, frightened that she might electrocute him again. "I know you want to have some benefit out of this too, and I won't deny you your share of the sum. You help me, and you get enough money to sustain yourself for a long time. You betray me, and you get a very slow, very torturous death. Do you understand?"

Evander nodded so vigorously, he almost sprained his neck. Iris glared at him for another moment before leaving and slamming the door shut.

****

The next day, there were no electrocutions, so Evander took advantage of the bed's comfort and slept in till Ruth came to meet him.

"We're coming along, then!" she said with relief, hugging him. "Oh, and Lesly arrived!"

"Shhh!" he whispered. "Lower your voice."

"Oh, I'm sorry. But she arrived and she's all better. Has her medicine and everything. Also, she listened to our plan and declared that it was bound to be a failure."

"Damn. I hate how savage she is. Did she suggest an alternative?"

The dingle had. As Ruth told him what the plan was, Evander realised how meaningless their previous one had been.

"Well, excellent," he said with relief. "Just make sure Iris doesn't see her before we can actually do anything."

"Oh, of course! She has turned into a tiny mouse and is in Mr. Bundleheckles' pocket. No one has seen her yet."

Evander nodded. A silence fell between them, and it was comforting, the lack of the need of having some kind of conversation going.

"Evander, I was counting yesterday." Ruth sighed helplessly. "I only have some weeks left now."

To a stranger, this might mean nothing; it may even confuse them. But Evander knew that it meant that Ruth would be departing to the *afterlife* after some weeks. The thought that Ruth would leave soon made his heart hammer like crazy against his chest. He knew he wanted to say a million things to her, but he couldn't exactly figure out what they were.

Chapter 27

"Don't worry," she told him, trying to hide her eyes where tears had begun to swell. "I've heard that it is a painless process. I'll be gone before I know it."

But I'll always know you're gone, he thought, but didn't have the courage to say it.

"Ok, time to go," the guard grunted, emerging from the doorway.

"What? No. We still have some—" Ruth began but was cut off as the guard grabbed her wrist and shackled it.

"Special orders today," he said gruffly and pulled her along as he headed towards the door.

"We'll be fine, Ruth!" Evander called out as she disappeared behind the door, and it slammed shut.

What did the guard mean by 'special orders'? Was it because they had to leave to retrieve the key? Yes, that must be it. So, Evander sat, waiting, for another guard to come and escort him, but an hour passed by, and no one arrived. The wait was monotonous, and there was a constant exhaustion in Evander's body these days (probably because of the electrocutions), so he let his heavy eyelids droop.

What seemed like the very next instant, Evander was startled awake by a sharp scream enlaced with affliction. When he saw Iris in front of him, watching him, savouring his pain, he had to ask her, because he was petrified that he already knew the answer.

"Whose voice is that?"

Another scream echoed.

"I think you know," Iris purred with satisfaction.

He did. He just didn't want to believe it.

"No, it isn't her," he said more to himself than Iris. "Ruth's dead. She cannot be hurt."

"Oh, is that so?" Iris said sardonically. "Well, as it turns out, she can be. She's a mere soul, a lesser being. Of course, she can be hurt. And right now, she is."

Evander's insides were burning with such abhorrence and wrath, he wanted to strangle Iris to death. He tried to, but realised his hands were shackled to his bed now.

Ruth hollered a third time.

"STOP IT NOW, YOU MONSTER!" he bellowed.

Chapter 27

"I will," Iris said earnestly, smiling malevolently. "But I need a promise from you... if you do so much as lift a finger against my commands, you will face the worst consequences and so will that girl."

"I promise I won't do anything!" he screamed as another one of Ruth's wounded shrieks filled his ears. "I promise, okay? Just stop this. I beg you, stop it."

Iris' face turned to show her pride and she sauntered off, locking the door behind her. Minutes passed, and Ruth didn't scream again.

****

"I'm so sorry, Ruth," he told her the moment she walked in the next day. "Are you hurting still? What did they do to you? I am so sorry for what happened. It's all my fault. I—"

"Oh, don't be silly," she said, attempting to smile but ended up wincing. "I'm fine. I'm alright. It wasn't your fault. Any of it. All I want you to do now is focus on the plan. Evander, we cannot fail. Because if we do, you'll be dead. And even though I'll be gone, I won't ever be able to forgive myself. But I swear, I'll do everything in my power to save your life."

"Don't worry about my death," he said. "It is probably the easiest punishment that awaits me if we fail. But we cannot. And we won't, I promise. We will get the jewel and you will kill Iris and her daughters."

Ruth nodded and as they embraced one last time, she bid him goodbye. He couldn't understand why, but the air was heavy with a sense of finality; this meeting felt like a final farewell: the last time they'd be together when they were both at peace.

Ruth wished him luck and departed.

As he let weariness take over his body, the only proper thought he could form was – 'I wish I had more time with Ruth.'

28.

EVANDER – A Deal with The Devil

He felt better than he had in a week – he was given fresh clothes and a delicious meal that consisted of all kinds of fruits, bread and chicken, something he hadn't had in a very long time. Mainly because his father always gave it to his brother Diego and sister Juliana. Also, he hadn't been electrocuted for two whole days, which was an immense bonus.

As Lucius – the guard who had first met them – escorted him out, pulling him by his handcuffs, he told Evander that they would be leaving soon and would use a chopper. None of what was happening was supposed to be exciting, and yet, he felt slight elation at the thought of being in a chopper for the first time. He had seen it in movies many times, and it looked so cool, the way the hero would get off the chopper, looking all serious and ready to fight. He felt childish for thinking this way, but he couldn't help it.

"What on Earth are you smiling for?" Lucius asked him coldly and he realised just then that he had been smiling. He stopped now.

"The food was good," he said.

"Well, she needs to keep you all fed and healthy, doesn't she? Because you'll get her the jewel."

"Right."

Lucius deposited him at the entrance of the hall he had first come to when they had arrived here. Iris was waiting for him there; the mere sight of her made his insides churn.

"Ah, Evander, my dear boy," she said as she turned and spotted him.

Evander suppressed a groan.

"How do you feel?"

"Alright. Thanks for not electrocuting me these last two days."

"Oh, I couldn't. I needed you to have enough energy to help me." She looked at him for a moment and then clucked her tongue. "You must think I am so despicable."

Chapter 28

He did. In fact, at the moment, with her skin slightly goldened by makeup and her outfit a soft blue, she surprisingly looked more human than ghost. She was human, of course, but there was too much evidence to support the contrary.

"Every person I ever met hated me, you know," she said, and for the first time perhaps, Evander could see a human emotion in those usually vicious eyes of Iris – sadness. "Caleb was different. He found me intriguing, and, not to mention, I wasn't a criminal when we fell in love. He made me the happiest person on Earth, until our son Malcolm died."

What she had just said hit Evander squarely in the chest like a punch. They had a son? Who died? How?

"Oh, of course, you don't know about Malcolm. How would you? You barely know Caleb."

"What happened to your son?" Evander asked. "If you don't mind me asking," he added quickly.

"Oh, I haven't talked to anyone about it for 15 years now." Iris took a shaky breath. "His birth involved many complications but when Astoria and Maxine met him, they were overjoyed. I was overjoyed. Caleb's happiness knew no bounds. Our family was so euphoric. Of course, it was all too good to be true. A couple of months after his birth, he was diagnosed with a terminal illness. Leukaemia - blood cancer. We only had a couple more months with baby Malcolm before he passed on."

Evander caught a glimpse of Iris' tears before she hid them and felt a pang of sympathy for her. She was a horrible person, but losing a child, especially when they were an infant, seemed like an awful ordeal for just about anyone.

"I'm sorry that happened," he whispered.

"He wouldn't have died, mind you," she said, her voice losing its injured tone. "He wouldn't have died had we had enough money for his treatment. His condition was diagnosed quite early, and we still had plenty of time for the necessary treatment. What we didn't have was money. And we would've had that too had Caleb agreed to bend a few rules. But he didn't. He wanted to stay the dumb, noble man he was. And because of Caleb's desperation to stay sinless, we lost our son. After Malcolm died, something inside me changed. It's like... I lost my

Chapter 28

humanity. All I knew was that my son was dead because of Caleb. All I felt was hatred for him."

Iris looked straight at Evander now, smirking savagely and losing any humanly qualities she had possessed for a few moments. "So, I got him killed. And believe me, I truly loved him. Yet, it didn't take me a second to have him murdered. You, Evander, are a stranger to me. Killing you as ruthlessly as possible won't be any problem for me. So, let's make a deal. You don't cross me or mess with my plan, and you'll live. What do you say?"

So that's what this was. Evander had begun to wonder why Iris was telling him all of this. He understood now. It had been just another way to threaten him. Scare the wits out of him. Iris' plan had partially worked. Now, he knew Iris was a selfish and merciless monster. She had just admitted so herself. She didn't care about her daughters or her husband. She simply didn't care. And someone like that can be very difficult to hurt. Evander realised he was shuddering because he knew Iris wouldn't spare him if things went sideway.

He was terrified, but he still wasn't going to back down; he couldn't. Besides, the beginning of their plan didn't even involve him - it was for Lesly to do.

But at the moment, all he did was nod. Iris grinned and nodded, and guards emerged to take Evander to the chopper.

"You're walking on thin ice, boy," she warned him as she was leaving. "Tread lightly."

29.

RUTH – The Unspoken Goodbye

The truck Ruth's and Mr. Bundleheckles' cage had been placed in was dark and housed strange stenches that had begun to give Ruth a terrible headache. Now, in the dark, when they were absolutely sure no guard was anywhere close to them, Lesly, in the form a small mouse, jumped out of Mr. Bundleheckles' pocket and climbed onto Ruth's palm.

"I saw Iris giving your cage's key to this large guard, the bald one," she whispered. "He's huge but pretty dumb. I'm positive I can get the key out of his clutches. Once you both are free, you need to take down as many men as quickly as possible. I must warn you - I saw quite a lot this morning."

Ruth nodded grimly and watched the mouse disappear in the darkness.

"Don't you worry, Ruth," Mr. Bundleheckles told her. "We're going to be fine."

"Yes. But if you make any attempts to back—"

"I swear, I won't," he said apologetically. "I have always been on your side, Ruth. Always. The moment I knew you were after my girls, I knew this had something to do with their mother. I had to help you because I have wanted to stop Iris ever since she turned into this selfish, greedy being."

"I don't know if any of that is true," Ruth admitted. "I don't think I can ever completely trust you again."

"That's alright," he said, nodding ruefully. "I shall prove my loyalty to you by getting you out of this mess."

Lesly squeaked through the darkness, zipping towards the cage, a golden key in her small paws.

"I took it right from under his nose as he snored."

She made a noise close to a giggle as she jammed the key in the cage's keyhole. The door swung open, and Ruth gasped disbelievingly. How had they managed this so easily?

She carefully got out, wary of the golden iron bars that could burn her on contact. Mr. Bundleheckles got out after her and for a moment they wondered if the truck was locked from the outside. The truck's

Chapter 29

doors swung open just then, and in a flash, Mr. Bundleheckles' powers had rendered the guards who had opened it unconscious.

They got out along with Lesly and realised they were in a dimly lit parking lot. There were no cars except the truck and silence pressed on them.

"Where do you think Iris is?" Ruth asked Mr. Bundleheckles.

"I'm not quite sure," he said, looking down the empty area. "Let's get out of here first. I'm certain they aren't much far away from here."

As they started walking towards the door in the far side of the parking lot, Ruth heard a soft thump behind her. She decided to ignore it, as anything dangerous would not be so close to soundless, and the group walked on until there was suddenly someone's voice booming around the area.

"I was certain I'd find you here," said the voice.

Mr. Bundleheckles and Ruth spun at once, alarmed and ready to fight, but the person in front of them was not someone they could use action against.

"Mythil?" Mr. Bundleheckles wondered aloud. "What are you doing here?"

"Finding evidence that you deserve to be tortured eternally in the *afterlife*," he said coolly, grinning.

Mythil didn't look any different from that night he had come to Ruth's home in Toronto to reprimand her; he still wore that same gown patterned with galaxies and his hair and beard were still perfectly groomed. The only thing different was his expression – he was smirking smugly, and his eyes glittered with joy.

"What?" Ruth said. She had no idea what Mythil was talking about.

"He's caught me red-handed, Ruth." Mr. Bundleheckles heaved a remorseful sigh and his face turned grave.

"Yes, I indeed have, Caleb," Mythil gloated. "And now, you shall never get my job. Ever!"

"I was never after your job, Mythil. You must know that."

"All I know is that you are an excellent liar." Mythil's tone changed to angry now. "How dare you break The Kingdom's rules and help your soul with

Chapter 29

her mission? You have interfered with her case far more than you can be forgiven for. You must face the consequences of your actions, Caleb."

"None of this is his fault," Ruth blurted out. Even though she still had her doubts about him, Mr. Bundleheckles had helped her immensely; she couldn't just let him get tormented for an eternity. "I begged him to assist me, Mythil. I swear I did! He didn't want to. He didn't—"

"ENOUGH!" Mythil hollered, enraged. "You should be grateful I haven't annulled your case already, you shameless child! If I didn't have to look into Caleb's termination process, that would have been my first priority. As it is, I am sparing you for you have very little time left anyway. Hardly 7 days, as I recollect."

"Th-that's not correct," Ruth stammered, doing the calculation in her head. "I still have weeks. You must be wrong, Mythil."

"Oh, *that* I never am, imprudent girl," he hissed impatiently. "The moment I understood you had been getting assistance from your head, I cut down the time you have on Earth. Now, you shall be banished to the *afterlife* in 7 days!"

"B-but you can-cannot do that," she ventured unsurely.

"Of course, I can! Now shut up."

Mythil stormed towards the group and pressed a golden devise to Mr. Bundleheckles' forehead before either him or Ruth could react. Mr. Bundleheckles looked like he had been tased as he fell to the ground, his body riddled with multiple spasms. In a matter of moments, he had fainted.

"NO!" Ruth screamed, petrified. "No, this cannot happen. Mr. Bundleheckles! Wake up!"

She kneeled next to his shivering body, and shook him as much as she could, begging him to get up, but there was no response at all.

"Don't waste your energy," Mythil said, grinning ear to ear. "He won't wake up now. Not unless I want him to."

"B-but this is wrong!" she managed as tears spilled down her face and her throat closed up. "You shouldn't do this, Mythil. Mr. Bundleheckles was a good person. He truly was. He only broke the rules

Chapter 29

for the greater good. He was never after your job. He never wronged anyone."

She realised as she spoke the words that they were, indeed, true. Mr. Bundleheckles had always been on her side. She could see it now – his attempt to make his daughters spill the truth by lying to them; his desperate search for Iris; his fatigue as he had tried his level best to help Ruth. He had always been there for her, looking out for her, supporting her, guiding her. How could she have been so blind?

"Please, Mythil," she pleaded still, even though her tears had made her vision non-existent. "Please, don't torture him. He was a good person. All his life, he had been good, moral. Mr. Bundleheckles was a noble man."

"Maybe he was." Mythil shrugged, returning the golden device to the folds in his gown. "But I am not. Ever since he entered The Kingdom, he has been nothing but a pain for me. He will have to go. There is no alternative."

Ruth found herself still imploring to the diabolical man; she was bawling, shrieking, and going on and on about what a great man Mr. Bundleheckles was, but Mythil wasn't staying to listen. Within moments, he hoisted Mr. Bundleheckles' body over his shoulder and disappeared.

At once, Lesly was by her side, telling her comforting things that brought no comfort, consoling her even though she couldn't possibly be consoled. All of this had been her fault. She never should've requested Mr. Bundleheckles' help. Now, all that awaited him was pain and suffering. The worst part was... after all that had happened, after all that he had done for her, Ruth hadn't even gotten the chance to properly thank him or say goodbye.

She hadn't said goodbye.

"Ruth, I think there is—" Lesly began when the parking lot's door in the far end swung open.

Iris was there, with at least 20 of her men. Her face was triumphant like she had hit some kind of jackpot but then it turned confused. She glanced around the huge parking lot, probably looking for something. Her men stepped inside, and Ruth wiped her tears and told herself to forget everything that had just happened. Because she needed desperately to focus now - her powers were useless if she couldn't concentrate. She braced herself - some part of her

Chapter 29

was beyond afraid of the many men she'd have to engage in combat with, but in truth, she could beat them so easily, she wouldn't even break a sweat. All she had to do was concentrate.

The brawny men towered in front of her, wielding lethal weapons; their faces looked conceited, like they had won this battle already. After all, to them, the frail little girl in front of them wasn't even worth their energy. Ruth was glad. She could use the element of surprise to her advantage.

The first man stepped closer to her, grinning and hefting his large sword with ease. Ruth composed herself, cleared her head and urged herself to focus. But suddenly, it wasn't the man who she saw: it was Mr. Bundleheckles. Smiling, cracking silly jokes, being the wise, noble man he was. Gone. Forever. Not in peace, either. In utter affliction. Anger surged through her veins, and she thought about how every man in front of her was somehow responsible for Mr. Bundleheckles' predicament. She didn't need to focus or concentrate anymore; her fury was enough.

Her hands rose involuntarily, and the man flew across the parking lot, hitting the wall with immense speed and dropping to the floor, unconscious. One after another, increasingly nervous men took the first man's place and met his fate. Ruth was enraged, and the spells seemed to be working by themselves in the back of her head; the fight was starting to seem a little too easy when out of nowhere, a wave of weakness washed over her. For a moment, her powers seemed to have vanished altogether and she stumbled backwards, overtaken by the sheer fatigue and pain that had popped up out of thin air. The third last man advanced on her and just as he was about to use his knife on her, she managed to push him away with a spell. Ruth summoned his knife and as he returned to attack, she slashed his neck with it; holding his gash, the man fell to the floor. The last two men exchanged nervous looks and looked back at Iris.

"What are you waiting for, you idiots! Attack her!" she commanded.

They came together, weapons poised to harm Ruth. The men's knives collided against Ruth's skin but didn't make as much as a scratch. They looked at each other, horrified.

"Didn't you know that I'm dead?" she asked feebly.

Chapter 29

The men turned on their heels and ran for the exit but before they could escape, Ruth tried to thrust them against the walls and succeeding, both of Iris' soldiers were on the ground, knocked out. In fact, all 20 of her men had passed out.

Ruth collapsed on the floor, drawing ragged breaths, the last bit of her energy abandoning her to her own devices. She was dead, a soul – she wasn't supposed to feel pain. Yet, it surged through her now. Was it because she hadn't had her elixir in a very long time? No, that wasn't correct. There had been plenty of times when she had forgotten to take the elixir; she hadn't felt any agony or weakness or lack of powers. What *was* the reason for her pain, then?

"Growing weak, are you?" Iris appeared in her zone of vision, smirking tauntingly at Ruth as she winced. "How pitiable."

She tittered, and began to tug on Ruth's arms with much effort, pulling her towards the truck that was some distance away.

"Oh, I was being stupid, wasn't I, Ruth? I didn't need all those men to take you down. It's actually even better that you're dead." Iris's upside-down face was beaming at Ruth. "All I have to do now is make you touch that cage. You'll burn and soon enough, be gone. I believe Evander has already retrieved the jewel. I can get going on my merry way after I finish him off."

"You are g-going to k-kill him?" Ruth stuttered.

"Well, of course! Or do you think I'm dumb enough to share my money with that piece of crap?"

Ruth realised that Iris had reached the truck now and in a moment or two, she'd surely be incinerated by the cage's golden bars and soon enough, Evander would be killed.

A flashback hit her like a blow – she was standing next to a bed covered with a white linen cloth; on the bed was Evander, looking tired and injured but relieved as he saw that she was alright in spite of her previous torturing. "But I swear, I'll do everything in my power to save your life," she had told him. She had promised him she wouldn't let him die. Even though wherever she was headed to she probably wouldn't be aware of any of this, Ruth just couldn't leave knowing that Evander was headed towards death.

Chapter 29

In spite of her weakness and complete absence of powers, Ruth garnered as much energy as she could, and gripped Iris' wrists tightly and hurled her towards the floor, away from the truck.

Iris was moderately fit, but she had to be at least fifty; this kind of a manoeuvre was likely to result in a few broken bones. As she landed with a loud thud onto the ground, she shrieked and just as Ruth lost all her energy again, she heard footsteps. Had the guards woken up? Or had some more arrived to finish her off?

"Ruth!" Evander's gasp resounded in the silent parking lot and Ruth managed to lift her neck to look at him.

He wore a soiled orange t-shirt and faded blue jeans. His aghast face and arms were peppered with cuts and bruises and his hair was ruffled. In his hands, he held something shiny – the jewel.

30.

EVANDER – The Curse Comes Alive

When he burst through the entrance, he saw two things in the gigantic parking lot - Iris sprawled on the ground, groaning loudly and Ruth, close to a truck, lying helplessly, looking like she was about to die.

"Ruth!" he yelled, desperate to know if she was alive or not.

As her head slowly lifted and she looked at him, he remembered that she had already died a long time ago. He always seemed to forget that. But now, as he did remember it, he remembered her last wish - to protect the jewel and avenge her parents. *To protect the jewel.*

Evander looked at the jewel he held so casually in his arms. It was the size of an orange, but glittered with the light of a thousand suns. Even though he had looked at it for a whole minute when he had

Chapter 30

found it, he still had no idea what its true colour was. Maybe it didn't have one at all. It looked so magnificently iridescent, gleaming even in the dull lighting of the parking lot.

He tore his eyes away from the jewel and found Ruth still looking at him. She wasn't speaking but her eyes screamed for help. He ran towards her, gently placing the jewel on the floor on his way. He slowly helped Ruth up, and she sat on the truck's edge, taking deep breaths and occasionally groaning.

"What's wrong?" he asked her.

"I-I am not sure," she said, panting. "I guess the fighting was too much."

"Alright. Just try to hold on for a little longer. We need to get out before more of her men get here." Evander peeped into the truck and saw that the golden cage that had held Ruth and Mr. Bundleheckles was empty. Lesly - a small grey mouse now - was napping next to it.

"Where's Mr. Bundleheckles?" Evander asked Ruth.

"Exactly my question!" Iris said from behind him. She had stood up and – much to his dismay – stopped groaning. "Where is that dear husband of mine?"

"Mythil took him," Ruth said to no one in particular, clutching Evander's hand tightly because she had lost her stability. She leaned on the truck's side, inhaling and exhaling like she had run a marathon.

"Mythil? That guy from The Kingdom? Why? What happened?" Evander asked her.

"I can't..." Ruth trailed off.

Evander held her palm tightly between both of his, afraid that she was slipping away from him somehow.

"Well, whatever." Iris scoffed. "I'll find him later. But right now, I must end you."

Evander turned because he was genuinely curious to see whom she was speaking to. She was looking right at him.

"You cannot kill me," he told her. "You need me to take jewel."

"From here, I am pretty sure I can use your dead body too." The idea seemed to amuse her. "Actually, you know what, boy? I am going to do exactly that."

Chapter 30

Iris whipped out her dagger and advanced so quickly, Evander barely had any time to dodge the blade whizzing towards him. He had been beaten up a good number of times by his siblings, but Evander had never been in real combat. In plain words – he was terrified of the knife Iris was handling so effortlessly.

He didn't *want* to fight either. Horrible as she was, Iris was pretty old. Evander couldn't bring himself to harm her in any way. All he could do was dodge her attacks and push her away. But she was very skilled, he realised as she persevered and attacked continuously, not giving him a second to catch his breath. Then, she slashed for about the tenth time, and this time, he hadn't been fast enough. The blade collided with his left forearm, cutting open a long, gaping gash that spewed blood on the floor as Evander fell. He yelled as his blood trickled into his palm, and excruciation pulsated in his bleeding gash.

"And now, you die."

Iris' makeup had worn off and she looked as albino and unhuman as ever as sweat beads trickled down her maliciously sneering face. She raised her dagger.

Evander didn't have the energy to keep fighting, and quite frankly, he didn't know how to, either. Maybe he didn't mind dying. How painful could it be, really?

"EVANDER!" he heard Ruth yelled from behind him but he couldn't get up to look at her. Even without looking at her, he could recognise the desperation in her voice. She had promised him that she wouldn't let him die.

Then, something bizarre happened. Iris' knife flew right out of her hand and landed on the ground some feet away.

This is my chance, a voice said in Evander's head.

As Iris turned to look at her fallen dagger in absolute bewilderment, Evander hoisted himself up and pushed her over hard and crashing to the ground, she let out a shrill "OUCH!"

Evander reached for the knife, not really sure what he must do after he had retrieved it. He couldn't kill Iris, could he? No, that was Ruth's job.

Chapter 30

On the ground, Iris turned over and Evander saw the reason for her cry of pain. She had landed on the jewel's sharp, pointy end. As Iris slowly sat up, she saw the jewel and put the pieces together.

"NO!" she exclaimed and for the first time ever, Evander could sense fear in her voice.

For a moment, he didn't understand what the problem was. But then he remembered what Iris had told him, Ruth and Mr. Bundleheckles when they had first arrived at her place. *It cannot be touched by anyone who has sinned in any way. If this happens, that person is cursed, and will soon be met by some awful fate.*

"But I didn't touch it," Iris whispered to herself, hyperventilating. "No. I-I just fell on it. I am not cursed yet. No, I cannot be."

The dagger slipped out of Evander's bloody palm and he walked backwards, towards the truck where Ruth was. She clutched his right hand like a lifeline and he found her ice-cold hand was trembling. He looked at her and she was so pale, her skin was almost translucent. Her lips were blue and her eyes were bloodshot as she tried to focus on his face. What was happening to Ruth?

"Make her touch the jewel," she said in a pained voice.

"I'd like to see you try." Iris had stood up pompously in front of them, and had lost all her fear. Cackling, she picked up her dagger and flexed her arms. "Nothing can beat me, you dolts. You think either of you could outfight me? Even this dumb ancient stone can do nothing to harm me. I'm invincible."

Without warning, she was running towards Evander, blade poised in her hand to impale him to death. Midway, she stopped dead in her tracks and lost grip on her weapon. The heavy blade clattered to the floor and Evander saw a wisp of smoke billowing from the jewel behind Iris. The smoke got thicker and thicker and morphed into the shape of a hand. Iris was still stationary, as if she had been frozen in place with a current; she was staring right at Evander unblinkingly, her eyes ajar in horror. The smoke-hand moved towards her and soon, had her in a chokehold.

She started to move again and her wrinkled hands clawed at the fog that had gripped her by the throat and lifted her off the ground. She tried to scream but

Chapter 30

nothing came out of her mouth as she struggled to breathe. Iris began writhing, as she probably realised that her end was near. But the hand didn't kill her. After a couple of what must have been unbearable moments for Iris, the smoke dissolved into nothing and Iris dropped to the floor and there was a loud 'crack' sound after which she began to groan uncontrollably. She coughed and gagged and tried to gulp in air but with her sharp cries of pain, the entire thing was too much, even to just watch.

Suddenly, the air around her body ignited itself, and bright red and orange flames glazed her body, every inch of it. The parking lot echoed with the resounding sobs Iris let out as her body burned, blackened and turned to bones and ashes.

31.

EVANDER – The Kingdom

He had seen a couple of movies back home that involved infernos that looked horrifying even on a screen.

What he had just witnessed was far worse than any of that.

As Evander watched the last flame extinguish itself, he couldn't wrap his head around the fact that the ashes in front of him were Iris mere seconds ago.

"Evander," Ruth mumbled almost inaudibly and he turned to look at her, wondering if she was as dazed as he was.

He found that she was dealing with something completely different – her body, face, everything seemed to have faded slightly. It was like she was transforming into nothingness. His heart leaped. Was she going to the *afterlife*? But there was still so much time for that, wasn't there? Or was it that she hadn't had her elixir in so long? Yes, that must be it.

Chapter 31

"I don't feel well," she told him as her grip on his hand slackened. "I must go to The Kingdom."

"Yes. But I don't know how to... where is it? Maybe I can—"

"Lesly," was the last word Ruth got out before she fainted.

"LESLY! WAKE UP!" Evander shouted into the darkness of the truck where the mouse had been asleep.

"Wh-what? Is everything—" Lesly awoke at once, and looking at Ruth, forgot how to speak.

"She said she needs to be taken to The Kingdom," he told the dingle. "You can take her, right?"

"I cannot take her if she isn't conscious, Evander," she said dubiously. "As it is, travelling all the way to The Kingdom can be energy-consuming. Maybe you should come along."

"Just a sec," Evander said and ran towards the jewel, sidestepping Iris' remains and stuffed the diamond safely in his pocket.

Soon, they were off.

****

The ride had been longer than Evander had anticipated. When Lesly landed, he realised he wasn't nearly as disoriented as he had been during the last Transformation trip he'd had with Lesly. He guessed it had something do with the fact that they had Ruth's magic too, even though she was unconscious.

He precariously placed Ruth on the ground and looking up, forgot how to breathe.

The palace that stood in the distance was so ginormous and dazzled with such a marvellous golden glow, Evander suspected it was the Sun itself, hidden away behind these clouds, accessible only to those who had transcended existence on Earth. And yet, by the miracle of magic, he was there. Blessed enough to be able to set eyes upon the majestic gold columns of the palace, the elegant domes that crowned it and the iridescent gems that were embedded in the intricate carvings on the cornices. The palace gleamed with such an otherworldly brilliance, Evander realised he couldn't look at it for too long without going blind. *The Kingdom of the Lifeless* towered before him, in all its ethereal glory.

Chapter 31

Between the palace's entrance – that was heavily guarded by men dressed in purple uniforms – and where Evander stood, was a heavy throng of souls. The scene was bizarre because they were all nearly transparent. If he tried to focus too much on one soul to see them more clearly, they disappeared completely.

"Come on," Lesly told him and he peeled his eyes away from the scene. "We need to get Ruth inside."

Evander nodded and picked up Ruth. She had gotten even colder than before and was almost completely transparent. He was so worried, his heartbeat wasn't returning to normal no matter how many times he had inhaled and exhaled. They somehow squeezed through the crowd and got to the entrance. The palace's humungous doors were closed; Evander could see his reflection in their mirror-like surface. His pale face was dotted with cuts and grime and his clothes were filthy and stained with blood. Blood that had mercifully stopped pouring from the gash on his left forearm. He looked drained.

"Reason for arrival?" one of the guards asked Evander. "Case number?"

"Ruth is extremely unwell!" Lesly yelled and the guard looked down at her. "She needs urgent medical assistance."

"And what is her case number, dingle?" he persevered stiffly.

"5096!"

The guard pulled out a device from his pant pocket and typed into it swiftly. After a couple of moments, he motioned to one of the other guards to come and carry Ruth inside. The massive doors swung open and Ruth was whisked away from Evander and instinctively, protectively, he ran behind her, past the guard who had questioned him.

But just as he placed a foot inside, an intense sensation of being shot with a million bullets at once pushed him backwards and made him plummet to the floor. He could feel the pointy metal of a bullet penetrating every inch of his back, every blood vessel in his legs, every nerve in his arms and every organ in his body. Suffice to say, he would've chosen being electrocuted over whatever the hell this was any day.

Indistinctly, he heard Lesly's muffled shout - "I'm sorry, Evander. I have to be with Ruth!"

Chapter 31

So he lay there on the floor, as extreme aching racked his body. He could faintly hear people shouting warnings to one another.

"He's an undead!"

"Get him out of here!"

"Why is he even here?"

Evander couldn't get himself to tell them that he wasn't a threat. The bullets had reached his heart. He went out like a light.

32.

RUTH – The Escape

Her eyes opened to see grey morning light seeping through the windows that illuminated the room. The ceiling was plain white and when she moved her head from side to side, she realised that so were the room's walls. The room was nothing fancy – just a white bed in the centre with a table next to it and some cabinets in the corner.

Ruth realised she was wearing a comfortable blue gown that looked like what a patient would wear in a hospital. She felt clean and relaxed and – to her surprise – not weak at all. She flexed her arms and fingers and found nothing was hurting.

The room's door opened and in came a woman wearing white clothes that looked like a nurse's.

"Look who's up!" she said cheerfully as she set down the tray she was carrying on the table beside Ruth's bed. "I bet you feel much better than you have in days."

Chapter 32

"I do," she said and smiled at the realisation that saying that took no effort at all. "Can you please tell me what had happened to me?"

"Oh, don't worry." The lady smiled affably as she helped Ruth sit upright and arranged pillows to support her back. "It happens to nearly all souls once they are close to their deadline."

"I don't get it," Ruth told her. Even though her body felt perfect as new, her memory and thoughts were still a little foggy. She couldn't remember what was the last thing that happened before she had lost consciousness.

"Well, whenever there is about a week or so left for souls to stay on Earth, their human body grows really weak and their powers diminish considerably. If they are small or don't have proper immunity, they may even need to be extensively treated," the woman explained. "Like you. You've been asleep for about 2 days now."

"Wh-what?" she asked, alarmed. "But, before...Mythil told me I only had a week. That means I have only 5 days now."

"Yes, my dear. I'm sorry for that."

"Do you know where Lesly is? She's my dingle. She—"

"Yes, yes, yes," the nurse said soothingly as she stroked Ruth's brushed and tied hair. "All this stress isn't good for you. Why don't you have the *Elixir of Death* and this fruit while I go get your dingle? I'll be back in a jiffy."

Placing the tray she'd brought on Ruth's lap, the nurse left, soundlessly closing the door behind her. Ruth drank the elixir and nibbled on the fruit. But it was difficult to eat now that she'd remembered what had happened before she'd collapsed.

Iris had just died and Evander had been trying to help Ruth. Iris was *dead*. That was at least one problem solved. Then she remembered Evander. Where had he gone? He couldn't have entered *The Kingdom of the Lifeless*. But had he even come here with Ruth and Lesly? He must have. Or had he returned home somehow? Was he alright? Ruth's brain was too muddled with unanswered questions. So much so, that it started to cause her a headache.

Chapter 32

Torturous minutes passed by and Ruth sighed with relief when the door finally swung open again and Lesly - in the form of a fluffy white dog now - leaped into her arms. They embraced and Lesly asked her how she was but Ruth was impatient now.

"Evander. Where is he?" she asked.

"He-he... actually, what um, happened—"

"Lesly. Out with the truth. NOW."

"He was taken into custody, Ruth," Lesly said guiltily. "I might have been able to stop it, had I tried, but I was with you."

"What was he even taken into custody for?"

"Trespassing. He's an undead. He's forbidden to be here. They'll hold his trial soon."

"Oh, but that isn't his fault!" Ruth said worriedly. "He came here because of me. We must tell them that."

"It doesn't matter, Ruth," Lesly told her. "He cannot be here. Whatever the reason."

"What will happen if he loses?"

"Not much," Lesly said, trying to sound reassuring. "They'll just wipe off his memory and return him to his last registered address."

"What do you mean 'wipe off his memory'?"

"They'll review his memories and erase off everything from the moment he met you."

Ruth's heart sank. Somehow, the idea of being forgotten by Evander was so heartbreaking, she couldn't even speak.

"We can still save him," Lesly said. "I'm certain I can do something."

"Yes. I should—"

"Ruth, you cannot stay here any longer to help Evander. I know you really want to, but you cannot. You must go to finish off Astoria and Maxine and return the jewel back to where it had been."

Of course, she had to do all of that. And she only had five days. Time was ticking away.

"Where's the jewel?" she asked Lesly.

"Evander gave it to me during our journey here. There's a bag outside the room. It has the jewel and

Chapter 32

Astoria and Maxine's current location. Evander had decoded it before, remember?"

Ruth nodded.

"All you need to do is go there and finish them off."

"I'm afraid she cannot do that," the nurse said strictly. She had been at the door, listening. "She is still quite weak and all of that seems like it would be energy-consuming. Especially Transformation. She's too ill to do that."

"But ma'am," Ruth said, "you don't understand. I—"

"I will not hear anything," she said sternly. "It isn't my choice or decision, young lady. It is required by the rules of The Kingdom that you stay under observation for at least 4 days after your arrival. You only have to stay here for 2 more days. Then you're free to go."

"Alright ma'am," Lesly told the nurse. "We'll do as you say."

Ruth shot her a look like, *What the hell are you doing?*

"Very well then." The nurse smiled amiably. "Just rest now. Okay?"

Ruth nodded and after a minute after the nurse had left, Lesly went and retrieved the bag from outside and handed it to Ruth.

"If they won't let you go, Ruth, you will have to escape," Lesly said urgently. "I know you aren't completely healed but—"

"I'm healed enough for this," Ruth said determinedly. "Do you know how I can get out?"

Lesly shook her head, looking like she was all out of ideas. So was Ruth. She needed to find an exit in this colossal palace that neither her nor Lesly had ever seen fully. Ruth tried to remember what it was like when she had been here for the first time, in The Kingdom. What she recalled immediately was the sheer chaos in her head and, to the contrary, the pure tranquillity in her surroundings.

When she had awoken, she was in a room much like the one she was trapped in right now. It was clean and white and golden and very jarring to her when the last thing she had seen was her parents' dead bodies in front of her. Ruth remembered being

Chapter 32

utterly terrified that maybe she hadn't died when Astoria strangled her and they had captured her somehow and put her there. That's when a man dressed in white ironed shirt and pants had entered the room and told her she was needed somewhere. The man had taken her to a room where there was another man waiting with a large computer. He had asked for Ruth's name and other details like birthdate and entering them into his computer, he had asked about how she was feeling about the way she had been killed. She had been flabbergasted, of course.

"Oh, right," the man had said, sighing. "So, you're dead. You do remember how you were killed?"

Ruth had nodded as she began to feel a little giddy. "W-what place is this?"

"It isn't as much of a place as it is a state of mind," the man told her and seeing how lost she was, started differently. "Never mind this place. After every human dies, they have two fates that await them. Either they go to the afterlife or their soul is sent back to Earth for a short period of time to finish off any important mission as long as no timelines are messed with. After that, the souls do go to the *afterlife* anyway. So really, there's only one fate."

After much explanation, Ruth had finally understood that she could use this opportunity to avenge her parents and herself. Now she remembered the many formalities she'd had to go through to get five months for her mission. But she also remembered how she had departed from *The Kingdom of the Lifeless*.

"Lesly, I think I have a plan," she said to her dingle, a candle of hope lighting up within her.

****

Lesly spent the next couple hours following souls around the palace disguised as a tiny white-and-black mouse. Ruth had instructed her to do that so that she could get a sense of where exactly Ruth's room was. She knew one of the many exits in the palace. It was the one she had used to first get to Bosque Tranquilo from *The Kingdom of the Lifeless*. But at the moment, as Ruth guzzled down some more of *Elixir of Death*, she was more worried about what exactly her location was. The palace was difficult to navigate not only because of its size but also because of its complexity; the last time she had been here, Ruth had almost lost

Chapter 32

her way with the innumerable staircases that popped out of nowhere and disappeared and the many souls that each had a different place to go to: some worked for The Kingdom and so had business to attend to but some were like Ruth – looking to flee somehow. So, Ruth guessed that if she could find someone like that with Lesly's help, she could escape too.

Lesly finally arrived after what seemed like forever. She struggled and made her way to Ruth's palm where she began in a hushed voice, "I think I know where we are right now."

"Yeah?" Ruth asked.

"The infirmary is one level above the floor where all the decision-making takes place. Like the policies and stuff goes on one level below."

"Okay. Where do the new souls arrive?"

"Not exactly sure about that," Lesly answered grimly. "But I did see a couple souls who looked very unsure going down five levels. I tried to follow them but I think they started to notice me so I had to leave. And of course, the courtroom where they finalised your case is ten levels above the infirmary."

"Oh," Ruth answered. "Is that where Evander will be taken?"

"That I don't know," said Lesly. "His trial will probably be conducted in a different place. But there are multiple courtrooms on that floor so I am not sure."

"I'm worried for him too, Lesly," Ruth confessed.

"Don't be," Lesly said reassuringly. "The prison is about 8 or 9 or so levels down from here. Once you get out, I'll go check up on him and fill him in. I'll testify in the trial myself."

"Oh, yes! That would be an excellent idea!"

"Probably not." Lesly sounded pretty stressed herself. She had done far too much for Ruth. And she was continuing to do far too much. Even though it was technically her job, Ruth didn't know if she could ever thank Lesly enough.

"Why? What's wrong?" Ruth asked her.

"It's just that... we're both pretty well-known for our knack for rule-breaking," she answered sheepishly. "You having erased Evander's memory before and me having shown you that vision of

Chapter 32

Astoria and Maxine. I think a testament from me is the last thing they will trust."

Ruth's heart sank even lower and dread engulfed her. Not only were things problematic for her but they weren't looking much better for Evander either. She felt like she sinking in quicksand and instead of pulling her out, everyone else except Lesly and Evander seemed to be handing her heavy things that were only making her go in faster.

"Anyway. I'll take care of Evander, I promise. Now, try to concentrate – this mission is extremely important," said Lesly and Ruth remembered that it was indeed. Not only for Ruth, but also for Lesly. "Can you try to recollect where you had gone from the courtroom after your case was declared active?"

She tried. It was hazy, yes, but it was only 4 or so months ago. Ruth could see herself getting out the doors, feeling elated as if she had been given another chance to be alive.

"Ruth, go down five levels in the elevator and find James. He'll help you out," she almost heard her lawyer's voice.

James had turned out to be a wonderfully polite gentleman who had helped and guided her throughout the process of going back to Earth; the rules, technical formalities and everything else important she needed to know, he'd told her. He knew her case inside out and had been incredibly supportive and kind to her.

"James," she burst out. "We need to find James, Lesly. He'll help me. I'm certain he will."

"Oh, James?" Lesly said, remembering. She knew him too. He had introduced Lesly to Ruth. "Oh, he's a good bloke, Ruth, but he likes to play by the rules. We don't need someone like that at the moment. He'd rat us out. We would probably be in more trouble than we are in without his involvement."

That's when the room's door swung open and in came the nurse who had told Ruth she couldn't leave until two more days. Lesly hid under Ruth's blanket.

"Oh, there you are! I was afraid you were constructing some sort of escape plan," the nurse said jokingly.

Chapter 32

Ruth gave a nervous chuckle as the nurse set her tray of food on her lap. "No. Cause that would be absolutely crazy."

"Right you are," said the nurse, smiling wide. "Don't try anything weird, okay? Our security is very tight. You'll probably just invite more punishment."

"Wouldn't wanna do that," said Ruth, trying to conceal the sweat that was trickling down her temple. She started to gobble down her food and after some minutes, the nurse left.

"We're leaving in a moment and we're going up five levels to find James," she told Lesly with finality. "He'll help us. He'll have to."

33.

RUTH – The Obelick

Lesly gave her the indication that the coast was clear and Ruth stepped out wearing the clothes Lesly had conjured for her; she couldn't wear the hospital gown she had on before. She didn't want anyone knowing she was a patient or that she was attempting an escape. She ran down the hall to the elevator and hoped it was empty. It wasn't.

"Greetings, fellow soul," said a man wearing burgundy pants and a deep violet shirt embroidered with soft pink flowers. "Where are you headed to?"

"Uh, my lawyer told me to go meet James," said Ruth, trying her best to sound honest as she pressed the button on the panel and the elevator shot upwards.

"Ah, James," said the man dreamily. "Oh, how sad he's been lately. That poor thing."

"Wh-what do you mean?" Ruth asked. "Why's he sad?"

Chapter 33

The man looked side-to-side as if he was afraid some invisible person in the elevator would hear him. "Oh, I hear The Kingdom's giving him a tough time," he whispered. "He's working day in and out and apparently, they have refused to send him into the *afterlife* for another 50 years."

Ruth didn't respond because she was starting to worry again. At first, she knew she could request James to make an exception, but now, she was unsure. What if he was so angry he didn't agree to help her at all? What if he did indeed rat Ruth out? What would she do?

"It's your floor, fellow soul," said the man, now grinning as if he had forgotten about James altogether.

Ruth nodded and got out and even though she wasn't thinking of it consciously, her feet somehow carried her to the room where James had been. Her hand rapped on the door and it opened a minute later.

James looked nothing like he did four months ago. His face had deepened worry lines and the dark circles under his eyes were prominent. Recognising Ruth, his face changed from tired to shocked.

"R-Ruth? Is that you? What are you doing here? Is everything alright? No one told me you were going to visit," he said, alarmed.

"Look, James, I really need your help," Ruth said, maintaining the tone of urgency. "Can I come in?"

He let her in and after locking the door shut, Ruth spilled out everything. How she had broken far too many rules and how she was there, trying to break a last one. And how his help was the only thing she needed now to avenge her parents and herself.

"I know you aren't one for helping rule-breakers, and I know you don't exactly approve of my decisions but I need your help, James," she pleaded as her eyes released her tears. "I need to get back here before they send Evander back. I barely have four days left now."

James took a seat on a chair next to a brown desk. "Well, you certainly took no regard of any of those tips I gave you before you left," he said, sighing. "And you certainly made a huge mess of everything."

"Yes, I know. I know. I'm horrible and I'll be punished later and I know I'll deserve it but I don't

Chapter 33

deserve this, James. Not being given the chance to kill my murderers."

"You know, Ruth," he began, his face wearing an austerely look. "Life isn't always right and wrong. Sometimes you need to do a little wrong to be right in the end. I get that. A month back, if a soul had come rushing to me, begging to help them escape, I'd have called the authorities and have them imprisoned. But I can't play by those same rules now."

"So... so you'll help me?" Ruth asked, sighing with relief.

"Oh, yes. But we need to get you out fast so that you're far enough when I tell them you escaped. Because I would need to tell them."

"Okay, got it. I'll run quickly. Just tell me where the exit is."

"Yeah... the exit. That's not possible."

"What do you mean?"

James thought for about a minute, then looked up and stared at a large wooden cabinet in the corner of the room. "I think that's the only option," he said, more to himself than to Ruth.

"What is that?" Ruth asked, looking at the seemingly ordinary cabinet.

"It's called an *Obelick*. You enter it. It burns you. And you're out of the palace. You will end up in a river from where you can use Transformation and get where you want to go."

"It burns me? Why? I-I don't get it. Can I not get out a physical exit?"

"Not unless you have a permit, Ruth," he said. "Every single exit is guarded by men armed to the teeth. And you are quite famous in The Kingdom for being a potential criminal. Whatever that is. They'll recognise and imprison you."

"Of course," she mumbled to herself. "Of course I'm a potential criminal."

"We use the *Obelick* when we need to escape quickly in terms of emergencies. Obviously, it isn't used often. I think the last time it was used was centuries ago. It may not work perfectly, mind you. But I am certain it will get you out of the palace. Which is what you want, right?"

Chapter 33

"Right," Ruth said. She knew this was the only way to get out but she was worried. If it didn't work, she'd be in far worse trouble. But what choice did she have?

She looked at the little mouse by her feet. "Should I do it, Lesly?"

"Looks like your only option, Ruth," answered the dingle.

"Okay. Alright. I'll go into the *Obelick*, James," she told him.

"Well, then, you better get going quickly." He walked to the cabinet and opening the doors, waited. Ruth looked dubiously at the empty blackness the cabinet held.

"Will it work?" she asked.

James smiled. "Only one way to find out."

"All the best, Ruth," Lesly told her.

Ruth steeled herself and stepped in.

34.

EVANDER – The Prison

When his eyes opened, it took them a moment to adjust to the darkness. Evander realised he was in some sort of prison. He was lying on a tattered mattress and was surrounded by rusted iron bars. The entire space inside the bars was smaller than a queen-size bed. He felt claustrophobic. He also felt clueless about why he was in another prison.

That's when a dim light switched on some feet above his head on the ceiling. A man dressed in a purple guard's uniform appeared and opening the prison's door, placed a plate of food inside. Before he could leave though, Evander snapped out of his daze.

"Hey, hey, listen," he said to the guard. "Can you, like, tell me what this place is? And why am I here?"

"What, you have amnesia or somethin'?" The guard scoffed and locked the door.

"Please," Evander pleaded. "I genuinely don't remember."

Chapter 34

"Well, this is *The Kingdom of the Lifeless*. Since you're an undead, you were arrested for trespassing. Your trial will be held in about an hour."

"Trial? What trial? I-I—" he started, confused and terrified. "Look I'm not a criminal or something. Don't kill me, please. I beg you, don't kill me."

"No one's killing you, lad," grunted the guard. "If you win the trial - which you won't - you will get to keep your memory. If you lose, your memory will be erased and you'll be sent back home."

Before Evander could even understand the full impact of what the guard had just told him, the guard disappeared, leaving him alone and petrified. He noticed that the gaping wound on his left forearm was completely healed now - no scar, nothing at all; probably fixed by the doctors in this place. He sat there, shivering and feeling disgusting, hungry and jaded as he pondered the consequences of setting foot into this rotten kingdom.

He was going to lose his memory. Maybe not all of it but most probably any memory even remotely related to Ruth would be wiped clean from his head. He'd forget Ruth. He'd forget this entire mission.

He'd forget the hope he had found when he had met Ruth. And maybe this time, the magic would be strong enough to keep his memories forgotten even if he saw any picture like he had last time. He'd be returned to his old home, or – more accurately – his former jail. Quite frankly, he'd much rather stay where he was: in this dim, dusty place crawling with flies that had begun to attack his bland, stale-looking food.

He also felt very nervous about the trial. He had read about them in books and seen them in movies, but he couldn't even guess how dreadful they'd be in reality. Especially a trial held in *The Kingdom of the Lifeless*. He had no idea what he could do to better his chances at winning this trial. Would he even get an advocate? Or would there really be an argument or discussion at all? He knew he couldn't lose. There was too much at stake: his memory of Ruth, Ruth's mission—

Wait. Where the hell was Ruth? The last time he recalled being with her was when she had been unconscious and he had helped bring her here. She and Lesly had entered the doors of the palace but he hadn't been able to. Perhaps Ruth was getting help at

Chapter 34

the moment – whatever medical assistance it was that souls could get. Of course, thinking of that made him remember her weakness right after Iris had died. What had caused that? He still didn't know. And by the looks of it, he never would.

He could only hope that she was fine now. She still had plenty time before she had to go to the *afterlife*. Her mission was nearly complete too. They had retrieved the jewel and Evander remembered giving it to Lesly to keep safely. Ruth had the jewel and Astoria and Maxine's location too; that is, if they hadn't moved yet. If Ruth hurried, she could easily return the jewel and hunt the sisters. Yes. That was it. Her mission was almost complete.

Or maybe, while Evander had been knocked out in this prison, Ruth had already done all of that and headed to the *afterlife*. But the idea didn't comfort him. He hadn't gotten to say goodbye properly. Besides, as it occurred to him, he didn't *want* to say goodbye to her. Evander had known from the moment Ruth had told him the full truth that their friendship was going to be brief. But now that its end was clear as day, now that her departure was closer than ever, Evander didn't want it to end. He didn't want her to go. It wasn't just about losing the only friend he'd ever had or about having to return to his tormenting home. It was *her*. Evander didn't want to lose Ruth.

"Evander," a small voice whispered and he jumped, scared out of his wits, his head whipping from side to side to see where the sound came from. But he couldn't see anyone – no guard or anyone else who'd say his name.

"Evander!" hissed the voice again, more irritated this time.

He tried to search for the direction from which the sound had emerged and was baffled to realise that it was the mattress he was sitting on. But when he looked for the source of sound, he found something completely different. A small white-and-black mouse stared at him with beady black eyes, inches from his foot. Evander flinched and moved away from the mouse; he couldn't remember if they bit humans or not.

Then, inexplicably, to his absolute bewilderment, the tiny mouse spoke in an enraged squeaky voice, "IT IS ME, YOU FOOL! LESLY!"

Chapter 34

"Lesly?" he said aloud, both relieved at her arrival and angry at his own stupidity. How could he not recognise her? Well, actually, she changed a *lot*, so Evander couldn't take all the blame.

"Be quieter," she told him in a hushed voice. "And listen. There have been multiple developments."

"What do you mean? Is Ruth fine? Where is she?"

"She is fine. She was slightly unwell but they treated her and she has escaped to return the jewel and finish off the sisters."

Evander sighed with relief and allowed himself a smile. She hadn't left Earth yet; maybe they could meet once before his memory is erased.

"Wait, what do you mean by 'treated'?" he asked Lesly. "Why was she unwell in the first place? Why had she fainted whe—"

"Ok, calm down!" Lesly cut him off vexedly. "Listen, this is too much, but bear with me. So, Mythil had come to that parking lot after Ruth and Mr. Bundleheckles had escaped their cage. He arrested Mr. Bundleheckles because he had been helping Ruth – which he is forbidden to do."

"So, where's Mr. Bundleheckles now? Is he here? Can we help him?" Evander asked because even though he wasn't a fan of the old guy, Mr. Bundleheckles had kept his promise – he had helped Ruth down to the last second.

"He... isn't here," Lesly answered sadly. "He's in the *afterlife*. Being punished."

"Wh-what?" he asked with horror. "Is there any way—"

"No. He cannot be helped anymore. Once souls move on into the *afterlife*, nothing can be done. But you need to keep listening now. Okay?"

Evander nodded, feeling nothing but horrible; he had never liked Mr. Bundleheckles, and now he was going to be tortured for however long eternity lasts. Guilt wasn't a strong enough word to describe how awful Evander felt.

"So, Mythil was really angry at Ruth for getting help from Mr. Bundleheckles and he reduced the time she has left on Earth. She has only about five days left now. Because of which her powers had begun to weaken. So she fainted."

Chapter 34

"Five?" Evander asked; maybe he had heard it incorrectly. "She'll leave in *five* days?"

Lesly nodded. And Evander felt his heart crumble into a million pieces he knew he'd never be able to put together again. Just five days. She wouldn't return soon enough to meet him before they erased his memories. He would never see Ruth again. Just thinking that was so incredibly painful, for a moment, he thought that maybe it would be better to have Ruth removed from his memories; then, at least, he wouldn't spend the rest of his life cursing his fate.

"Time to go," said the guard, appearing in front of the door and unlocking it.

"For the trial?" Evander asked as Lesly hid under the frayed fabric that was supposed to be the blanket.

"No. For my daughter's birthday party," the guard said sarcastically. "Of course for the trial, you nut."

He entered and cuffed Evander's hands and as they stepped out, Lesly managed to catch hold of Evander's pant leg which she climbed on and as the guard and Evander walked, reached Evander's shoulder.

"Don't answer or make any noise," she whispered into his ear, making him flinch. "The trial is going to be tricky, but I'll help you. I can give a testament as a witness. There are just a couple of formalities I need to look into first. Don't worry, okay? Just be honest. And respectful. Don't speak unless spoken to. You have done nothing wrong."

Then, the weight of the miniscule mouse disappeared from his shoulder and he walked on, the guard tugging at the cuffs that dug into Evander's wrists. As he passed the other prisons, he saw the awful condition their inhabitants were in – some with scarred and damaged faces and bodies, some just sitting in a corner, oblivious to the world, and all of them absolutely filthy and skeleton-like.

"How long will the trial last?" he asked the guard as they stepped into a very pretty crystal elevator. As the thing shot upwards at high-speed, Evander had a rush of adrenaline coursing through him. Maybe he could escape. But, more accurately, he couldn't. Not with all the magic they had here.

"Well, your case is pretty simple," the guard answered, his face wearing an apathetic expression. "Shouldn't be more than thirty minutes. Honestly,

Chapter 34

boy, I don't even get why they waste time with trials for cases as straight-forward as yours. Wouldn't it be more efficient to just erase your memory and send you back?"

Evander didn't know what to say. Maybe this guard didn't know just how important certain memories could be. Maybe he didn't care. *The Kingdom of the Lifeless* certainly didn't care either.

Evander knew he was doomed.

35.

RUTH – An Unattainable Memory

When the mind-numbingly unbearable burning sensation started to dissipate, Ruth remembered that she did know how to breath. She took a deep breath and the simple act burned her insides; she realised her scorching skin was itching badly but she didn't want to do as much as move a muscle until she was sure she was out of danger. So, she waited for as long as it took for the tingling the fire had left to completely ebb. Then, she tentatively opened her eyes to see pale yellow light surrounding her. She was submerged in water that reached her calves. *It's the river*, she thought and was suddenly overjoyed. *I'm out of the palace!*

She looked around her and found the glittering golden palace was 500 metres or so to her right. This was her chance. She had to leave. So, even though escaping *The Kingdom of the Lifeless* had been a painful

Chapter 35

and tiring experience, she knew she couldn't stop to rest. She concentrated and found that Transformation was much difficult now than it had been when she had first learnt it. Still, Ruth persevered because she could hardly give up now, and much to her relief, in a couple of minutes, she had turned into a maple leaf.

****

As she transformed back into her human form, Ruth was aware of only one thought – "Finally, I will avenge my parents."

She took a few wobbly steps and plummeted to the ground. Transformation had taken its toll. She lay there, in immense exhaustion, as the aching left her body. Ruth drew in deep breaths and tried to hoist herself up. She couldn't. She could feel heat behind her eyes and soon, a tear trickled down into her hairline. She felt so drained. So impossibly done with everything. After 17 years of nothing but ease, comfort and happiness, all of this was unnecessarily hard. She didn't want to get up; or return the jewel; or kill Astoria and Maxine. She didn't want to do anything. She let her eyelids droop and the blackness engulf her.

Ruth was too much of a mess to understand whether the vision that followed was a dream or a memory. She saw the living room in her parents' house, the one she had lived in her entire life. A much younger version of Ruth sat on the mustard yellow couch. Ruth was fiddling with a Rubik's cube, and as she continued to work on it – her eyes intense with concentration – her mom, Veronica, arrived from her bedroom. She wore a floral pink dress and a matching pink hairband holding back her gorgeous auburn locks; this is what Veronica always looked like in Ruth's head. Her emerald eyes sparkled with warmth.

"Oh, honey, are you still on that?" she asked, as she disappeared into the kitchen and filled a glass with juice.

"Mom, I think I've almost got it," Ruth said, still distracted with the cube.

"Well, I'm sure you're going to get it if you try hard enough." Veronica set the glass of juice on the table next to the couch. "What about your homework?" she asked as she settled down next to Ruth.

Chapter 35

"I finished it in school."

"Well, alright. Have your juice, okay? And your father and I were thinking... maybe all of us can go out this evening, watch a movie, shop, have dinner at one of those fancy restaurants you've been wanting to try out."

"I have a test coming up," young Ruth told her mom, her eyes still glued to the cube she had almost solved.

"Yes, I know, my love, but this coming week, your father and I will have a lot of meetings to attend and work to finish off. So, I figured we could have some nice family time together before that."

Ruth watched her young self finish a last move and there was the cube in her hands - all its colours perfectly aligned. Young Ruth let out a shrill "YAY!" in triumph, jumping on the couch, and Veronica beamed at her, a smile spread across her face.

"You did it!" she said, her voice reverberating with happiness as if she herself had achieved something unbelievable.

"Yes! I did it!" Ruth shrieked with happiness and hugged her mom tightly. "I did it!"

"Well done," Veronica said. "Oh, your dad is going to be so proud. Wait till he sees that solved cube. The look on his face will be priceless."

"Yes! And then we can go celebrate!"

Veronica laughed with joy, and pulled young Ruth in an embrace. "You bet we will."

****

As the vision slipped away from Ruth, her eyes opened at once, and she registered the multiple tears that had soaked her cheeks.

She'd never get that again.

She'd never hug her mother, or celebrate with her father. She'd never become a doctor. She'd never chat with Avery or drink coffee with Gracie, or watch football matches with Noah and Steve. She'd probably never even see Evander again. Ruth had lost her life.

And Astoria and Maxine were the reason.

Ruth found the energy to stand up. Astoria and Maxine had taken far too much from her. And while

Chapter 35

Iris had been rightfully punished, her daughters' penalties were still due. Fuelled with fury more intense than ever, Ruth walked towards the place where Mr. Bundleheckles had told her the jewel had been before, where Iris had found it. The house that it had been hidden in was about 10 miles or so from the house Iris had been living in.

The building looked exactly like Mr. Bundleheckles had described it – completely demolished. Ruth let herself wonder only for a moment what could possibly have happened to Ravenwood for it to have been rendered this way. Shaking off the irrelevant thought, she carefully walked into the house, and the moment she opened the rotting door, she knew she was in trouble.

She could hear voices, many of them. They were coming from the downstairs level of the house. Ruth looked at the flight of stairs that lead downwards at the right of the living room; there were people here. What people? Were Iris' men back to get the jewel's money? Ruth was certain that this was it.

After double-checking that the jewel was still with her, safe in the bag, she rushed down the stairs. And when she reached the ground floor, she found something far more terrifying than Iris' men.

36.

RUTH – The Jewel

Undead.

Seven of them stood in the dimly lit room before Ruth. All their agitated chatter died down instantly when she arrived; they gawked at Ruth in utter bewilderment and she stared back in shock, certain that she was about to break a million rules of The Kingdom.

"Ruth... Forbes?" said a man she hadn't noticed before.

He appeared from the shadows and walked up to stand in front of her. To her absolute horror, she recognized him. He was Elijah Nelson, a friend of her parents'. She knew him very well; he'd come to her house for Christmas and Thanksgiving and her parents liked him very much. He worked for the museum that looked after the jewel Ruth had in her bag.

"Is this really... you?" he asked, dazedly. "Ruth?"

"Ye-yes, it is me, Uncle Elijah," she managed.

"But this isn't possible," he said incredulously. "I attended your funeral!"

"I-it is quite a long and complicated story," she said embarrassedly.

"I'm sure I can keep up," he said, eyeing her suspiciously.

"Elijah, that isn't important," a man dressed like a guard with an ugly scar across his cheek said authoritatively. "The jewel is missing. It was supposed to be moved to the new location today and it isn't here. What should we do now?"

Ruth wasn't exactly contemplating the consequences of her actions when she opened the bag and took out the jewel. It glistened in her hands even though there was next to no light where she stood.

"She has the jewel!" she heard a man scream in terror from the back of the room.

"She's the thief!" another one said with triumph.

"She must be imprisoned!" a third yelled.

Ruth lifted her eyes from the jewel and looked at a dumbstruck Elijah, whose mouth hung open. She

Chapter 36

handed him the jewel. "Take better care of it," she said. "And don't worry. The people who had stolen it have been rightly punished."

Elijah stared at the jewel like it was made of stars. "None of this makes any sense at all," he mumbled to himself.

The guard with the scar on his cheek snatched the jewel from Elijah's hands and placed it carefully in a metal box that was locked shut and its key was kept in another metal box that had a digital lock. Surely, it was impossible to steal the jewel as long as it was with these guys. The two boxes were put away in a larger gold-coloured box that two guards carried up the stairs. The rest of the guards followed them and the only people who remained behind were Ruth, Elijah and the guard with the scar.

"Ma'am, my name is Ryan," he said, looking very concerned and relieved at the same time. "I need to know why the jewel was with you. And who these 'rightly punished people' you just mentioned are."

"You have the jewel, right?" Ruth said, trying her best to dodge the question. "All you need to do is focus on that. I'm not really important. You should be grateful that I brought it to you. I could've used it, you know."

"You are literally 17, Ruth," Uncle Elijah said harshly. "I am not buying any of that. Tell me the truth now!"

Ruth flinched, not because she was afraid but because she had never imagined that Uncle Elijah would speak to her that way. But she knew it wasn't his fault. He deserved to know the truth. But she couldn't tell him. She had already put Evander through so much because he knew the reality; Ruth couldn't possibly do the same thing to Uncle Elijah.

"I'm really, really sorry for this," she said earnestly and thrust out her hands.

The next moment, both the men had collapsed on the ground. She had erased their memory the best she could, and she was pretty confident that her magic had improved because if the spell is done correctly, it usually renders the undead unconscious. She rushed up the stairs now; she had to erase all the other men's memories too and flee as fast as possible before anyone could come to.

Chapter 36

The men were loading the gold box in the trunk of a big black SUV. As they shut the trunk and got seated in the car, waiting for Elijah and Ryan, they noticed Ruth. She drew in a deep breath and thrust out her hands again, trying very hard to ensure the spell worked on all of them. If there was any error, she could end up getting unimaginable punishments in *The Kingdom of the Lifeless*. Even though the car was quite far, Ruth could see that the men had fainted in their seats. She ran to the car and checked. They were all unconscious, but she couldn't be sure about their memories.

But there was nothing she could do about it because she was running out of time. Uncle Elijah and Ryan could be coming to the car at any moment. Ruth dug out the diary that was in her bag and flipped to the last page. There were the coordinates that she needed to travel to next. She was, finally, going to meet Astoria and Maxine.

She concentrated hard and in a moment, she was a fleck of dust.

37.

EVANDER – The Verdict

He had been expecting a massive courtroom, filled with tons of people, jury, an array of lawyers and the air enlaced with dread and tension. So, when the guard who had escorted Evander from his prison opened a pair of black doors down a long empty hall after getting off the elevator, Evander was surprised.

What awaited him – instead of the grim court he had anticipated – was a small room with only 5 people in it. A large black oak desk stood in the middle of the room. On one side of the desk was a large bald man with satiny brown skin and a grey beard, wearing black velvet robes and having an expression that said, 'I'm done with my life'. On the other side of the desk was a man and a woman dressed alike in formal pant-suit; they stood up to greet Evander with a curt nod and a tight smile and made room for him on their side of the desk. Two women stood against the wall of the room, a notepad and pen in their hands.

Chapter 37

All their expressions of extreme apathy made it clear that this trial was the last thing they cared about.

The guard uncuffed Evander and left the room.

The large bald man cleared his throat and heaved a sigh. "Please have a seat... Mr. Lennon," he said with a heavy voice.

Evander did.

"Sir, I am Andy Diaz. I'll be defending you," the man on Evander's left told him with a respectful smile. "Can you tell—"

"Your honour," said one of the standing women, addressing the large man. "Respectfully, I think we all have better things to do than be here. This trial is simply meaningless."

"I do agree," said the woman sitting on Evander's right. "Mike and Cole saw him trying to enter the palace. He is very obviously undead. I simply don't get why we should waste any time—"

"Because I deserve to keep my memory," interrupted Evander even though he had been clearly instructed by Lesly not to do exactly that. "I get that y'all probably don't give a damn about me. Why would you? It's only your job. But for me, those memories are more important than anything I have ever owned. You cannot just take them away."

"Mr. Lennon, you are forbidden to speak unless spoken to," said the judge. "And you certainly don't have any right to tell us what to do."

"I do have a right to preserve my own memories!" shrieked Evander, standing up and losing his patience. He'd had enough of these horribly insensitive people. "I know you care very much about your kingdom's secrecy, but believe me, I have literally no reason to go around blabbing about it to anyone. If you're afraid that I'll tell another undead about any of this, you're wrong. I promise. I'll take this secret to my grave."

"Mr. Lennon, I'm afraid we have certain laws," the judge said grimly, rubbing his bloodshot eyes tiredly. "Which strictly dictate not to make any exceptions. Especially when the soul who you tried to enter with, Ruth Forbes, has a reputation of breaking rules as she pleases. Furthermore, just a couple of hours ago, she escaped from the infirmary even though she was supposed to stay there for two more days. Now, while she is going to serve some kind of sentence in the

Chapter 37

afterlife for her recklessness, we cannot just let you go either. Even though you knowing about *The Kingdom of the Lifeless* and arriving here is entirely *her* fault."

"But, your honour," Andy said. "We have a witness. She needs to make her testament."

"Ahh, yes." The judge sighed again, his shoulders slumping forward; he looked exhausted. Evander couldn't even guess how many trials this place held. But by the looks of it, the number was large. "The dingle. Bring her in."

Evander plumped back onto his chair as Andy pressed a button on a device and the black doors behind Evander opened. And at first, he couldn't see anyone when he remembered that Lesly had changed into a mouse. The mouse sprinted inside the room as the doors shut.

"Why is she so tiny?" the judge almost groaned.

"Lesly, if you could please turn into a bigger animal so that speaking with you is easier," said Andy.

Lesly did – she changed into a fluffy white cat and hopped onto Evander's lap.

"So, Lesly, could you please tell us—" started Andy but was cut off by the woman on Evander's right.

"Oh, this is rubbish. What will this dingle tell us, your honour?" she said furiously. "She helped Ruth with all that rule-breaking and she has broken quite a lot of rules herself. Ruth Forbes is her first soul too; she is highly inexperienced. Her testament means less than nothing. I say, we sentence her a good punishment too."

"Ma'am, quite frankly, I don't care much about what happens with me," Lesly snapped at the woman, trying very hard to hide her anger. "But this trial isn't for me. It's for Evander and he is innocent. He has done nothing but help Ruth with her mission—"

"Which is forbidden," broke in the woman.

"—and be a perfectly selfless human being," Lesly continued like the woman hadn't spoken at all. "He deserves no punishment whatsoever. I promise you that he won't open his mouth even if it meant being killed. I know him. I know him better than any of you. Evander is someone you can trust."

He was flabbergasted. Not only at Lesly's sass, bravado and complete ignorance of her own advice

Chapter 37

but also her last comment. She trusted him. And she was ready to fight with the authorities of *The Kingdom of the Lifeless* to save his memories. Evander had never been this touched before. Now, more than ever, he didn't want to lose his memory; he didn't want to forget what it felt like to have a friend, to have someone who's got your back, to have someone who thinks you're worth fighting for.

"Well, that's a lovely speech, fellow dingle, but I am afraid it's too much of a breach of courtroom etiquette," said the standing woman, who had spoken earlier.

"So is interrupting the opening statements of the defendant, Barbara," Andy said bitterly.

"ENOUGH!" The judge yelled and Evander winced. "I think I have heard all that I need to hear."

"Your honour," pleaded Lesly. "I'm very sorry for my behaviour. And my rule breaking. I know Ruth and I will have to pay for it and we will totally deserve all of it, but I implore you to not give the same treatment to Evander."

"He won't be punished, dingle," the judge answered, downright annoyed at this point. "He won't feel a thing."

"But it would still be immoral and unjust," Lesly insisted, and Evander was glad because suddenly he had lost his ability to speak. "Erasing his memories is a punishment to him. Something he doesn't even deserve. Please, your honour. I'm begging you. You can increase my punishment by tenfold. But please, don't do this to Evander."

"That's it." The judge stood up and took in a deep breath. "I'm sorry if this is like a punishment for you, Evander. But our Kingdom would come crashing down if we broke and followed the rules as we wished, driven by emotion. I'm compelled by the laws I helped make and I *cannot* break them. No matter how trustworthy you might be. No matter how important those memories are to you. They will have to be erased. I really am sorry."

Evander felt a piercing sharp pain where his heart was.

"Sara, Barbara," the judge said, pointing at the standing women, "you two take care of him. Everyone else leaves the room right now."

Chapter 37

The doors opened behind them, and the judge, Andy and the woman on Evander's right departed. But Lesly stay put on his lap.

She looked at him and her yellow cat eyes had tears in them. "I'm so sorry, Evander. I failed you. I failed Ruth."

He scratched the back of her ears and put on a smile, which felt like the hardest thing in the world. "You didn't fail either of us, Lesly. Don't blame yourself for what's about to happen. You tried your best. Please remember that. I am glad I got to meet you and be your friend. If I was allowed, I would never ever forget what your friendship and support mean to me. Thank you so much for everything."

As if unable to be there any longer, Lesly jumped off his lap and bounded out the doors.

He was all alone, once again.

"This won't hurt a bit," said Barbara, thrusting out her hand.

38.

RUTH – The Assassin

The desert was as gorgeous as the last time Ruth was there. Only this time she was too exhausted to fully take in its beauty. She collapsed on the sand that had just begun to cool, but she was determined now. Determined to finally give those sisters a taste of their own medicine. And right now, even though her body was hurting in places, she ordered herself to get up and look for them.

As she walked on through the chilly desert, a haunting possibility hit her. What if Astoria and Maxine weren't here at all? What if they had moved on to a new place? One that Ruth had absolutely zero clues about? There was no way she could figure out the new location's coordinates. Not without Evander. The thought pulled her up short. She stood still, gazing into the distance as she let Evander drift into her mind. He was probably facing his trial right now as she searched for her murderers. There was no way he was going to win it. There was no way Lesly would

Chapter 38

be able to convince anyone that he was harmless even though it was the truth.

The Kingdom of the Lifeless had a lengthy rulebook but the most important one was quite simple – 'Do not let any undead gain knowledge about *The Kingdom of the Lifeless.*' Ruth was to blame for the fact that Evander had tried to enter *The Kingdom of the Lifeless*. But they wouldn't just let him leave. They may not chastise him, but she was sure that his memory would be completely erased, like Lesly had told her. Even though a part of herself kept saying, *It doesn't matter, it doesn't make a difference*, it wasn't true. It *did* matter; although she wasn't going to be here long enough to mourn about it. But that wasn't the point, was it? Ruth just couldn't wrap her mind around the fact that Evander would just return to his cage-like home and resume living his old dreadful life, being tortured, oblivious to the fact that she had ever been a part of his life.

Suddenly, Ruth snapped back to reality because she heard sounds: low voices conversing, muffled by the loud wind. Her head whipped to her right and in the distance, at the bottom of the large dune she was standing on were two figures. As they drew closer, Ruth dropped onto the sand, trying her best to watch them while staying hidden. Surely, it was them.

She didn't really want to until she had more of an advantage with the element of surprise but Ruth rose, completely revealing herself.

They gasped as they realised it was her, the puny, skinny little girl they had killed. They were only about ten feet away now and Ruth could easily hear Maxine shriek, "Oh my god! How the hell did she get our location? I thought Dad was leading her away from us!"

"Don't worry," Astoria replied, cracking her knuckles. "I can handle her."

"You dimwit, you already killed me!" Ruth yelled above the wind and realised she was grinning ear-to-ear. "You couldn't hurt me to save your life!"

"RUN!" Maxine said to her sister and they started off away from Ruth.

Ruth's grin wavered as she realised that if they did outrun her, they could indeed escape. She had to get to them. And fast too.

Chapter 38

She precariously inched down the dune and ended up slipping and falling in the sand, face-first. But she stood up and began running again. The sisters had a head start of about 30 meters or so and it dawned on Ruth her calves weren't exactly going to cooperate with her high-speed chase. Yet, Ruth ran for what it was worth, which was, quite a lot. The biting wind cut through her clothes as her legs burned. The distance between Ruth and her killers was dwindling but she didn't slow down. Not for a fraction of a second. Running had never been her strong suit but as she reached out and yanked Astoria's filthy blonde hair backwards, Ruth was proud of herself for being able to outrun two people who were literally running for their life.

Ruth was jaded, yes, but her powers hadn't given up on her. Yet, at least. A small tug from her was enough to tip Astoria's muscular build downwards, to the ground. She fell and groaned as she hit the sand. Ruth instantly trapped Astoria in a headlock.

"Maxine! Help me!" Astoria pleaded; it wasn't easy for her to speak with her air supply cut off.

"Ruth, I know we wronged you but do you really wanna be a murderer?" asked Maxine, a note of panic in her voice, her already pale face completely decolourised now, sweat running down her temples.

"Funny how the tables turn, huh?" Ruth asked Astoria, tightening her grip around Astoria's neck, chuckling wryly and completely ignoring Maxine's senseless attempts at preserving her sister's life. "Now, you'll realise what it felt like to be me, and my parents, who were doing nothing but their job."

Astoria gagged; her lips were turning purple.

"Please!" her sister begged, tears forming in her menacing black eyes – eyes that she had gotten from her mother Iris. "Please don't kill my sister."

"Oh, so you can see your sister?" Ruth asked in sarcastic surprise. "But you couldn't see my mother? My father? You couldn't see an innocent 17-year-old?"

In answer, Maxine just sobbed.

"Why are you still standing here? Run. Maybe I'll spare you if I'm too tired to chase after you."

But instead, Maxine did something that surprised Ruth. She grabbed Ruth's neck from the behind and pulled really hard. The motion caused Ruth no pain

Chapter 38

at all but made her loose her grip on Astoria's throat. She escaped Ruth's grasp and just as Ruth grabbed Maxine's wrists and flipped her over her head and she slammed into the sand, Astoria began to run.

"See?" Ruth asked Maxine as she positioned her hands on Maxine's neck. "She didn't hesitate for a moment before abandoning you. If you'd run when I told you, maybe you could have lived. Well, it's too late now."

Ruth twisted Maxine's neck with enough force to snap it. The sound of breaking bones echoed in Ruth's ears and Maxine fell to the ground, still as a stone, dead as a skeleton.

Ruth looked to her right, where Astoria was running as fast as she could dare. Ruth immediately knew she couldn't run all the way over there. The combat had tired her incredibly and the pain that had arrived after Transformation was getting worse. If she didn't do something right away, she'd lose Astoria, perhaps forever, and her actual murderer would roam free on Earth even after she had departed to the *afterlife*.

Her knees buckled and Ruth lost her balance as she thrust out her hands in Astoria's direction and chanted the spell under her breath. This spell had always been a particularly difficult one, and it definitely wasn't easier now, what with Astoria's resistance and Ruth's lack of energy. Yet, it was almost as if she was pulling some invisible string attached to Astoria's back; Astoria was slowly moving backwards - towards Ruth - in spite of struggling hard. Her hands had begun to hurt because of the strain but Ruth persevered. She had given up too many times before; she knew this couldn't be one of those times.

Astoria stumbled backwards and fell on her back a few feet away from Ruth. Every muscle in her body complained but Ruth stood up and made her way to a panting and bewildered Astoria.

"Wh-what happened?" she asked Ruth, an aghast expression on her face that was slick with sweat.

"I'm dead, remember? All thanks to you."

Before Astoria could try and make the stupid decision of running again, Ruth caught hold of her throat and squeezed as tightly as her feeble shivering hands would let her. Astoria wouldn't go without a

Chapter 38

fight, of course, and so, she clawed at Ruth's hands, raked her nails across Ruth's face but none of it made any difference. None of it mattered because as seconds passed, Astoria was closer and closer to death and Ruth was closer and closer to avenging her family. Pretty soon, Astoria's hands dropped onto the sand and her amber eyes dilated. In a matter of moments, her blinking stopped and her chest was utterly still now.

Astoria had just breathed for the last time.

39.

RUTH – The Afterlife

Ruth woke up after what felt like a long time. Her body felt stiff and uncomfortable, like it wasn't her own but borrowed from someone else. She didn't feel good and she was fed up of being so used to feeling like that. Exhaustion and agony were default for her body now. She wanted to feel something good – like energy coursing through her or the comfort of tucking yourself in after a long, tiring day.

Her eyes slowly adjusted to the slanting rays of sunlight that were pouring over the fractured world. Ruth sat up and blinked until she could finally see things clearly – the sun that hung in the sky, lovingly exuding warm orange light, the pristine golden sand and the dead bodies.

Ruth flinched and crawling on her knees, moved away from Astoria's very dead body. That's when she noticed the sharp pungent stench that poisoned the air. Ruth coughed and gagged as she stood up and

Chapter 39

managed a couple of steps away from the people who would have been alive if it hadn't been for her. Who would have been alive had they not murdered three innocent people. Ruth's initial disgust at her own actions ebbed into a rare and almost foreign feeling of satisfaction. Elation, even.

She looked at the dead sisters for a long time, dealing with an array of conflicting emotions and thoughts. Finally, she realised she couldn't handle this anymore - dealing with this kind of baggage. Ruth was only 17. She was too young. She deserved peace. She deserved happiness. And maybe the *afterlife* was the only place she could get those things now. She had no idea how long she had been passed out after the exertion had overpowered her. Maybe she was closer to her ultimate fate than she imagined. But still, she wanted to go there by choice, not tied up in handcuffs that would only hurt her more. So, for what would be the last time, Ruth turned into a sparrow.

****

The palace stood only about ten feet in front of her when she landed. The throng of chattering souls standing between Ruth and the palace's front doors silenced at once when they noticed her. Their faces changed to show recognition: eyes widening, mouths dropping open and loud gasps escaping those mouths. Ominous whispers spread through the crowd like wildfire as they gawked at Ruth, making her feel like she had committed a crime. Which, according to these people, of course, she had.

She stepped forward and the souls made way for her even though they were flashing her scowls and disapproving looks. She'd respond, but the last thing she cared about was what these souls thought of her. When she finally did reach the gigantic glistening, golden gates, the guards looked at her and recognized her instantly. Ruth supposed they would arrest her. But they just looked at her with a sad expression as they opened the gates, as if they felt pity for her. The thought angered her.

"Don't look at me like that," she blurt out with a heavy, croaky voice. "Like I'm a broken doll or something."

"Oh, you aren't broken. Yet," said one of the guards and laughed; the other snickered. "Use the

Chapter 39

elevator and head to the 25th level. And, uh... try not to take any detours this time."

When Ruth did enter the humungous hall, adorned with gold and carvings and tapestries and all those magnificent things she didn't care for anymore, she located the elevator and headed straight towards it. She punched the '25' button so hard, the tiny crystal cracked slightly. Before she could do as much as sort her emotions that were running so high, the silver-mirror doors of the elevator opened and forced her to get out and face the consequences of all the wrong decisions she'd had to make to do the right thing. That's what she told herself as she took in the scene – *I did the right thing. I did what I had to do.*

An army of people dressed in ironed white, black and grey pantsuits, wearing grim expressions on their faces were standing there, clutching laptops, notepads and even scrolls. She stepped out feeling defenceless and attacked. She wondered if they were all really there only for her, to question her, to bombard her with very true allegations and to sentence her to an awful *afterlife* that had no trace of the peace and happiness she had been yearning for.

"Ms. Forbes," said one of the women at the front in a stiff voice. Her clean brunette hair fell in an elegant curtain around her square face; her eyes bore into Ruth's unnervingly. "It is time for your trial."

"Right now? I just—"

"The trial of any soul planning to depart into the *afterlife* is held a day before their due date," said the woman indifferently. "So, in theory, your trial was supposed to be held yesterday. But, as it is, you have arrived only now. So, I suggest we get started as the trial will last at least 3 hours and with the formalities, I doubt we'll have any breathing time before you go into the *afterlife*."

The explanation's summary was this – Ruth was leaving Earth that very day, probably in a matter of mere hours; she also had a ton of punishment to face. She wanted to jump into a big monologue about how even though she had broken many of The Kingdom's rules, she hadn't caused any tangible harm; she had simply done what needed to be done to avenge her family. But she didn't have the energy. Besides, at this point, she frankly didn't care about her future prospects. What she did care about was Evander's

Chapter 39

memories and how her last wish was being a part of them.

"I don't care what you do to me. But please, don't erase his memories." She realised she was pleading and tears were escaping her eyes again. "He means more than anything to me. Don't make him forget me. Just please—"

"Who is she talking about?" asked a boy at the back of the group. He looked small and scrawny with orange hair and a pale freckled face, wearing a shirt he hadn't tucked in properly. He looked younger than Ruth.

"The undead, Roofus," said the brunette woman at the front exasperatedly. "Evander."

"Oh," was all Roofus said as his face turned from baffled to slightly disappointed. Maybe even a little sad.

"Ms. Forbes," said the brunette woman. "The undead's trial was held about three days ago. The appropriate verdict was passed and his memories were erased. He was sent home yesterday."

For a minuscule moment, Ruth thought she was a part of a computer simulation and was facing a bug that had been overlooked during the programming. Because what this lawyer woman was telling her was obviously a mistake. Wrong. Not true. Because how could Evander forget her? How could he go back home and resume his old life? It didn't make any sense to her.

No matter what, in her head, she had always believed that this accident that was him discovering her truth would cause his life to take a turn for the better, like hers had. He had given her hope and strength and made her feel alive; he had made her laugh and taught her empathy in a very different sense than what she believed it to be; he had made her feel grateful for her life; he had given her so much. But she had failed in doing the same for him. Because for him, his life hadn't changed one bit. He was back at square one and he didn't even know that he had ever been anywhere else.

Ruth wanted to say things. Yell them. Yell how the inane judge had passed the wrong verdict; yell at Lesly how she hadn't done her job well enough; yell how everything in her life was far from fair. But she found

Chapter 39

she couldn't. She couldn't make a single sound as the brunette lawyer woman described the trial's procedure while escorting her to the giant courtroom where a multitude of people had garnered to watch her be sentenced to her fate.

She saw the wonderfully painted high walls of the atrium; she saw the mixed reactions of the people that were ogling at her; she saw the stack of papers on the table beside which she was told to sit. Ruth saw everything but didn't register any of it. Because she simply didn't have the ability to think of anything except Evander.

All Ruth could think of was how he had never seen a single moment of true happiness; how his big heart had given her something to hold onto when her life was spiralling out of control; how he had selflessly agreed to help and hadn't given up even when the stakes had skyrocketed. She could see his face clear as day: his electric blue eyes that always seemed to be blinking too fast, the lean bridge of his nose, the elegant curve of his cheek, and his bedazzling smile that showed once in a blue moon. She could hear his voice: slightly low, clear and often sarcastic. She wanted to hear his voice again; she wanted to see his face again. She wanted to feel his supportive and reassuring presence beside her as the trial began and people started to speak one after the other in an orderly fashion while the room held its breath.

So, Ruth sat there, mulling over everything that had happened in the past 5 months, trying to ignore the voices that were speaking around her. Suddenly, she realised someone was shaking her.

"Ma'am I cannot defend you if you just sit there like you're made out of stone," said the woman who was shaking her. She looked old and wise with her sleek glasses and a grim expression. She looked irked too. "I don't think you heard me clearly before. I'm Samantha Delvis. I am your defendant. And, as you must know, you haven't left me much to work with. So, do as I say, okay?"

Ruth nodded.

The next couple of hours were a blur of standing up and speaking a bunch of lines Samantha had given her and answering a series of senseless questions and watching Samantha and the brunette woman converse very intensely. Ruth said what she was told to, did as she was told and basically acted like a robot,

Chapter 39

for as long as they'd allow her. She suddenly wasn't very worried about having to serve a dreadful sentence. She didn't care. About anything, now. She just wanted to be done with all of this. Disappear. Into thin air. Only, that wasn't possible.

After what must have been about 4 hours since Ruth's trial had begun, the judge managed to silence the humungous courtroom. You could hear a pin drop.

"Now, after much analysis and a careful examination of the witnesses and evidence presented, the jury and I are ready with our final, irrefutable verdict," said the judge, an old, wrinkled woman who looked shrivelled in her oversized black velvet robes. "Ruth Forbes, case no. 5096, will serve 5 years of physical as well as psychological punishment in the *Gehennalocus*, after which she will be sent to the final stage of the *afterlife* – *Caelumlocus*."

The crowd erupted into grumbles of disagreement and even loud objections about how this sentence wasn't enough for an offender like Ruth and how she didn't even deserve to head into *Caelumlocus*. That's when she understood what the fancy new word

'Caelumlocus' meant. It was the final stage of death – the stage when you just cease existing; no one really knew what it felt like, but it was supposed to be the peaceful part of the *afterlife*.

The protests soon died down, though, because the judge had literally gotten up and left along with the jury. The people who were calling for Ruth's blood a second before got bored and departed too, leaving behind half a dozen lawyers who were packing up their things and a very apathetic Ruth.

"Aren't you happy?" asked Samantha. She was beaming at Ruth. "I got you less than half of the punishment you would have gotten ordinarily!"

"Oh, did you? Well, that's excellent. Thank you," Ruth said in monotone and stood up, heaving a sigh. "Do you know where I'm supposed to head to next?"

Samantha gleaned through a number of documents before telling Ruth she needed to go to the 57th level. Ruth nodded and they exchanged a brief farewell and the next moment, Ruth found herself on the 57th level, her eyes searching for the room she is supposed to enter. A door to her far right opened and a woman in her early twenties stepped

Chapter 39

out; she had ginger hair and an aura of warmth as she smiled amiably at Ruth.

"You must be Ruth Forbes," she said with a Spanish accent, walking up to Ruth. "I am Celia Vergara. Pleased to meet you." She held out her hand and Ruth commanded her own hand to shake it.

Celia guided her down the hallway and they entered another room – this one buzzing with din: papers being stapled, documents being printed, files being stacked into shelves. Ruth was told to sit at a table where she signed document after document, not bothering to read what the pages said. Finally, she was told to hold out her right wrist, where Celia pressed a red-hot burning stamp on her tattoo. When the stamp lifted, her previous tattoo was changed to an itchy and painful one that looked like clouds trying to conceal a sun.

"Excellent," Celia said happily. She took a seat next to Ruth. "Now we just need those documents to be approved and then I can escort you to the place from where we send souls into the *Gehennalocus* – the former part of the *afterlife*."

"That's where I'll be punished, right?" Ruth asked neutrally.

"Yes. You'll stay there for 5 years before they erase your memories entirely." Celia looked at Ruth with sympathy before saying, "I'm truly sorry, Ruth. We aren't really allowed to meddle in any soul's case but everybody knows about yours. And I do agree with many others that your punishment isn't justified. You don't deserve it."

"What does it matter," Ruth said, running her thumb over the tattoo.

She wanted to tell Celia that the person who actually didn't deserve their fate was Evander; that he should have gotten to keep his own memories. But she figured that telling Celia would make no difference. In fact, it dawned over Ruth that nothing would make any difference now. Nothing mattered at all.

To say Ruth was entirely present for whatever followed that minute conversation would be inaccurate. She didn't even remember any of it when she was being dressed by another soul whose name she couldn't recollect. Then, she was at the front of a big, clean white door. She felt pretty clean herself in

Chapter 39

a pristine floral yellow dress and sky blue slippers, with her hair pulled back in a ponytail.

"Yes, we're all done here," said a voice joyfully from Ruth's left. "You can open the door and enter the *Gehennalocus*."

Ruth realised the voice was addressing her. And she understood the time had come. The door to the *afterlife* was right in front of her, waiting to be opened.

But before she did open it, Ruth forced her foggy mind to clear and tried to reflect upon her life. Her loving parents whom she was ecstatic she had managed to avenge; her cosy little home where she had created innumerable memories; her friends with whom she had shared so many unforgettable experiences. And Evander. Who didn't even remember her.

Ruth regretted a lot of things, like not taking all the risks she could and enjoying the smaller moments her life had gifted her but mainly, she regretted meeting him. She regretted giving him any kind of hope that would always be just out of his reach. She wanted to go back in time and change all of that. But at that moment, all Ruth could do was wish Evander all the luck and happiness in the world and hope that he'd find a way to escape, to live the life he'd always dreamed of, to be the person he'd always wanted to be.

Goodbye Evander, was Ruth's last coherent thought as she twisted the doorknob open.

40.

EVANDER – Back in Paradise

The day arrived with emptiness and daze. Like all the past ones had. Evander sat up on his bed and watched the sun rise in the azure sky through the window.

It was a fine Saturday. Not only because Julio and Bella were away at a vacation but also because Juliana and Diego needed to attend an exhibition for two whole days and that meant Evander had the house to himself. He wasn't entirely alone, though. After his detour three months ago, his loving father had assigned his own bodyguard Miguel to Evander. But it was more than evident that Miguel wasn't there to protect Evander; he was there to keep Evander imprisoned.

Evander looked at his bedside table and found the day's list. He picked it up and read through the 48 items. 48 tasks that he needed to finish by the end of the day. Evander would always think how a prison would be more peaceful than his home every time he was done reading his list. But then he would dismiss the baseless thought because he hadn't ever actually been in any prison; he had no idea what that would be like.

Evander got up, took a shower, got dressed and entered the kitchen, hoping to have some breakfast before getting started on the day's chores. Instead of a quiet and empty kitchen, he found Miguel, his large, brawny bodyguard who always looked like he was regretting his life decisions.

"Looking to escape?" he asked Evander, stuffing salad in his face.

Evander laughed. "Looking to have a slice of bread before scrubbing all the dishes clean all by myself."

"Good."

"Like I even have anywhere to go, Miguel. Come on. You know better than that," Evander said as he brewed a strong doze of coffee.

"Well, I know what your father told me. That you left three months ago and landed outside the front door 5 days ago unconscious, claiming you didn't remember the last 3 months at all. Now, isn't that shady?"

Chapter 40

"Man." Evander sighed. "Didn't my father tell you that the doctor said I have amnesia? I don't even remember leaving. I don't remember the damn solo trip Juliana keeps telling me I was fortunate to have."

"Or so you say," Miguel said, narrowing his eyes at Evander as he drained his coffee mug. "Just know... I will not hesitate to harm you if you try anything strange."

"Just know... I won't," Evander answered, mimicking Miguel's tone.

Flashing him a threatening look, Miguel left and Evander started on the dishes, feeling more lost than he'd ever been in his entire life. He thought about that chilly evening four days ago when he had awoken on the front steps of his home with his backpack, with his family surrounding him, gawking at him like he had come from a strange planet. They had, obviously, reprimanded him immensely in ways that made him wince even now; they had also attacked him with a gazillion questions that he'd had no answers to. He remembered sleeping in his tattered bed that night, deprived of dinner or a drink of water, trying to remember the past 3 months. How? Why?

What had happened when he had returned from the trip he didn't recall anymore?

Evander finished off the last dish and began the mopping, wondering how he'd been lucky enough to have his stuff with him, still. He knew he must have taken his backpack with him for the trip, with his passport and Visa and whatnot. Luckily, surprisingly, he hadn't lost any of it.

Of course, no one in his family understood his dilemma of not remembering a thing. His father had taken him to a doctor but it was only to confirm if he was saying the truth. Julio was as befuddled as Evander when the doctor had told him that Evander had amnesia, and would probably never recall whatever it was that he didn't remember at the moment. Although, Julio and everybody else had gotten over it really quickly. After a couple of days had passed, they acted like the entire thing hadn't even happened. Evander couldn't do that. So he had tried asking Diego.

"Well, Dad asked me to go get you. You were in some village, outside a hut's door and I picked you up and we returned," he had answered.

Chapter 40

"But I don't remember that, Diego," Evander had miserably told his brother.

"And I don't care, douchebag."

So, obviously, that conversation had been of no help at all. Like the other conversations Evander had tried having with the rest of his family members. No matter what they told him, it didn't help him be convinced of why he couldn't remember such a long period of his life.

Evander had a tugging sensation that this had happened before. That he had been hopelessly searching for something he didn't remember even in his past. A strange feeling of déjà vu was overwhelming him, because no matter how hard he tried, he just couldn't recall a single thing.

Hours passed and Evander ticked off one item after another from his never-ending list. By lunchtime, he was sweaty and exhausted as he filled up his plate with all of the leftovers and sat down to have his meal.

"How many tasks left?" Miguel asked, appearing out of thin air and making Evander jump.

"About 27."

"Good."

"You know, you don't have to be such a jerk to me all the time," Evander said, annoyed. "That's not what my father is paying you for. Besides, my life is pretty miserable as it is."

"It's for a reason," Miguel said unsurely, slightly thrown-off by what Evander had said.

"Oh, is it? What did they say it was? Why do you think I am treated this way in my own house by my own father and siblings?"

For a moment, the burly guy was dead-silent.

"They never told me but I assumed it must have been something pretty terrible," he finally said sheepishly.

"Of course they didn't tell you. They couldn't, without making themselves look like ruthless sociopaths." Evander scoffed and took a big bite of his sandwich.

"What do you mean?"

"Don't humour me," said Evander. "I know you don't care. No one does."

Chapter 40

"Well, it's part of my job. I need to know," said Miguel, sounding almost human for the first time.

Taken aback, Evander set down his half-eaten sandwich and tried to think of way to explain it without making Miguel think his family was diabolical. Then, he gave up because it was impossible.

"My birth had complications," he began. "They couldn't save my mother. So, my family blames me for her death. They've never said it explicitly, of course, but it's always been pretty clear. Always since I spent my 6th birthday all alone, locked up in the attic."

He didn't want to say that last part but it just slipped out. That's when he realised that this was the first time he had spoken this out loud. The feeling was liberating - something heavy seemed to have been lifted off of his shoulders.

Miguel stared at Evander in disbelief. "You're making that up."

"Kinda wish I was, man," he answered and resumed devouring his sandwich.

"Th-that's awful." Miguel sighed and sat on the couch across Evander. "I am sorry for you."

Evander just shrugged his shoulders as he continued eating.

"Can I help you in some way?"

"I don't know, Miguel," Evander said. "You're being paid to keep me locked up here. I don't see how you can help me. Just be nice, maybe?"

Miguel nodded and Evander went off to clean his dishes and finish up the rest of his tasks.

It was close to midnight when Evander was finally able to collapse on his bed. Exhausted, he was ready to drift off into a hopefully tranquil slumber. So, when his eyes closed and the tendrils of fatigue pulled him under, he didn't resist.

41.

EVANDER – Someone called Home

Dreams had always been a traumatic ordeal for Evander. Sometimes, they'd bring him agonising flashbacks that caused him to wake up screaming and loathing his family. Sometimes, they'd bring an alternate reality of what could have been had his mother not died. Sometimes, they were about him going out into the world and finding out that his family had always been right – he was a good-for-nothing idiot, and wouldn't ever make a good writer. But sometimes, his dreams were simply strange and meaningless; this kind he particularly liked, because they were so far away from his dreadful reality.

That night, as he fell asleep, he had a bizarre dream. A very realistically bizarre dream. At first, he thought he was standing in the middle of nowhere. Then, the hazy fog that glazed his surroundings lifted and he realised he was in a big empty room. He looked around, hoping he'd meet someone or find something that made sense. But he didn't and as time passed, he was starting to grow bored of his pathetic life; even his dreams were monotonous.

Then, suddenly, out of thin air, popped out two people. Evander jumped, terrified as he looked at the people more carefully. The man looked about 40 and wore beige pants and a pale blue t-shirt. He didn't look dangerous at all. The woman with him was no different. She wore a flowing yellow skirt embroidered with floral designs and a violet blouse. Her hair was a beautiful auburn. Both of them smiled at Evander so genially, he thought they must know each other. But he couldn't place them at all.

"It's been quite some time since I've seen you, son," said the woman, wiping off a tear. That's when Evander noticed her eyes – vibrantly emerald and making him feel like he had seen them before.

"Yes, of course," said the man, nodding in Evander's direction with slight disappointment. "He doesn't remember us, Veronica."

Was the confusion on Evander's face that clear?

Chapter 41

"I-I am sorry. I actually just—" began Evander apologetically when Veronica cut him off.

"Oh, don't apologize, dear! You have no reason to say sorry. In fact, we both owe you an apology, as well as a big, big thank you."

Thank you? Apology? What was she talking about? Evander had never met these people. And just when he had decided that this dream was some lame trick his brain was playing, a blood-curdling bout of aching racked his head so suddenly, he was blind-sighted for a second. He doubled over, sure that the pain's intensity would consume his whole being; fortunately, it didn't. He righted himself.

"Boy, are you okay?" asked the man with a look of concern.

"He's trying too hard to remember, Dylan," Veronica said, looking just as worried.

As his blinding ache went down a notch, Evander realised she was worried for *him*. And so was the man she had just called Dylan. They were concerned about *him*. As if they cared. He had never been treated this way before.

"Oh, okay," Dylan told Veronica. "Let's not wait any longer."

"Evander," began Veronica, tearing up, "no amount of thanks can ever convey the gratitude we feel for you for helping our daughter through thick and thin. Agreeing to help her almost got you killed and you knew that that was a possibility but you agreed to help her anyway. We're so immensely sorry for the trouble we put you through. We cannot tell you just how thankful we both are."

What daughter? What help? Evander's mind was going berserk with every word Veronica spoke.

"Avenging us and herself was the only thing she truly wanted, Evander," Dylan said, his hazel eyes filling up with tears. "And if you hadn't been there for her, supported her, motivated her, she wouldn't have been able to do it."

"Sir, I'm sorry but I don't know what you're talking about," Evander finally said.

"That's okay," Veronica said soothingly. "You don't need to know, understand, or even remember. But we had to do this. More importantly, our daughter had to do this."

Chapter 41

"Ma'am, I don't know who your daughter is."

That's when the girl appeared next to Veronica, out of nowhere, just like Veronica and Dylan had. Her straight black hair was tied back like her mother's and she wore a white dress patterned with flowers. Her almond-shaped hazel eyes looked exactly like her father's, but they were bloodshot and puffy from crying. They looked familiar, her eyes, and that tired look they had. She looked at him for a long time in silence and so did he, because now, he was certain he knew her, or at least once had.

Then, a short, strangled sound between a whisper and a gasp escaped her mouth. And she released the breath she seemed to have been holding. A single tear trickled down her cheek as her hand rose to touch Evander's cheek. The soft palm of her hand was slightly trembling. She lightly gasped and after a moment, stroked his cheek with her thumb. Evander wasn't used to being touched (probably because his family treated him like an untouchable) and yet, this gesture didn't threaten him or make him flinch. Instead, it comforted him.

"He's real," the girl whispered in such a low voice, Evander had to strain his ears to hear her. "All of this is real."

"Yes, sweetie, it is," Evander heard Veronica say, sounding pleased, but he just couldn't take his eyes off of the girl's.

The pounding returned to his head, now much, much worse than before, making him feel like his brain was literally being sliced and scorched over and over and it was sickening, but he held his ground as well as the girl's gaze. Because he realised that he did know those eyes, and very well too. He knew those tears and the anguish that the girl's sceptical voice had. As moments slipped by, Evander realised he knew the girl too.

BAM!

There was a flash of blinding light in his head and his eyes shut as he tumbled backwards, his knees turning to jelly. He hit the floor and as his eyes slowly opened to see bits of sunlight dancing around, he remembered. He remembered everything.

Chapter 41

"Evander," he heard Ruth's anxious voice as she rushed to him, clutching his hand. "Ar-are you okay? What's wrong?"

"Nothing," he said and smiled, even though it hurt. "Nothing's wrong now, Ruth, because I remember it all."

An array of emotions went through her face, but the one that stayed was that of sheer joy, the kind he'd never seen on her face before. Her smile was so impossibly stunning, he was afraid he was going to faint just looking at her. All those memories surged through him now - the ones he could never have afforded to forget but *The Kingdom of the Lifeless* had erased anyway. In that moment, Evander felt what could only be described as a feeling of being home.

He managed to sit up and Ruth pulled him in an embrace and her sweet lavender scent was wafting into his nostrils again. When they pulled apart, Ruth's face was covered with tears.

"I never got to thank you," she said, sniffling. "For risking your life a hundred times over just to avenge mine. For making me realise that in spite of what happened, I had so much to be grateful for. For making me feel alive, even in death."

"I wanted to thank you too," he said, wiping her tears. "For making me realise I did deserve happiness, even though my life began with my mother's death. For making me understand that I am not worthless, in spite of what I was raised believing. For making me see that even though my family was hurting, they were wrong to hurt me. And for teaching me that it's okay to trust. That it can be good again."

Evander realised he was tearing up too now. This wasn't just 'thank you'. This was good-bye. But how do you say good-bye to someone you have come to think of as home?

He didn't have the strength to say it. He never would. And, as it turned out, neither did Ruth. Because she said nothing. She simply nodded and wrapped her arms around his neck and didn't let go.

Until the blackness dissolved her, and she slipped away, as he tried to hold onto her. He couldn't.

42.

EVANDER – A New Beginning

He woke up, panting like he had run a 5k. He looked around, and found he was in his room, not the big hall. The realisation disappointed Evander; the sight of his room and the sense of reality that accompanied it confirmed only one thing – he'd never see Ruth again. Maybe in his dreams, but his dreams would never again be like the one he had just had. Because even though it had happened in his head, Evander was certain that it had been real. What Evander was entirely uncertain of was how the dream had even come to him. He was supposed to have forgotten anything even remotely related to Ruth, and he had. Then how on Earth had that dream managed to enter his head?

Evander sat up and took a few gulps of water from the bottle next to his bed. He checked his clock; it ticked to 6:13 am. It was morning and soon, he'd have to get up and moving with all the work. But he didn't have the energy for it. Although he had slept for about 6 hours, the dream had caused his brain to be extra active, which resulted in his current weariness. He wanted to go back to sleep, to dream of Ruth again, and maybe this time when he woke up, she'd be there, right next to him.

But he didn't. Instead, he got up and took a shower and began with his day, trying his best to tick off every item on his list as fast as possible (luckily, there were only 29 today). So, he swept every inch of the floor and got done with the laundry and the dishes and preparing his and Miguel's meals and everything else that he was expected to do. Miguel didn't chat with Evander and he was glad, because he didn't have time to waste.

By 7.30 in the evening, Evander had successfully completed all his work and dinner and bid Miguel goodnight as he headed off to his room to shut the door tightly and start packing.

Packing. Because after Evander had woken up from the dream that he so yearned to be reality, he had understood that even though Ruth wasn't with him, a part of her would always be. He didn't know how his brain had shown him that dream and revived its own storage, but all of that had happened for a

Chapter 42

reason. The reason was that life is too short – it's too short to tolerate being punished when you're not guilty, it's too short to not be everything you want to be, and it is definitely too short to believe you're unworthy of being happy. Because having his brain tampered with had caused this very important epiphany to fade away, something had made those memories return to him. He didn't know what it was but he knew this – he wasn't just going to waste his life even after unknown forces had gifted him this miracle.

In fact, as Evander stuffed his clothes in a suitcase he had managed to sneak from his father's room while cleaning it, he realised that it simply wasn't a choice anymore. Leaving his 'home' or not wasn't a choice because he wasn't going to see Ruth again. He needed to do her justice by doing this for himself. It was what she wanted. She wanted him to run away, leave and never return. And Evander was going to do just that. He just had to wait for the right moment.

As he finished packing, he carefully put away the suitcase just in case Miguel showed up at his door for whatever reason. He charged his phone. While he was meticulously cleaning his siblings' rooms, he had managed to collect whatever cash he had found lying about. Then, he had realised that the sum of money still wasn't enough to get him anywhere away from Mexico. So, he had stolen a good amount of money from his father's secret stash; it was *supposed* to be a secret but Evander had lived with Julio for too long to not know his habits inside out. He carefully secured the money in a dusty old duffel bag he had found in the attic some years ago, along with his passport and Visa. Then, he waited.

Hours passed and at 10.03 pm., there was an unexpected knock at Evander's door. He hid anything that could seem suspicious, composed himself and opened the door.

"What's up, Miguel," he said a little too casually.

Miguel looked at him for a moment and then said, "I wanted to have a word with you."

"That sounds serious," Evander said, closing the door and sitting beside Miguel on the bed, hoping that whatever this was, it would be wrapped up soon. "Everything alright?"

Chapter 42

"No, Evander," Miguel said earnestly with a hint of sadness. "Everything isn't alright. Ever since you told me the reason your family treats you this way, I've been thinking if I'm doing the right thing by doing their work. Why should I keep you locked up here?"

Because it gets you paid, was Evander's first thought but he didn't say it. Maybe Miguel was just emotional enough to actually help him run away. Evander had to play this right.

"Uhh...I'm not sure," he said and smiled wistfully. "It's just my fate, Miguel. I was destined to stay here like a prisoner, work like a slave and be treated like a murderer."

"But why?" Miguel's voice had genuine pain. "When I was your age, I used to go around working in other people's houses and they'd pay me for doing half the work you do. And they were *strangers*, Evander. And here you are... being behaved with like this... by your own *family*." Miguel's voice had something more than mere sympathy: it had disgust and anger and hopefully just enough hatred to result in empathy.

"Yeah, I agree. It's awful," said Evander. "But there isn't anything you can do, Miguel. Your hands are just as tied as mine."

As Miguel took in what Evander had just said, his face changed. Suddenly, he appeared to be thinking really hard. "I don't think that's entirely true."

Jackpot. Evander couldn't believe he had such excellent manipulation skills.

"What do you mean?" he asked, pretending he had no idea what was going on.

"There's just the two of us here till tomorrow morning. I'll help you run away in exchange for some money," Miguel said.

"How much?"

"How 'bout 3000 bucks...?"

"I don't think I have more than 2000."

Miguel's eyes shone. "Alright. It's more than what your father was giving me, anyway. I'll help you. Start packing. I know a guy who can take you to the airport. You do have enough money for the ticket?"

Chapter 42

"Depends on where I go," he said, realising he had put in no thought about where he was supposedly running off to.

"What do you mean? Do you not know where you wanna go?" Miguel asked like Evander had gone insane.

"I mean... I didn't even think I'd get to escape this prison today. How would I know where to go?"

"Have you never thought of running away? You must have some idea about where you would go if you did leave this place."

"Not really. I had assumed that my father would eventually let me live by myself. I assumed I'd find some town far away from Mexico City."

"You cannot make that mistake, Evander. I know your father. He's insane. He could send men after you, to hunt you down."

"You really think he wants me to be here that bad? I don't think he'll care that much. When I had disappeared for 3 months, what had he done, anyway?"

"He told me the police investigation ran for a couple of months but then they gave up. So, yeah, I guess, he wouldn't care all that much."

"Well, ironically," Evander said, "that's actually a huge relief."

"You still shouldn't be here though," Miguel said. "Mexico? Really? You can be anywhere in the world and you want to be here? Where you suffered all your life?"

Miguel did have a point. Evander had about 5000 Mexican peso. He could easily buy a ticket and find a place somewhere in the cheaper parts of the US. And who knew, maybe that would be far more beneficial for his writing career too.

He thought about where he had always envisioned himself being when his life had finally turned around. He wasn't sure. But the one place he had always been fascinated about was New Orleans. He had read about it in some fantasy and horror books. It was a beautiful city, humming with architecture, music, good cuisine, and vibrant culture. Or maybe it wasn't as amazing as painted by fiction, but when Evander had read those stories, he had been only 10. He had dreamed about going to New Orleans, even if it was

Chapter 42

just a little vacation. Now, it didn't need to be a little vacation – he could decide where he wanted to spend his entire life. And maybe New Orleans was more expensive than he could afford, but he'd figure out that grownup stuff later, right? At the moment, he had to get the hell out of Mexico.

"I'll go to New Orleans," he said with finality, grinning at the idea.

Miguel smiled at him in approval. "What about the money for the ticket?"

Evander googled and found that the tickets weren't that expensive: it was a 7-hour flight. He had enough money to cover a one-way ticket, no problem. Of course, the money wasn't his to take, but Evander didn't care. Besides, he was pretty sure at least half of it his father had earned illegally; furthermore, Julio wasn't exactly a noble person – stealing from him made Evander feel no guilt whatsoever.

He ran to his father's room and collected every last bill that wasn't locked away; the sum was just enough to pay Miguel and pay for the ticket and have some left when he did get to New Orleans. He told Miguel to call his friend after an hour, when 'he was done with packing'.

Miguel left to pack his stuff as well. Evander wondered what Miguel was going to do now. He had worked as Julio's bodyguard for 10 years now - he'd accompany Julio in his office and on business trips. Where was he going to go after betraying his boss of 10 years? Surely, he couldn't stay here, or Julio would ruin his career just to spite him. But maybe the money he was taking from Evander was sufficient for him to move somewhere else as well. Evander found it strange how easy it had been to make Miguel his friend instead of someone standing in his way. Hopefully, Miguel wouldn't change his mind before the hour ended.

He checked his suitcase and duffel bag repeatedly, wondering if he had left something behind. Then, he remembered. He rushed to the corner of his room. It had a broken floorboard, which allowed a small space to be created in the floor. In this hole, many years back, Evander had hidden his diary. The diary in which he had started to write a story, the one he had given up on finishing. He took the diary out of the hole and wiped the dust off of it surface. On its

Chapter 42

leather, he had used scissors to inscribe his name – 'Evander Lennon', followed by a very ambitious 'A Future Author'. His fingers ran over the words and a smile broke out on his face. Finally, he was going to live his dream. He may not become a writer right away, or even for years, but at least he knew he was taking a step in the right direction.

Stuffing the diary in his suitcase, there was nothing left to do but wait.

****

At about 11.30, Miguel came to Evander's door to tell him it was time to go, his friend would be coming soon. As they gathered their things and headed to the door, Evander told Miguel to go on and wait outside for him. Once he left, Evander turned and looked at his former home one last time. He didn't have one fond memory in this place, except the ones he'd made reading and writing stories. He he'd never felt any safety or peace here, especially as long as his family was anywhere around. Evander realised he was incredibly relieved when he thought about how he was never, ever going to be in this place again. He twisted open the doorknob, and found leaving was one of the easiest things he had ever done.

Outside, he stood beside Miguel. After waiting for another twenty minutes, a battered, old and dented cab with scratched black paint showed up at Evander's doorstep.

"Thank you so much for helping me out, Miguel," he said. "You don't know how much this means to me."

Miguel affably patted Evander's shoulder. "I just... couldn't sit quietly and watch something so wrong," he said. "And thanks to you too... for the money," he added.

"Where will you go from here?" Evander asked him.

"Back to my hometown," he answered, his tone nostalgic. "But don't worry about me. Julio won't be able to hunt me down."

They exchanged a final goodbye and Evander got seated inside the cab as Miguel took off in another direction in his own car. The driver introduced himself as Camilo and started off with the speed of light. Evander tightly clutched onto his suitcase and

Chapter 42

duffel bag, hoping the ride wouldn't end up giving him any more injuries or pain. He had seen enough of both of them.

At what must have been 2 in the morning, Camilo stopped the car with a jerk, awakening Evander from his nap.

"We're at the airport," Camilo grunted, rubbing his eyes tiredly.

"Okay," Evander said, getting out of the car. "How much do I need to pay you?"

"You're a friend of Miguel... the ride was free."

"Thank you so much, Camilo," Evander said earnestly, astonished by how kind people can sometimes turn out to be. Kindness was something of a foreign trait to him.

Camilo nodded, turned the car around and left.

****

When he approached the lady at one of the counters at the deserted airport, he was told that the next flight to New Orleans would be at 6 am. So, he bought the ticket, carried on with the check-in procedures and when everything was done, he sat on one of the benches with some other people who were either waiting for flights or loved ones.

Waiting was torturous. But Evander dozed off multiple times and before he knew it, it was time to board his flight. He had gotten a window seat, luckily, and after settling down and the flight taking off, the sky was clearly visible to him. The first rays of sunshine had just begun to wash over Mexico City. The very first sunrise in his new life. As the sun rose, the warmth and comfort of its light reminded him of Ruth. Her name made him smile.

Ever since her existence had returned to his brain, he had busied himself with plans of escaping and while running away was important, that wasn't the only reason he was keeping himself busy. The real reason was that he didn't want to think of Ruth - because thinking of her meant missing her. Which was the worst form of hell on Earth.

But now, in the silence interrupted only by someone's snoring or chatter, he let her enter his head. Evander relished her memory; he relived every single moment they had shared. He was so glad his memory had inexplicably returned. Because had that not happened, he would have been in his father's

Chapter 42

house, sleeping, waiting to get up the next morning and continue with his cursed life.

In fact, as he thought back, he realised that so many other things had been essential for him to not have ended up there. Had he not met Ruth, and strived to discover her secret, none of this would have happened. Had he not agreed to help her, none of this would have happened. Had that middle-aged tribal man and woman not helped him in those woods, none of this would have happened. That's when it struck him! The man and woman were Ruth's parents! Veronica and Dylan. When Ruth had explained her truth to him, she had said that her parents had already moved on into the *afterlife*. So, if they had, how had they helped Evander by coming back to Earth?

Another item added to the long list of things Evander didn't know and would probably never understand. What he did know was that he was grateful. So very grateful for the life he had ahead of himself. Because multiple times, he was very close to being killed or to being a prisoner forever. What lay ahead was neither of those two fates. Evander felt ecstatic.

It would be incorrect to say that he hadn't lost anything. He had lost Ruth and Mr. Bundleheckles and had no idea where Lesly was; he had left his family behind and even though they had been horrible to him for as long as he could remember, he knew he'd think of them sometime in the future. In the future, he'd regret many things but right now, as the plane carried him to New Orleans, Evander could feel only one thing – the delicious taste of freedom, something his wretched life had always been empty of.

But his life was no longer wretched. It was destined to be difficult, full of bumps and potholes and thorns that would make him bleed. But now, it was full of possibilities. It was full of opportunities dying to be grabbed. Evander couldn't wait for this new chapter of his life to begin.

Epilogue

He stares at the blank screen in frustration. Why is this so difficult every time around?

Evander turns to look at his bookshelf. Its top level is lined with seven books – books *he* has written over the last twelve years. His eyes fix on the first one from the left – 'Back From The Dead'. Suddenly, he forgets about his current project, which feels less like a 'work-in-progress' and more like a constant frustration.

He stands up and walks to his bookshelf, taking the first book he has ever written off of the shelf and examining it's cover. It has a girl with silky black hair, gorgeous hazel eyes and she is shooting what seems to be flames out of her hands. It is Ruth, on the cover. The book is about her, of course. Needless to say, she was all Evander could think about when he finally reached New Orleans, 12 years ago.

There is a sudden scraping sound that startles Evander and makes him drop the book. He turns toward the sound and finds a grey Scottish Fold cat on his windowsill. He has always adored cats – they are fluffy, silly and hilarious. In fact, for the longest time, he has been planning to adopt one, so seeing this stray right outside his window – which is weird because his apartment is on the 8th floor – he has no option but to let her in.

The cat enters curiously and makes a strange motion with its head – as if looking around the room.

"What are you looking for, kitty?" Evander asks, shutting the window and scratching the cat behind its ears. "Scraps of food?"

The cat meows for a moment and then breaks into speech – "Evander, it's me. Do you remember me? Probably not."

He jumps back, terrified of the adorable creature who somehow speaks. But just as his heartbeat has begun to rise, Evander remembers the cat's words – "Evander, it's me."

"It's me, Lesly," the cat says just as he's reaching this conclusion himself.

This is even more jarring than a speaking cat.

"Lesly? How can it be you? How did you know I was here? How did you get—"

"Oh, you *do* remember." She sighs. "You still ask so many questions," says Lesly with a hint of a chuckle in her cat-voice. "Well, to answer some... I got help from a friend and looked up your location in The Kingdom's database. It wasn't so far from where I need to go next so I figured I'd pay you a visit."

"How do you remember me still? After 12 years?" he asks, awestruck at the effort Lesly had put in to get to him.

"You're one of the most incredible people I've ever met. And I've met tons of people - dead and alive. Of course, I remember you. Wait, how do you remember *me*? The Kingdom had your memory erased," she adds confusedly.

Evander smiles and grabs a chair. "It's a long story."

****

When he's done narrating all that had happened after the unfortunate verdict was passed 12 years ago, a silence falls between them. Perhaps, Lesly is too overwhelmed to respond.

"Maybe both your questions have the same answer," Lesly says, thinking hard. "I think I understand why Veronica and Dylan were able to help you without actually returning to Earth. And how you got that dream."

"Really? How? Why?" he asks, desperate to know the answers to the questions that have been bugging him for more than a decade.

"Well, when souls move on into the *afterlife*, a part of their essence remains on Earth. So, pretty much every soul that ever lived on Earth has left behind a fraction of their essence."

"What does that have to do with anything?"

"Veronica and Dylan left parts of their essence behind, and when Ruth - who still hadn't moved on into the *afterlife* - required help, that essence found a way to help," Lesly says. "Then, when Ruth moved on, her and her parents' essence helped bring your memory back. I don't know how they did it, or how it actually works, but their connection to you must have been really strong for it to have happened successfully."

"So... their essences helped me get my memory back?" Evander asks, beyond befuddled.

Lesly smiles. "Think of it this way - a lot of the things we think are fate or luck are really actions of these essences trying to help or sabotage us."

"I know I've probably said this a million times by now, but, that doesn't make much sense."

"Death, the *afterlife*, The Kingdom of the Lifeless and its ways are somewhat funny - they don't always work in a sensible fashion, Evander. Believe me, I know souls who have been working at The Kingdom for decades and still have no clue about what's really going on."

"Sounds like a glitch in the system," Evander jokes.

"It indeed is."

"Do you get to see the souls in the *afterlife*? Like Ruth?" he asks with child-like hope.

"I don't think you really understand what the *afterlife* is," she says. "It isn't like a room you can just enter. And Ruth's not just waiting there. After her trial, she was sentenced to 5 years of punishment, after which she moved on into *Caelumlocus*, the final stage of the *afterlife*. There, you stop existing. Your soul is reborn as somebody else's. What remains of your essence is lost. Ruth has moved on, Evander. In every way possible."

So that's what happens when you die. There's no eternity of torture or forever of peace. You just... stop existing.

And that means that not only is Ruth dead, but that she is completely gone. 'In every way possible.' That's not what happened in Evander's book, though. In his book, Ruth's character found a way to come back to life and live her life to the fullest. In his book, she had to burn herself to return to Earth. And when she did, she rose from her own ashes, like a phoenix.

"What are you thinking about?" Lesly asks him gently, as if he's a fragile glass vase that her voice has the capability of shattering.

"Phoenixes," he answers, not wanting to tell her how foolishly hopeful he had been while writing his first book. Hopeful that maybe, Ruth would return to him one day, having risen from her ashes.

"Oh," she says, probably surprised his reply wasn't simply 'Ruth'. "They're the ones that come back to life, right? Like, on their own?"

"Yes," Evander says. "They're mythical, of course. But, according to legend, when a phoenix dies, it ignites and burns to ashes. Then, it is reborn from those very ashes, brand new and stronger than before."

Lesly seems to think about that. "Isn't that something," she finally says, rivetted with the idea. "We're all phoenixes, if you think about it. In our own way, we're always rising from our ashes. That's the only way to survive, I think. You have to burn to be invincible."

Wow. I've never thought about it that way before, thinks Evander. He realises Lesly is absolutely right. Hadn't he burned a hundred times over in that childhood pile-of-bricks of his? Hadn't Ruth, when she was assassinated? And hadn't they both come out the other side stronger? But, Ruth's strength didn't matter now. Not in the *afterlife*, where she had simply stopped existing.

"So, that happens with everybody?" he asks, shaking his head and deciding it's best not to mull over Ruth's non-existence. "The going to the *Caelumlocus*? Do all souls end up there?"

"Not really. If you've been too bad a person on Earth, you could be sentenced to an eternity in *Gehennalocus*, the place where the punishment takes place. Ruth only spent 5 years there, because she was sinless and lucky enough to get a good lawyer to soften the blow of her rule-breaking. But for most criminals, like murderers, rapists and people like that, *Gehennalocus* is as far as they'll ever go in the *afterlife*. They never get to go to *Caelumlocus*."

"So, they really are there, still? Iris and her daughters? In *Gehen-gehlocus*— In hell?"

"Yes," says Lesly. "And they will be there for a very long time. Being punished for their sins."

"What about Mr. Bundleheckles?" Evander asks.

"I thought you hated him," Lesly jokes.

"I did," he says, "when I thought he was hell-bent on killing me. But he was on our side all along, wasn't he?"

"Yes. Which is why even though Mythil wanted him to be punished for eternity, he wasn't. After spending a decade in *Gehennalocus*, his trial was held again. And it was decided that he had suffered enough for disobeying The Kingdom's rules and because he hadn't caused any real harm, he was allowed to go into *Caelumlocus*."

"That's great!"

"Yeah. One of his friends got promoted to a judge, so he reopened Mr. Bundleheckles' case. Otherwise, someone's sentence being changed is a very rare phenomenon."

"How do you know all of this in such depth? About Iris, her daughters and Mr. Bundleheckles?"

"Well, I've been a dingle for 12 years now, Evander. You make friends. And we all help each other whenever we can. Sometimes by finding stuff out about certain souls, or undead."

"What's being a dingle like?"

Lesly falls quiet, licking her paw like she doesn't know how to answer his question.

"Most of the times it's awful," she says finally, with a wounded tone. "I have been assigned to many different souls, who died in many different ways and return for a number of reasons. With each soul, it's a different kind of sadness. Being amongst the dead is painful in unimaginable ways."

"I'm so sorry, Lesly," he says, feeling like an idiot for asking her anything. "But now that you know where I live, you could drop by once in a while and we could chat and maybe it'll cheer you up."

She smiles. "I'd love that."

They just sit silently because Evander has run out of questions to ask Lesly, and he knows he will upset her if he asks anything personal.

"How did you leave, though?" Lesly asks him, after the pause becomes too long. "And come here, to New Orleans?"

"I ran away after I got that dream," he tells her. "My bodyguard, Miguel helped me catch a plane to New Orleans. The next few years were really difficult. I had to work multiple jobs and sleep hungry a lot of nights. But, you know, I found friends who helped me and after struggling for about 7 years, I worked really hard, and now I'm a best-selling author!"

Lesly beams at him. "Ruth always told me you deserved your happy ending. I'm so glad you got it, Evander. I am so proud of you."

Evander smiles back, trying to hold in his tears. "Thank you."

"Well, I should get going now," Lesly says. "I'll come again!"

"See you soon," Evander says, opening the window.

He watches the cat leap from one pole to another and disappear in the trees. He closes the window, and wiping his tears, walks back to the shelf, picking up the fallen book and taking a long hard look at the girl who was supposedly Ruth.

At least he had helped fulfil her last wish.

Placing the book back in its place, Evander walks back to his desk.

And before he can doubt himself, words start flowing right out of his head and onto the screen.

Acknowledgements

This endeavour would not have been possible without the infinite support of my parents, Nilima and Mayur Mandhane. In spite of my writing this book through the hardcore academics of Grade 12 and preparation for Engineering, they encouraged me to pursue what gave me the most happiness – storytelling.

I also could not have undertaken this journey without my grandparents, Usha and Omprakash Gattani. The idea for this story came to me back in 8th grade. All I had done then was write a page about it. But after writing my debut novel, my grandparents pushed me to pen-down this idea too. There would be no second book without them.

Milton Keynes UK
Ingram Content Group UK Ltd.
UKHW020134021224
451809UK00020B/245

9 789348 199485